Let Love Be Enough

By Robyn Nyx

2022

Praise for Robyn Nyx's work

Never Enough

"Nyx's debut is an entertaining thriller with two well-realized heroines. But readers who can handle the gory content will find it well balanced by plenty of romance and copious amounts of sex, as well as a solid cast of supporting characters and some insightful handling of contemporary social issues." ***Publishers Weekly***

"If you are a sucker for fast paced, gritty crime thrillers that will make you neglect your household chores and read way past your bedtime, well fellow book lover, this is certainly the story for you." ***The Lesbian Review***

The Extractor Trilogy

"Nyx balances the task of developing emotionally complex characters and creating a plot that is well paced and full of action on a grand scale. The story is captivating, and the best part is that it's the first in a fantastic trilogy." ***The Lesbian Review***

"I genuinely couldn't have predicted what did happen though, and urge everyone to read this trilogy if not for the imaginative story, then for the intensity of how people's actions affect not only their own lives but the lives and feelings of others. So good! Robyn has perfectly captured all that moral uncertainty between doing the right thing legally and then doing the right thing morally." ***LesBiReviewed***

"The redemptive power of love is a huge take-away from this book. There were more than a few times where I found myself on the verge of tears while reading some of Landry's conversations with her best friend Delaney." ***Victoria Thomas***

Music City Dreamers

"Fans of the show Nashville will love Music City Dreamers by Robyn Nyx, for its angsty drama involving megastars and aspiring singers, songwriters and record executives. This is also not the stereotypical Nashville of bros and whiskey you often see on CMT." ***NPR***

"I really enjoyed this story and I am so glad Ms Nyx made this foray into lesbian romance. She has captured the passion and intense emotions of the two women, as well as weaving a fascinating story." ***Kitty Kat's Book Blog***

The Golden Trinity

"Ms. Nyx tells an awesome story with real characters, and that to my mind is the goal of a good book." ***Lesbian Reading Room***

"What an excellent book and I demolished it in one go! I had such a great time reading Uncharted and would be happy to pick it up again tomorrow. The pace was perfect and felt like I was on the adventure with Chase and Rayne. For the last 30% of this book, my heart was in my chest with all the excitement." ***Les Rêveur***

The Copper Scroll

Holy hotness, batman!! Chase and Rayne's sexual and emotional chemistry flows onto the page. This isn't an experience you want to miss. Just make sure you read the first book before this one. It's just going to make the experience all the better. This book really is jam-packed with action, adventure, and romance. I really hope this isn't the end of the 'The Chase Stinsen' books because I am not ready to let these characters go just yet. ***Les Rêveur***

Nyx has the ability to get you into the heads of her characters, and Chase and Rayne are no exception; and I loved that she showed us that not everything in life is always black and white. I've already re-read it twice. I thought The Golden Trinity was good, it had my heart racing, and I was awash with adrenaline in places, but The Copper Scroll surpasses it. I'm just waiting for Book 3 and the film series. ***The Lesbian Review***

Dead Pretty

"The relationship between CJ and Dak is really cute and wholesome even though it's really sexually charged, it takes a lot of talent to create that balance." ***The Lesbian Review***

"A fantastic combination of crime and love story twisted together in a well balanced flow. Nyx's writing is power and beautiful." ***The Hyperactive Bookwork***

"Robyn Nyx is a wordsmith that takes you on a roller coaster ride of emotions and drops you off at a HEA, but only after you've bitten your nails down to the quick." ***Mayra Luria***

LesFic Eclectic Volume One

Robyn Nyx has put together a fantastic collection, and brought to us some amazing new talent as well as stories from some of our already loved and established authors in the genre. Engaging readers with new writers is always fantastic, and the new writers included in the Lesfic Eclectic are all absolutely brilliant." ***LesBiReviewed***

LesFic Eclectic Volume Two

"I have read the seasoned writers before such as Anna Larner, Robyn Nyx, Brey Willows, Jenn Matthews and Anne Shade as always blew me away with their storytelling. A little something for everyone is the tagline across the cover, and I couldn't agree more. I highly recommend grabbing a copy of Lesfic Eclectic, a bottle of vino and taking one story at a time." ***Les Rêveur***

LesFic Eclectic Volume Three

"Having read the previous two volumes, I wondered if volume three would still achieve the same delightfulness as its counterparts but, truth be told, it's the most magical one yet." ***Queer Literary Loft***

By the author

Dead Pretty

The Chase Stinsen Adventures

The Golden Trinity (Book One)

The Copper Scroll (Book Two)

Music City Dreamers

The Extractor Trilogy

Escape in Time (Book One)

Change in Time (Book Two)

Death in Time (Book Three)

Never Enough

Edited by Robyn Nyx

LesFic Eclectic Volume One

LesFic Eclectic Volume Two

LesFic Eclectic Volume Three

Let Love Be Enough

By Robyn Nyx

2022

Butterworth Books is a different breed of publishing house. It's a home for Indies, for independent authors who take great pride in their work and produce top quality books for readers who deserve the best. Professional editing, professional cover design, professional proof reading, professional book production—you get the idea. As Individual as the Indie authors we're proud to work with, we're Butterworths and we're *different*.

Authors currently publishing with us:

E.V. Bancroft
Valden Bush
Michelle Grubb
Helena Harte
Lee Haven
Karen Klyne
AJ Mason
Ally McGuire
James Merrick
Robyn Nyx
Simon Smalley

For more information visit www.butterworthbooks.co.uk

This trade paperback is published by Butterworth Books, UK

Previously published as Never Enough, this version had been re-edited with over three thousand words deleted, and seven thousand new words added.

Cataloging information
ISBN: 9781915009210
Credits
Editor: Jan Stone
Cover Design: Nicci Robinson
Production Design: Global Wordsmiths

Acknowledgements

A huge thank you to my editor, Jan. You keep me going with your insightful edits and your unerring faith in my voice. A huge thanks to my amazing proofer, Margaret Burris. Her hard work is a wonderful help in producing the final product. And I'd like to thank my dedicated team of ARC readers for their encouraging and enthusiastic reviews and for taking the time to read my words. Your early love of my books gets me through the initial panic of every new release.

And finally, thanks to my readers, new and old; I hope you enjoy this story as much as I enjoyed writing it. I love you all.

Dedication

For my buddy of all things, Brey.
Love will be enough for all
we're going through.
I promise.

Chapter One

"ALEKSANDRA, COULD YOU TELL me what your organization, Safe Bornes, does?" Madison Ford pushed the microphone closer to her interviewee and smiled, though it was the last thing she felt like doing. The bile this Oxford-educated Russian woman was peddling sickened her.

"We destroy lives." Aleksandra tilted her head and smirked. "You're the only American I've ever met that could pronounce my name properly. Did you know that it translates as 'defender of mankind?' I was born to do exactly that. I am protecting regular Russians from anti-democratic militants who would overthrow our way of life if they are allowed to go unchecked."

Madison glanced at her colleague, Geva Doyle, who was busy capturing pristine images of the motley crew of young people in the room. Without words, they communicated their disgust for these people. Aleksandra had requested this interview with both of them following the trans feature they'd produced which had won them both a Pulitzer. She wanted to show them how misguided they were. She was adamant she could relieve them of their liberal attitude toward trans people. All they had to do was come to Russia so she could *educate* them.

"And if you don't protect 'regular Russians,' what do you believe will happen?"

"Three-quarters of the Russian population believe that transgenderism is a mental illness. There is some truth to that, but more, it is a flagrant disregard for morality. If we fail to fish for and catch these hooligans, we are complicit in the destruction of our traditional values. If we stand by and do nothing, we are allowing a minority to shape the future of our society." Aleksandra stood and grasped the shoulder of one of her protégés as her speech grew more impassioned. "This desire to change what you are is a weakness in Western culture we Russians will not propagate. We will not allow this notion to infiltrate and infect our nation. God chooses what you will be, not you and a doctor who will butcher you for money."

Her gang clapped and howled their approval of her words. Aleksandra looked directly at Madison, clearly expecting her to be convinced by the zealous sermon. She looked somewhat disappointed in Madison's lack of positive reaction.

"Is he the new recruit you spoke of yesterday?" Madison gestured to the guy Aleksandra held by the shoulder. He was bouncing on his heels in excitement for the "hunt" they were about to embark upon.

"Yes, yes. This is Kulik. We're grooming him to lead a new faction in Smolensk. When we're on the safaris like tonight and he's close to his prey, he is calmer than this. But really, he wants to kill them. Put them out of their misery. They think they are not what they are supposed to be. We will help. We will end them."

The easy way with which Aleksandra spoke of murdering a fellow human being made Madison shudder. It was all she could do not to violently hurl all over them. Who were they to dictate what a person felt and knew deep inside themselves to be true? "Do you believe you have the right to end someone's life?"

"We're not killing them. Not yet. We make them see what they're doing is wrong and give them the opportunity to change." She shrugged and motioned for Madison and Geva to follow her. "Come. Let us go on safari and you can take your pictures. Kulik is going to act as bait. He already has someone on the hook." Aleksandra waved Kulik's cell in the air before pressing it into his hand and slapping him on the back. "He's very fond of the urine humiliation. He likes to drink light beer in preparation. He gets irritated if I don't let him, but I won't be allowing that tonight. You don't get to see that."

I don't want *to see that.*

***

A staggering three quarters of the Russian population believe that being trans is a mental illness, an aberration not to be tolerated. It is a country whose economy is faltering, where pensions and salaries barely cover the cost of living. It's a

```
nation nurturing a healthcare system
that fails those most in need, and an
educational establishment which is
forsaking their younger generations.
How is their government combatting
these shortcomings? By igniting a
conflict among their people and fueling
a horrifying hatred of trans people,
distracting them from focusing their
anger on the real culprits of their
misfortune and disquiet—the Russian
regime. "It's hunting season, and we are
the hunted."
```

Madison recalled the terrifying statement from a Russian trans woman she'd spoken to earlier that day, before they'd spent three hours with the Safe Bornes and witnessed one of their terrifying hunts. She stopped typing and took a sip of the Swedish vodka she'd been nursing since beginning her article. She pressed the glass to her lips and looked out the window of her hotel room in St. Petersburg, Russia. As she'd traveled the world, building a reputation as a highly respected journalist, Madison had seen all manner of unseemly activity and witnessed countless acts of inhumanity. The brutalities she'd observed over the past week were just as heinous, and that they were happening so openly made them even more distressing. She clenched her hands tight then stretched them out before continuing.

The gentle knock on her hotel door was a welcome distraction. Madison uploaded the unfinished article to the cloud, closed her MacBook, and answered the door. Geva stood before her, bottle in hand.

"I have vodka." She raised the bottle for inspection.

"I have a deadline," Madison said, vaguely rueful. She often hooked up with Geva in times of extreme stress, like genocides, natural disasters, and civil unrest. Their relationship, the very essence of casual, was originally born of Madison's desperate need to feel a connection in such turbulent surroundings. Not that she'd had to persuade Geva. She admitted a long-term crush on Madison, one that started way back before they'd worked together on the trans feature.

"We always have deadlines. We always find the time."

Geva's voice was soft and in direct contradiction to her appearance. Years of harsh winds and unprotected exposure to the sun had given Geva a complexion beyond her actual lifetime. She had a rugged look about her, which, accompanied by her always windswept, dirty blond hair and sharp, blue eyes was an attractive combination. Their encounters had become so regular that it wasn't unusual for their rooms to be adjoining.

Geva was right. Madison had what she came to this democratically forsaken country for. She could write the article tomorrow on the thirteen-hour flight back to L.A. She stepped aside to allow Geva entry. "Then by all means, join me."

Geva caressed her hip gently as she slipped past to place the bottle beside Madison's laptop on the glass desk. She followed, craving more of her touch. This country was infecting her, and she needed it washed from her blood. A screaming, body-flushing orgasm would do just that.

Geva sat on the chair Madison had just vacated, topped up her glass, and offered it to her. She filled her own and tapped the lid of Madison's MacBook. "What's next for you?"

Madison took the drink and sat on the edge of the bed. "I've been talking with someone who claims to be part of a big organ trafficking organization. I'd planned to have some downtime after this in L.A., and this guy is based there, so I'm going to follow up and see where it leads. Plus, my agent wants me to do an interview with Elodie Fontaine. She's doing good things with her celebrity, raising awareness of the extent of human trafficking in the States. Seems to be a certain symmetry in it all." She sighed deeply. Right now, she just wanted some release. Their time with Aleksandra and her gang over the past few days had taken an emotional toll. If she were honest, the thought of diving into something as heavy as organ trafficking was the last thing she wanted to do.

Geva leaned forward and put her hand on Madison's knee. "Maybe you should take a break. You've been pretty full-on for a while now. When was the last time you went on vacation?"

Madison laughed. "That's not a serious question, is it? You British people get way too much vacation. Only us Americans know what it is to work hard." She raised her glass and emptied it quicker than she would've liked. This trip had affected her more than she cared to admit.

She stood, placed the glass on the desk, and pulled Geva into a familiar kiss. Her dalliances with Geva were decadent indulgences necessary to keep them sane in these crazy realities. In daily life, this wasn't her style at all. One-night stands, spontaneous sex, fucking with no emotion, that was the playground of Hollywood stars like Elodie Fontaine. Although she'd grumbled about it to her agent, Madison had to admit she was looking forward to that interview. Elodie was an intriguing actress whose work Madison enjoyed, and her involvement with the TIP office and humanitarian work made her even more interesting. She seemed like someone content and satisfied with her life. Madison wondered what that would feel like, to be at peace. She pulled herself back into the moment and concentrated on Geva.

A powerful knock on the door of the adjoining room jolted them from their kiss.

"Is that your room?" It was past midnight. In countries like this, calls at this time invariably meant trouble. Geva put her finger to her mouth, and Madison went quiet. They heard the door being kicked in, Russian voices shouting aggressively, and tables being turned over. The adjoining door between their rooms was kicked inward, and they were confronted by five of the Russian politsiya, batons in hand. The tallest of them strode forward, smiling maniacally.

"Madison Ford and Geva Doyle?"

Madison saw recognition in his face. His question was rhetorical.

"Why?" Geva took a step to place herself between Madison and the menacing intruder. "What can we help you with, Captain Dudko?"

"What you can do for me, Ms. Doyle, is pack your bags and leave." He eyed her with obvious distaste before casting his gaze to Madison. "Ms. Ford, it is in your interest to do the same. There is no need for either of you to…make a scene."

Madison touched Geva gently on the arm and came forward. "Isn't it a little late for an official police welcome, *Ment* Dudko?"

Dudko laughed at Madison's slang honorific. "Garbage? Ironic, I think you would call it, considering your engagement with the garbage of *our* fine country."

"Indeed. Are you a member of Safe Bornes too?" Madison's challenge was dangerous, but this was the man who had ordered the capture and torture of a politically active lesbian pop group. She couldn't, and wouldn't, bring herself to feign politeness.

"You think you are humorous, Ms. Ford, but neither you nor your humor is welcome here."

Dudko motioned his officers forward. Two of them moved toward Geva with cuffs in hand. Madison instinctively tried to stop them, but the other two politsiya rushed forward and fixed Madison in their grasp. "She's a British citizen. You can't do this." She watched helplessly as Geva was roughly hauled back to her own room. Dudko slammed the door shut behind them.

"And you, Ms. Ford, are an American citizen."

Dudko invaded Madison's personal space. She heaved at the stench of stale plaque on his breath.

"But I care not for your Western origin," he closed his bony fingers around her throat, "or your militant liberal views. You would do well to avoid my country in the future."

Madison shifted uncomfortably in the trio's tightening grip. "You're aware it's against European law to threaten a member of the world media corps?" She swallowed hard against his leather-gloved palm pressing against her esophagus.

He laughed again before striking her with his other open hand. "This is not a threat, Ms. Ford. It is a statement for your consideration."

He released her and wandered over to the desk. The officers holding her turned her to follow him.

"You are a danger to our democracy. You are guilty of a number of illegal acts, including inciting subversion. I could throw you and your photographer friend in prison for your crimes against this country." He opened her laptop. "If I were to seize this computer, Ms. Ford, I strongly suspect I would find you guilty of further transgressions." Dudko slowly unscrewed the top from Geva's vodka bottle and began to pour the contents onto Madison's keyboard.

She surged forward, pulling against her captors. "This is outrageous."

Dudko cast an instructive glance to his sergeants, and they pushed her arms farther behind her back, forcing her onto her toes. She watched, powerless to defend her Mac as it suffered a less than noble death, spluttering electronic expletives at its tormentor.

"Though you may think me an illiterate savage, I am fully aware of your reputation for fearless and perceptive writing, Ms. Ford."

Dudko lifted her laptop by the corner of its screen and held it high above his head. Madison closed her eyes. The hotel was an old castle, and its floors, though littered with plush rugs, were age-old stone. She couldn't watch.

"I enjoy your other work, but you should be more careful of your environment. One slip. One accident..."

He released the MacBook and it dropped to the floor, smashing the screen. She winced as if he'd damaged a piece of her. Once more, he moved close enough for her to study the pockmarks on his weathered face, and his dark, shark-black eyes fixed on her. In the adjacent room, she could hear more equipment being smashed. Geva would have to replace her entire kit bag when she returned to England.

"And suddenly, some other great writer is composing your obituary. My sergeants will help you pack your belongings. You have an early flight back to your debauched homeland, Ms. Ford. I would hate for you to miss it. You would not like the way I entertain visitors who overstay their welcome."

Sharp pain flashed across Madison's cheek when Dudko struck her again with the back of his hand. She snarled as if to retort but clenched her teeth to keep the words from escaping, lest she enrage him further. He clearly had no respect for her citizenship or the slight protection being media provided. Rotting in his jail wouldn't get her article written so she could show the world what was really going on in his country.

"You have something to say, Ms. Ford? Your particular brand of bombast rhetoric is bursting to get out, yes?"

Dudko's officers applied a little more pressure, and Madison winced. She could see he was desperate to arrest her. No doubt it would be quite the promotion-sealing action, to arrest a gay foreign journalist. Madison tongued her busted lip and managed a smile through the twisting pain in her arms. "None but the lonely heart shall know my sadness, Captain Dudko. I have nothing to say." The words left her mouth despite her desire not to anger him more. Fortunately, it seemed the Tchaikovsky reference eluded him, and he strode away, confident in his victory.

She was shoved toward the wardrobe by the goons he'd left behind. Her hand shook as she reached to open it, so she clenched her fist and stretched it out. She didn't want to show them her fear. *Play along, and I'll get through this. And we'll still publish this article when we're safely home.*

Chapter Two

"Elodie? Should I get the phone?"

"No. Don't touch it." Elodie would've used the woman's name, except she couldn't bring it to mind. She'd picked her up hours earlier at the opening of another superclub but had been more than a little intoxicated, and the music had been too loud to hear much else. She was terrible with names, but she did remember it was something to do with a famous song. There'd been a choice of potential playmates, of course, as there always was. And this one hadn't disappointed, not physically, anyway. Invariably, Elodie was disenchanted with the level of interest they showed in her beyond the bedroom and the inevitable request to get them a screen test. Elodie had no doubt the question of acting was imminent.

She slipped across the bed to reach for the phone and shivered as the satin sheets went from body-warm to bare-cold. The shiver went a little deeper when she saw herself on the front cover of *HumanKind* magazine beside her phone. The World's Most Beautiful Human for the fifth time in nine years. She ran her hand through her hair and made a mental note to see her stylist today. She hated it when she couldn't feel the warmth of the sun or someone's hand directly on her neck. She'd have her head shaved if it weren't for the fact that her adoring fans loved her trademark style. There was something empowering about short hair, particularly since the vast majority of Hollywood's darlings wore theirs that much longer. She was flipping off the norm, and they loved her all the more for it.

"If you're not calling to tell me I've won another Oscar, I'm not interested."

"Elodie, I have two opportunities for you, and I just had to share them right away. First, I have a must-do meeting for you this week with the big new company in town." Paige Bailey, Elodie's agent, always seemed shrill and hurried.

"A must-do meeting with an unproven studio?" She hated being told what to do. There was only one person who'd ever done that, and she was long dead now.

"Um, well, it's a great opportunity with all the writers' strikes going on. FlatLine is the only studio beginning new work. It's an adaptation of one of your favorite books…unless it's not one of your favorite books anymore, and you didn't tell me."

"Calm down, Paige. You'll give yourself another heart attack." The woman lying beside her giggled. *Jude! That's her name.* "Which book?"

"I can't remember the title. Or the author. It's the one with the Russian woman who has to become an assassin to save her daughter. She dies in the end."

"*A Glass Heart's Requiem*, yep. But it'll only be interesting if they stick to the original ending and don't make it Hollywood schmaltzy romance." She reached over and squeezed Jude's breast. "What's the second opportunity?"

"I've pulled in a favor with Madison Ford's agent and got you an interview to discuss your work with the TIP office and human trafficking. It'll raise awareness like you want and serve as potential publicity for the human trafficking film you want to get financed."

Now she was interested. Elodie's work with the government's department to combat human trafficking globally had quickly grown from a desire to do something good into a passion for helping people, and she was devoting more time and money to it than Paige liked. Making profitable use of Elodie's time didn't include so much volunteer work, and fifteen percent of zero wasn't the way to make her happy. Paige was a typically heartless bitch of an agent, but she was Elodie's heartless bitch of an agent, and in this town, primarily that's what she needed. "That's a real coup. How did you manage that?"

"Hollywood revolves around favors," Paige said. "You know that. And most of them originate from dark, poorly kept secrets."

"Intriguing. Now I really want to know how you did it. Why don't you come over and bring some breakfast? I'm hungry." Elodie caught Jude's eye, and she recognized that look. She saw it over and over when they wanted her to live up to her infamous sexual appetite. One day, she hoped someone would see what else she could offer.

"We'll check your schedule and see when you're available. I'm pulling in a huge favor to get Madison to do this. She's in Russia right now, covering gender and war or something, so we'll schedule it as soon as she's back on US soil. She doesn't do celebrity interviews, so I expect there'll be no room for discussing your movies."

"You've done great, Paige. And I wouldn't want to talk about Hollywood with a reporter of her caliber anyway. It'd be a waste of an opportunity to get my human trafficking work an even higher profile. What time is it?"

"Ten thirty."

"Swing by at twelve then."

Jude traced her fingers slowly over Elodie's hip.

Elodie smiled. "Make that one."

"Of course."

"Then I'll see you later." Elodie ended the call, stretched out, and kicked the covers down to her waist. "What're you doing all the way over there?"

"Just waiting for my cue when you'd finished. You know, love interest enters stage left." Jude sidled over to nestle on Elodie's chest and began to trace her fingers over Elodie's stomach.

Elodie ignored the love reference. She recalled nothing about Jude that would keep her interested beyond breakfast. "I thought you were waiting on tables, not waiting for your big break. Why didn't you say?"

"You didn't seem interested in too much conversation last night, of the small talk kind, anyway."

Elodie grinned as she recalled the filthy words she'd whispered in Jude's ear while she fucked her. "What makes you think I'd be more in the mood for conversation now?"

"If you're not, I'm sure I can amuse you in other ways." She traced the veins along Elodie's forearm with her nails.

"What do you have in mind?"

"Maybe you could do that thing you did last night…I'm pretty sure I could take it again."

Elodie closed her eyes and mentally pictured it. Jude *had* been delightful. Elodie didn't know whether she was a good actress or not, but she was exceptionally talented in bed. She caught hold of Jude's arm and used her body weight to shift her onto her back. Elodie knelt over her and pinned Jude's arms above her head. She positioned her breasts close to Jude's mouth. "How much do you want it?"

Jude smiled as she lifted her head and pressed her mouth around Elodie's left breast. She tongued her nipple and wrapped her legs around

Elodie's waist, pressing her wet pussy to Elodie's stomach. Elodie couldn't resist a small grin and pushed against her. Jude dropped her head back to the pillow.

"I want it bad."

Jude's lips were full, flushed with arousal. Elodie loved to see that on a woman. It was an unavoidable biological response to their own raw sexuality.

"Please fuck me."

Elodie smiled wickedly and laughed. "No."

Jude unwrapped her legs and sank into the bed. She pushed herself farther up so her pussy lay beneath Elodie's breasts.

"Please. I need you inside me. Fuck me, Elodie."

Elodie caught hold of Jude's hair and leaned hard into her soft body. "Later, little one. I need to shower." She removed herself from the entanglement and headed for the bathroom, deliberately swinging her ass for Jude's benefit.

As Elodie brushed her teeth, she thought about the new script Paige was bringing over. It could be a great part. Better yet was the interview Paige had secured with Madison Ford. She was in a journalistic league all her own. She was fearless and always in pursuit of justice. She'd recently won a Pulitzer Prize for a stunning feature charting the female-to-male transition of her fellow actor, Troy Donovan. On the set of her last movie, Elodie had heard Troy's tale of him and Madison getting together in graphic detail, and for some reason, didn't want to believe it. The woman was principled and professional. Surely she wouldn't jump into bed with one of her story subjects.

Elodie respected her attitude and the way she handled herself and those around her. *I'd like to handle her*. Her beauty matched her intelligence and tenacity. She'd read much of Madison's work. Her articles about famine, war, and poverty had touched Elodie deeply and made her think about being more than just an actress. But it was her articles on organ trafficking in the States that prompted Elodie to do something useful with her own fame. Since she'd started that work, she'd vaguely wondered if Madison would ask for an interview. But despite her involvement with the "Decade of Delivery" and her work combating human trafficking and organ sales in L.A., Madison had stayed well away.

Elodie had no right to garner any special attention from Madison, she knew that. She wasn't doing anything with enough impact to warrant *any* attention from Madison at all. No doubt an actor was far from her radar, but still Madison remained a distant ideal of someone who might interest Elodie beyond one or two nights of wild, mind-blowing sex. Maybe all Madison could see was the intricately created façade of Elodie Fontaine, the movie star. Sometimes, Elodie wondered if she'd worn that mask for so long, she didn't know how to take it off…even if someone came along that made her want to try.

She stepped under the rainforest shower and took a moment to enjoy the warm blanket of water that fell on her body. She concentrated her thoughts on the impending interview with Madison. Another perfect chance for Elodie Fontaine to promote Elodie Fontaine. She knew Paige would insist on certain topics, things to ask, and things not to ask. But Madison would push different buttons and ask personal and probing questions.

It wasn't like Elodie was ever lost for something pertinent to say. People always marveled at her eloquence, that all too rare ability to know precisely the right words for every occasion. She'd never been caught out by some half-wit hack. She was always in control, of herself and of others. Often, they just didn't know it. Madison Ford, though, was a different prospect. She was no hack. Elodie didn't care that Madison had agreed to interview her so her agent could repay a favor. She was just glad she'd finally get the chance to meet her.

Drying herself off, Elodie was confident she would be inspired as always. She dropped her towel to the floor and padded back to the bedroom. She half expected Jude to be gone, but a quick glance at the bed proved otherwise. Jude had fallen asleep on her stomach with her legs wrapped around a pillow, raising her pert ass from the bed. Elodie approached the bed quietly and took the time to watch the gentle rise and fall of her breathing. She loved to watch the naked body of every woman she came across in Technicolor detail, but Jude was too thin for her own good. She looked almost fragile, and Elodie wondered how she hadn't damaged her last night. She turned her attention to the shape of her ass and the way it smoothed down to the back of her legs.

She exhaled slowly and deeply. Elodie knelt beside her, slipped her arm underneath Jude's stomach, and pulled her up onto her hands and knees. Before Jude had fully woken, Elodie was inside her, quick and smooth. Jude gasped for breath as she thrust into her. She felt her try to fall back to the bed for support, but Elodie held her firm and pressed their bodies together.

When Elodie removed her arm from beneath Jude's body, she stayed in position, apparently resisting the temptation to sink into the forgiving softness of the bed. Elodie grasped Jude's neck to bring them face-to-face. She kissed her, and her mouth cushioned the force with which she fucked Jude. She wanted Jude unable to concentrate on their kiss. She wanted the throbbing to be so intense that the rest of the room blurred and all but paralyzed her. Elodie wanted Jude to relinquish control and allow her body to respond without her will, without limitation.

She stopped kissing her and focused on their rhythm and the feel of her fingers inside Jude and enjoyed the physical intimacy. She pushed in harder and watched Jude's body respond. Jude's breathing quickened. She became even more vocal and pushed her ass back at Elodie, practically daring her to go harder, faster, deeper.

Elodie deliberately slowed down, again watching Jude's body and the way she sank toward the bed, probably both thankful and hateful of the abeyance in pace.

"Please," Jude whispered.

"Please what?" Elodie kept her voice calm and soft, despite the raging need to bring Jude to orgasm.

"Please. Don't stop."

Elodie laughed quietly. She wasn't about to stop, not before Jude had given her whole body and mind to the act. To her.

Elodie responded to the plea, to the moment, and most of all, to the sex. They fell onto the bed, and Elodie knocked Jude's hands from under her, crushing their bodies together, becoming as complete and as close as they could be. Jude writhed beneath her weight, the restriction clearly driving her pleasure still higher. As Elodie continued to fuck her, hard and deep, Jude fast approached a shuddering completion. Her breaths became shallow and quick, her body convulsed, and each slight movement of Elodie's fingers inside her pushed her closer to the edge. Jude plummeted over it, her body trembling and her mouth wide open, her pussy contracting tightly around Elodie's hand. She bucked wildly beneath Elodie, who simply held her close and waited out the surrender.

Jude finally lay still. Her breathing slowly returned to normal as occasional tremors beginning from her core coursed through her body abruptly. Elodie withdrew, rolled back onto the bed, and smiled. Jude's abandonment of her own self-possession and her complete release to the intoxicating pleasure of their sex was refreshing and welcome.

It was refreshing and welcome every time.

Chapter Three

"I'm finding your choice of car quite ironic right about now, Carlos. What do you think?" Therese Hunt looked at the captive man with disdain. He was strapped into the front seat of a Ford Escape. His clothes were dirty, torn, and bloodied, his face swollen and bruised. Therese's crew had been thorough when they'd worked him over. Therese liked that about her small but trusty crew. They took their jobs seriously. They knew if they didn't, they'd have to answer to her. And no one wanted a private audience with Therese.

Carlos swallowed with difficulty, and Therese saw the resilience and hatred in his eyes, felt it as he spat into Therese's face. The blood, saliva, and mucus dripped down her nose and onto the unlit cigarette in her mouth.

Therese's jaw involuntarily tightened. "Spitting is such a disgusting habit, Carlos. You should know by now how much I dislike it." She took a deep breath, removed the cigarette, and rammed it into Carlos's mouth. "I was going to spare you this one last agony." Therese saw the panic in his eyes. "But I find my compassion can be so fleeting, so momentary. People should take advantage while they can. They—you shouldn't test me with useless acts of defiance." She stepped away from the car. "Cate." She flicked her eyes to the trunk.

Cate opened it and pulled out an older man, bound and gagged. She brought him to Therese and kicked him to his knees.

Therese watched the two captives exchange looks she found satisfyingly desperate.

"Please, God, no. Not my dad."

Therese pulled the gag out of the kneeling man's mouth.

"What are you doing with my son?"

Therese smirked at the obvious terror in his voice and cuffed him upside the head. "Shut it. Explain to your dad why you're here, Carlos." Therese chose to ignore the fury and hatred in his eyes, although she always enjoyed that part, too. "You owe it to him. He deserves to know why he's going to die tonight." The kneeling father grunted, and Therese hit him again. "Tell your dad how you've afforded to buy him a nice house with a pool."

Carlos looked at his father. "I work for a criminal organization—"

"Worked," Therese corrected him, clenching her jaw in barely controlled anger. "Explain to your dad how you've betrayed me. How you've decided that, despite the fact I've paid you handsomely for the past decade, you've sold me out. Explain exactly why you're both going to die here tonight, in a disused parking lot in a dirty part of town, far from where you've been living on my dollar."

"Please, Therese, you don't need to do this. Not him."

Therese scoffed. "Don't I? I should let you both go?" The rage inside her rose. She'd built an empire from nothing, established a nationwide business that had made whelps like Carlos into something special. And yet, here she was again, reprimanding an errant employee for an unforgivable act of betrayal that had jeopardized her whole operation. "Do I look like a fool? If I don't kill you, if I don't slaughter what's left of your family, what message does that send to everyone else on my payroll?" She kicked out at the trembling man at her feet. Sympathy eluded her. She only felt wronged, unnecessarily wronged, and Carlos had to pay for that, along with his dad. And then Therese would visit her right-hand woman, Natasha.

Usually, they'd share moments like this. Therese had discovered long ago that ending someone's life was both addictive and highly sexually charged. Killing someone never failed to make her horny. She and Nat always fucked each other senseless after they'd killed someone. Therese had been told it probably had to do with her childhood, the way she'd been used and abused by her adoptive parents. She smiled, remembering that was the last pearl of wisdom that particular therapist ever delivered.

"You don't have to kill my dad. He doesn't know anything. He can't harm you. I'm begging you, Therese, please let him go."

Therese watched Carlos dispassionately as he began to sob. She shook her head. Crying was weakness, a failure to control emotions. She thought Carlos was better than that. "Tell your dad what you've done, Carlos, or I'll make you watch while I peel the skin away from his body." Therese withdrew a caping knife from its sheath on her belt. She grabbed a handful of the man's hair, yanked his head back, and pressed the blade to his exposed neck.

"No! Please. I sold her out, Dad. I tried to tell the Feds about her operation."

"Tell your dad what operation. Tell him what you've done to afford his house." Therese pressed the blade harder, and his thin skin sliced enough to release blood.

"We deal—"

"You dealt, past tense."

"I dealt in human organs. We sell—"

"Sold, you don't do it anymore. Your choice."

"We sold them to the highest bidder."

Therese looked down at the man and saw the horror on his face. She always enjoyed that moment of realization when loved ones inevitably disappointed each other. Even as they stared death in the face, familial frustrations were still ridiculously important. "Don't worry, *Dad.* He finally had an attack of conscience. After ten years of reaping the rewards from the death of 'innocents,' he decided to try to put a stop to it. Isn't that right, Carlos?"

"I don't know what else you want me to say."

"Why don't you tell your dad how you'd sometimes personally source those organs just for fun? How you'd find a woman in a bar…and be honest, Carlos. Your dad should know what his son really is before you die." Therese enjoyed this: dismantling someone piece by piece and watching them squirm. Carlos deserved it. His dad, not so much, but she really had no choice, or she'd be seen as weak.

"I'd go to bars sometimes and pick up a girl. I'd bring her back to a hotel room, and my crew would take her down."

"See, *Dad*, your loving son liked nothing more than to exercise his power over women by sealing their fate. He's a closet misogynist disguised as a perfect straight guy. What do you think of your faultless son now, *Dad*? Now that you know everything he's bought for you over the past ten years was bought with blood money. Literally, blood money."

"I don't want to believe it. Please, Carlos, please tell me it's not true."

Carlos hung his head, and Therese could practically see the shame dripping from his forehead along with the sweat from the merciless L.A. heat.

"I'm sorry, Dad. I'm so sorry."

Therese slowly nodded, satisfied she'd fully destroyed the illusion of the ideal father-son relationship Carlos had always bragged about. There was no perfect family relationship. They were all shams. People went to their graves in wretched ignorance, thinking their loved ones were faultless. Therese hadn't suffered that particular artifice since she was five, when her real parents decided she was old enough to sell into sexual slavery.

"Say goodbye to your father."

"No! Please don't—"

But before he'd finished his plea, Therese had drawn the deadly blade across the kneeling man's throat, and she held him there while his life flooded from his neck. She flicked her attention from the fast-disintegrating Carlos to the beautiful deluge of thick red fluid pumping from the laceration she'd created. She watched it saturate the sea-green shirt the man was wearing, enjoyed the patterns it made as it ebbed ever downward.

"Élan vital. Taken away so easily."

Cate dragged the dead man to the car and carelessly slung him in the backseat like a sack of groceries. Carlos thrashed in his seat, trying to free himself. Therese's assistants doused the car in gasoline and trailed a path to her feet. Cate handed her a matchbook.

Therese looked at it and saw it was from her favorite restaurant. She recalled the halloumi and hummus burger she'd had last time she was there with Nat. Maybe they'd go there tonight after they'd worked up an appetite from fucking. "I hope your brief moment of piety was worth it." She lit the match and casually dropped it to the ground. It ignited the gasoline and coursed toward the car in a blue-green sublime swagger intent on slaughter. Therese stepped back from the intense heat but watched in fascination as it engulfed the vehicle and its two occupants in flames that danced dramatically. Carlos's screams were mildly pleasing. She'd murdered enough people with fire to know that it was a particularly painful death. It was up there in the top five of her homicidal repertoire, along with skinning and acid. But you couldn't beat a knife; it made death so very personal.

Therese turned away as Cate handed her a lit cigarette and her phone. She dialed Nat as the gas tank exploded. She rolled her eyes at her crew whooping and hollering like it was the Fourth of July.

"Meet me at my place in half an hour. I've just finished dealing with

Carlos."

"And now you're coming to deal with me?" Nat asked.

Therese took a long draw on her cigarette. "In your favorite way, yes."

Chapter Four

"I love the script. It's brilliant. It's so dark and intense. You want to hate her, but it turns out you really shouldn't. I'm impressed you want to stick to the writers' original ending, given that the heroine dies. That's not your typical Hollywood movie fare." Elodie allowed her enthusiasm free rein. She hadn't been this excited about a project for a while.

"Ah, is that a problem? You don't want to die at the end of the movie?"

Elodie smiled as the project's director, Al Fox, tugged on the edge of his mustache. "I've got no problem with the ending at all. It's refreshing."

"When I read the book, I found myself rooting for Elya too. Sure, she's done some bad things, but she's been driven to those for a very powerful reason. Once our audience knows that, they'll know she shouldn't be punished for a love that self-sacrificing." Al slapped the table, and the glasses on it shook. "But it did make me wish for a happy ending and for Elya and Kim to survive so they could raise Elya's little girl together. But you just know that Elya has to die for all the bad things she's done. It's the ultimate self-sacrifice for her little girl, making sure she can lead the life Elya never had the chance to."

Elodie nodded. "That's exactly right. If you can convey that feeling of redemption throughout the whole film, I think you're onto something."

"That's where you come in. That's your job."

She laughed. "That simple, huh, Al?"

"Hey, you made audiences love a cop-killer. This'll be a piece of cake."

She tapped the table. "How come I don't have to test for this?" She addressed her question to Jules French, aka, *the money*, seated at the end of the table. Though he'd introduced himself at the beginning of the meeting, he had said nothing since and had yet to participate. Elodie thought that strange, given that it was his company and his very first movie. She liked to earn a part. She loved to test against other actors because the competition made her performances even better.

"The project wouldn't have proceeded without you on board, Ms.

Fontaine. You simply had to be Elya Charinov. You were the only actor I had in mind while reading the screenplay, and I couldn't get past that. I realize that's not the way Hollywood usually works, but it's the way it will work here."

Jules had become more animated as he spoke, and Elodie found his passion infectious.

"I did get it right, and you weren't drawn to playing Kim?"

"Not for a second. Elya is the challenge, hands down. Kim is an all-American girl, fighting the good fight. Elya is more tragic. She's dark and lost, drowning in the immorality of what she's doing. The tragic anti-heroine is always a tough sell." Elodie was already in deep. The character excited her, and she *had* to play her. "Who do you have in mind for Kim and the three male parts?"

"Lela Darvis or Kiana McIntyre for Kim, choices one and two," Al said. "Todd Capron or Twist Wayans for the Russian, Rory Meliz or Rock Docherty for the Chinese guy, and it has to be Brad Carlton for the Italian."

"That'll be a great cast if you can get all your first choices," Elodie said. Lela was a real babe. They'd enjoyed some fun times on previous sets. "I can't wait to get started."

"Can I assume our proposed remuneration plus royalties is sufficient, Elodie?"

She smiled as Jules slid a copy of the contract across the table toward her. "It's more than sufficient." Elodie signed in all the tabbed places since her lawyer had already approved it.

"You would have done it for less?"

"Of course, but my agent would've killed me. She's on commission."

Jules laughed. "Then I hope this will be the first of many projects together."

Elodie was no fool. She'd wait to put pen to paper with FlatLine again until the project was finished, and she was satisfied with the result. Three-picture deals had never been her style, and the days when she made a film to put clothes on her back and food in the fridge regardless of the movie's quality were long gone. She hadn't done a movie she wasn't proud of for over ten years, box-office hit or no. The same couldn't be said of some of her contemporaries, many of whom only cared for the paycheck. "One at a time, Jules, one at a time."

Chapter Five

"I STILL CAN'T QUITE believe we've been deported from Russia." Madison shuffled her butt in the economy class seat on Flight BA 236 from Moscow to Heathrow. They'd been accompanied by the politsiya on their transfer from St. Petersburg to Moscow to ensure they boarded their flight. They needn't have wasted their time. Madison didn't want to spend another minute on Russian soil.

"You said we were taking a risk with this one. And I doubt Aleksandra will be happy with your finished article. We need to hope she stays in her own country and doesn't come searching you out."

Geva often had a relaxed take on any situation, and Madison wished she knew how she did it. "I know, but I was hoping I might be wrong. Something inside me hoped that *we'd* be the ones educating *her*."

Geva laughed gently. "You know better than anyone that minds like Aleksandra's can't be changed. You can't reason or argue with someone that fanatical."

"That will never stop me trying. For the one in ten thousand that might see things differently, it's worth it." Madison smiled though Geva was right for the most part; Madison had very personal experience that people found change difficult. No matter how many times they promised they would. "I just don't get how a second world country can be traveling backward at such an alarming rate. They've got Babin distracting the Russian people with rafts of antigay and transsexual legislation when it's the Russian regime that's responsible for their misfortune and disquiet. They've got a faltering economy, a failing healthcare system, and an educational establishment forsaking their younger generation. They're focusing their anger on the wrong people. It won't be long before he takes them into another pointless war for the sake of his ego. Why he's not been assassinated yet, I don't understand."

"You don't have to convince me. Have you considered a change of career? Perhaps you should be moving into politics?"

Madison sighed. "Like I could do anything else."

"What we do isn't forever. Over seventy of us were killed and nearly forty jailed in the last year alone. No one would blame you for moving on."

"Moving on?" Madison frowned. "How did we get from the Russian government being a complete cluster fuck to me giving up the job I love? I got into this kind of journalism to make a difference. A near-death experience in Afghanistan didn't stop me, so I'm not about to let a jumped-up police captain end my career. He doesn't get to win even though he thinks he has. Sometimes the pen isn't as mighty as the sword, but history's written into books, not stabbed."

"Are you okay, madam?"

Madison looked toward the whispering flight attendant and forced a smile. "I'm fine. Thank you."

"Can I get you both a drink?"

Madison's smile became genuine, though she was skeptical rather than pleasant. The question made her think of her father. He believed any problem could be solved with drink too. But it was never just one drink. "A bottle of water would be great, thanks."

"I'll have the same," Geva said.

"Certainly." The attendant was carrying an armful of magazines and offered one to Madison. "Perhaps you'd like to take a look at this? I love *HumanKind*, and the *Sexiest Human* issue is always my favorite."

Madison nodded and smiled politely, glad of the distraction. Her passion for the job could get a little too intense at times. Madison accepted the proffered magazine, and the attendant gave another copy to Geva. On its cover, movie star Elodie Fontaine's features were flawless and her intense, deep green eyes stared up at her. Precisely sculptured, short blond locks contrasted against her tanned skin and framed her face. She had an enviously sleek physique that was the result of years of free climbing in Utah, where she'd grown up. This would be a pleasant diversion from her not-so-quiet rage. "I'm going to read for a while and take some time to calm down."

"I'll be skipping to the photo section. Purely for professional purposes, obviously," Geva said and winked.

"Obviously. It has nothing to do with the subject at all."

"Of course not."

Madison smiled and began to flick through the pages, heading straight for the same section. *What does it take to be the World's Most Beautiful Human?* For Madison, and thousands of other women around the world, the appeal was clear. Elodie seemed confident and cocky in a sexy way, and she exuded an unusual self-assured energy. The result was undeniably attractive. She was physically flawless, and her genealogy had been particularly blessed with a seemingly ageless complexion.

Madison had first seen her in *Night Deeds* when Elodie was just twenty-five. Her portrayal of a single mom's battle against neighborhood drug dealers was an intelligent and courageous performance. It involved some heavy makeup and she put on thirty pounds for the role, evidencing a lack of vanity and a depth usually absent in Hollywood's biggest stars. Subsequent interviews she'd read with Elodie left the question open as to who she really was. Was the Elodie the public knew the real thing, or simply a cleverly designed construct to keep her fans happy?

Madison inspected the magazine's contents and something akin to guilty pleasure rippled through her as she flicked through to the eight-page spread. Madison had to applaud Elodie for her career longevity, despite her sexuality. She'd managed to engineer a meteoric rise to become the darling of Hollywood *and* the movie-going world, and she hadn't done it quietly. She hadn't stayed in the closet while she established herself and proved her mettle as an actor, rather than a one-hit wonder. She hadn't played it safe and confirmed her celebrity status with a die-hard fan base before she'd come out. She'd been completely open right from the get-go, and in doing so, she'd given new meaning to the phrase "out and proud." It seemed her absolute disregard for the establishment sealed her status. Women flocked to her. Men wanted to emulate her success in the bedroom. Producers and directors wanted her in their films. Actors were desperate to work with her. Elodie Fontaine had been bestowed with far more than her fair share of the *it* that people talk about, the *X factor* sought in new talent. She was magnetic and rumored to be absolute dynamite between the sheets. Madison had seen plenty of tabloid gutter press articles featuring kiss and tell stories by enough women to prove it.

As Madison thumbed through the glossy photos once, twice, and a third time, she pondered her decision to acquiesce to her agent's request for her to interview Elodie. Perhaps Madison's credentials made Elodie's people think an interview by her would lend veracity to Elodie's acting career. If that proved to be true, it would irk her a little. Madison would make sure this interview was purely about Elodie's humanitarian work, and she'd be steering well clear of any discussion of her movies. She wouldn't be used to promote Elodie's career. She was only interested in her work outside the studio.

"It's a shame you don't need a photographer for this interview." Geva motioned to a particularly stunning shot of Elodie relaxing in a chaise longue by a deep sapphire pool.

"Is Elodie Fontaine your type?"

"Isn't she everyone's type?"

Madison tilted her head. "You make a salient point. Anyway, I think they've already got a photographer, but I would've thought a fluff piece like this was beneath you."

Geva raised her eyebrows. "I would've thought the same about you, but you're still doing it."

"Not by choice. Hollywood favors have been exchanged, according to Dom. I haven't spoken to him in any depth about it yet, but I don't expect it will take too much time."

"And then you'll be investigating the organ trafficking lead?" Geva closed her magazine and shifted sideways on her seat to face Madison. "What happened to your downtime?"

Madison avoided Geva's intense stare, knowing it was borne from a kind of love. "I wouldn't know what to do with myself if I did stop working. Stories don't care for my vacation schedule. I go wherever they are whenever they're there. You're exactly the same."

Geva narrowed her eyes and huffed. "So I guess the next time we'll meet will be on your next foray into world affairs?"

"You're more than welcome to drop in on me in L.A." For a brief moment, Madison wondered if Geva needed more than she was offering, more than Madison could offer any woman. They hooked up when they were working together intensely, as if the process got more than creative juices flowing. Being in such close proximity to another inspiring, talented woman was incontrovertibly erotic. But her longer-term relationships had been far less successful.

She'd sought therapy after a series of disastrous codependent relationships. That had predictably pointed to her childhood and the past she'd never shared with anyone for fear of being seen as an attention-seeking victim. She threw herself into her work instead, and that was an easy excuse as to why her attempts at intimate connections never went the distance. It wasn't that she wasn't open to a life partner, she just didn't think she'd be able to find someone who'd accept her for all she was, all the brokenness, rather than the Madison she projected in her work.

She almost always felt love of some kind, but she was never really *in* love. She didn't feel capable of it. Inevitably, something would ruin it, and it would probably be her. The romantic ideal of perfection, the "getting everything from one person," a soul mate, was the stuff of fairy tales she'd never really believed in. Her parents saw to that. Geva was a pleasant distraction from that reality.

"I'll see how my schedule opens up. *National Geographic* wants me in China next, photographing pandas. Should be a nice change of pace as long as I don't piss the Chinese off like we did the Russians."

Madison laughed. "That's our mission, Gee. If we're not doing it, who will?" *And if I'm not doing it, I might actually have to address the emptiness.*

Chapter Six

It was the steel briefcase that made Therese smile. It wasn't a smile of mock sympathy for the predicament of the man in front of her. It was a smile that came from the knowledge that the briefcase contained a half million dollars. Nat exchanged pleasantries with their new client and settled him on the Italian leather sofa Therese had handpicked after her first successful heart sale. Therese thought only of that money and the next identical installment she'd receive when this man's wife turned up for the cadaveric allograft.

Her smile broadened as she recalled learning that term on the same day that she'd killed her adoptive parents. As she watched them slowly suffocate on gas fumes in their own car in a suicide she engineered, Therese had glanced at a newspaper on their dashboard. The headline proclaimed there was a growing epidemic in something called transplant tourism.

When she was watching their last moments of death, she'd wondered if she'd let them have it too easy. After all they'd put her and the other kids through, maybe she should have made them suffer a whole lot more. Maybe she should have taken a knife to them and cut off the source of their evil, taken away their power. But she knew this would be better. This would be clean and easy. The cops wouldn't be looking for anyone, not once they searched their house and found all the photos, the videos, and the "entertainment room." She'd still gotten to enjoy the terror in their eyes as they asphyxiated, as they realized this was the end for them, and that one of the kids they'd shamelessly sold over and over again was responsible for their impending death. Until then, Therese hadn't killed anyone, but she was instantly addicted to the feelings of power and absolute control that night. Looking into someone's eyes as they took their last breath was exhilarating, and she'd been enjoying it ever since.

When she was sure they were dead, she took the paper and sat on the hood of the car to read the article. Organ transplants from dead bodies was a booming business, and she'd quickly decided on a new career path away from the sex industry she'd been forced into and the drug gang she'd ended up in. She'd decided that being in the commodification of human bodies would suit her. It seemed to be a trade far less dangerous than her current occupation and far more lucrative. She'd been proven right, and here she was again about to make a million-dollar deal.

"These are your options again, Mr. Lucas. As I said before, we've taken your wife's blood type and body size and matched her to these five choices."

Therese watched Nat lay out the five information sheets of potential heart donors as casually as if she were offering him swatches of paint colors for his study. Mr. Lucas, if that was even his name, studied them, carefully read the details, and took in the photographs. She and Nat exchanged a weary look as he examined each one, even though he'd seen them before. She couldn't fathom what he was looking for, and she didn't really care. Glad-handing the client had always been one of the most tedious parts of the job. She'd heard too many sob stories to give a shit anymore, not that they had ever bothered her when she'd just started out. None of them came close to matching her history. Most of these people were just rich assholes who believed their lives were more important than the people Therese killed to order. She was the eBay of human organs.

"Could I take these to show my wife? I think she'd like to make the final decision."

"No." This was the kind of vacillation Therese simply couldn't tolerate. Nat had already couriered the documents a week before this, their first and only meeting. He should already know whose life he was happy to end. "If your wife wanted to have the final say, you should've brought her to this meeting. I think that given her One-A status, she's far too ill for that, so you should just make the choice for her. They're all excellent quality donors, and there's not much between them. It's simply a case of which one appeals to you."

He huffed and motioned toward the photographs. "You make it sound simple."

"That's because it *is* simple. You have the money to end your wife's suffering. She's got less than a month left if you don't do something about it, and that's why you're here. We *are* making it simple for you. All you have to do is pay and choose a donor." Therese sighed, beginning to lose patience. "After that, we'll look after everything. You're paying for an all-inclusive transplant package, Mr. Lucas. Natasha mentioned you had concerns about why we were more expensive than our competitors, and this is it. Other organizations don't show you where your product is coming from, and our aftercare facilities are second to none. For the rest of your wife's life, she'll have annual checkups, access to a dedicated doctor, and all the medication she'll need, no questions asked."

He looked down at the donor sheets again and pushed one toward Nat. "That one...please."

The way he stumbled over the word made it clear he wasn't a man used to saying please for anything. That in itself was satisfying. These people were almost as bad as the people her adoptive parents used to sell her to. *Does that make me as bad as them?* She dismissed the thought as quickly as it had intruded. She didn't have to justify anything she did to anyone.

Nat picked up the donor sheet and nodded. "Good choice, Mr. Lucas."

"I wonder though, what happens to the rest of her organs?"

Nat gathered the rest of the donor sheets and glanced at Therese.

"That's not your concern." Her abruptness clearly unsettled him, and she smiled. "Unless you're in the market for lungs too? Are you hoping to preempt a future problem?"

Nat's body shook a little with suppressed laughter. Mr. Lucas pursed his lips. Not only was he averse to saying please, but he also clearly wasn't a fan of being made to look like a fool.

"This is a serious situation. I'm not sure I appreciate your humor, Ms. Hunt."

"You don't have to, Mr. Lucas. You just have to appreciate that I know what I'm doing and that your wife doesn't have to have the heart of an executed Chinese prisoner."

This time, Nat didn't manage to hold her laugh, and Lucas glared at her.

"Natasha will courier the remaining details to you. You'll have to make your own travel arrangements to Cuba, but we'll take care of everything else. After the procedure, you and your wife will be back home in DC within two months."

Nat opened the door to signify it was time for him to leave. Lucas went to shake Therese's hand, and Therese clenched her jaw.

"She doesn't shake hands, Mr. Lucas," Nat said quickly.

Every time someone offered their hand, Therese was assailed with an image of her parents selling her for another debauched night of pain and greeting the buyers with a practical handshake, like the business they were doing could have been conducted on Wall Street. She'd broken every finger in each of her parents' hands after she'd paralyzed them with succinylcholine chloride, the same stuff they'd used on her for the buyers who didn't like it when she fought back. She never had decided which was worse. The ones like that, or the ones who enjoyed it when she fought back, so they could hurt her even more.

By the time Therese had pulled herself from that train of thought, Lucas was gone, and Nat was in front of her, her hands gently holding Therese's face. She knocked them away and the look that flashed briefly across Nat's dark brown eyes was a familiar one. It was accompanied by feelings Therese had neither the time nor the inclination for. Sentimentality was a dangerous thing in her business, and emotional intimacy was something Therese failed to understand the relevance of.

"While I was showing Mr. Lucas out, I took a call from Reed. He thinks Carlos sent out a second package."

"He did what, now?" Therese's anger pushed for attention. It didn't take much to rile her, but any threat to her business made her even quicker to temper. Nat took another step back.

"He's been looking into where he couriered his package from. It turns out Carlos mailed two packages at the same time, on the same account. He's hoping it might be something else, but he wanted to let you know before…before you did anything rash."

"Rash? RASH?" Therese took a deep breath and reined her tone back to the guttural menace she knew Nat loved and hated in equal measure. When she used it this way, Nat wasn't a fan. "Does he mean rash, as in killing someone who might still be withholding some vital information? Does he mean that kind of rash?" Therese took a step closer to Nat, grabbed her wrist, and yanked her forward. She stumbled into Therese, who caught a handful of her long brown hair in her fist. "Who the fuck would he have sent another package to, Natasha?" Therese pulled her close and snarled into her ear, "You knew him better than I did. You even fucked him once." That fact still irritated her. "How did he think?"

"I…I don't know. Maybe to his family or a close friend."

The fear in Nat's voice registered. From a young age, Therese had trained hard to disguise her own, and it was something she heard in the voice of every single person she'd ever killed. It disgusted her. But professionally and sexually, Nat had proven her worth time and again. Therese didn't want to kill her if it could be avoided.

She released Nat and seized the suitcase as she walked away. "Make sure Reed finds out. Or tell him he'll be joining Carlos."

Chapter Seven

Madison set her Zoom H6 in the center of the perfectly dressed table in the fancy restaurant Paige had chosen and sat facing the door to await the arrival of her interviewee, Elodie Fontaine. She'd been unsettled since returning from Russia, as she often was when she came home after a challenging assignment. When she'd experienced it early on in her career, she'd wanted to believe it was just the disparity between the chaos of the worlds she briefly inhabited and the relative calm of her apartment. She soon came to realize it was the emotional strain getting to her. She'd cultivated a hard, ice queen reputation and worked hard to maintain it. In a profession where women were outnumbered by men two to one, Madison didn't want to be seen as weak or emotional, and so she never let it show. As far as everyone around her knew, she was detached from the horrors they reported on, and it made her a better journalist because of it.

She touched the scar just below her right collarbone. The pain of a gunshot wound had been intense, but she hadn't wept or screamed. Her father had impressed upon her that, no matter the physical or emotional agony, crying was a weakness. And he gave her plenty of opportunity to perfect his ethos.

Madison took a deep breath and tried to push the unpleasant thoughts away. Her therapist kept telling her to be present and available in the moment, rather than residing in her head where her demons were disturbingly willing companions. The principle was solid. The follow-through was thus far proving impossible, but for the most part, people were too self-involved to realize. Except partners. They noticed, which was why Madison had taken a giant step back from relationships.

Focus. She didn't want to get caught up in the black tar today. She was looking forward to meeting Elodie and discovering who she was beneath the movie star façade. As if on cue, an ostentatious sports car pulled up outside the restaurant. Madison had no idea what make or model since cars didn't concern her. It was matte black and probably cost more to insure than her own car cost to buy. A sturdy pickup truck came in close behind. What Madison assumed to be Elodie's bodyguards were out and by her car to help her out. She tipped down her sunglasses and looked into the restaurant. She didn't disappoint. She was just as beautiful in the flesh as she was on screen. Madison smiled. A few days ago, she'd been interviewing some of the ugliest people in the world on the inside. Today, she was interviewing the sexiest woman on the planet. She didn't get many days like these, where the emotional strain of her chosen profession was negligible.

Madison tentatively raised her hand to wave and catch Elodie's attention, but saw the host sidle up to her and the two striking female bodyguards. He showed them to Madison's table, and she started to rise from her seat to greet her.

"Don't stand on my behalf. I'm not royalty."

Elodie smiled, and Madison could see how hundreds of women had fallen into her bed. Her smile was open and engaging, sexy and inviting.

"You *are* royalty to us, Ms. Fontaine."

Madison tried not to visually react to the host's toadying remark. One of her bodyguards was less subtle; she curled her lip and raised her eyebrows almost high enough to touch the bangs of her hair. They waited until Elodie was seated before they moved to the table behind and ordered drinks.

Elodie ordered an iced chai latte and waited for the waiter to go before she offered her hand to Madison. "It's really nice to meet you. I'm a big fan of your words."

Madison was impressed by her firm handshake and flattered by the compliment. "Thank you. Unsurprisingly, I like your work too."

"I'm glad to hear that. All interviewers say it, but your pedigree means I actually believe you."

Elodie laughed gently, and Madison noted how her green eyes sparkled mischievously. She shifted the mics on her digital recorder so that one pointed toward each of them. "I'll press record, and we'll talk as if we were having a regular conversation. I'll make some notes too, so please ignore that. Does that sound okay?"

"Of course, that's fine."

The waiter returned and placed Elodie's drink on the table. Madison saw him try to catch Elodie's eye, but she simply offered him an empty trademark smile. The difference between that one and the one she'd given to Madison was glaring.

"What I'd really like to do with this interview is show the world the Elodie Fontaine that's not quite as well publicized as your movie persona."

Elodie laughed, and Madison acknowledged she was beginning to find it infectious. She had an easy humor and smiled like a woman who didn't care about wrinkles and laughter lines.

"And what do you mean by that?" Elodie asked, sounding a little indignant.

Madison smiled, hoping that Elodie wasn't serious. "There's a lot of material out there about you. Big talk show interviews, *many* kiss-and-tell stories." Madison instantly regretted her emphasis but continued without hesitation. "There are glossy magazine shoots and countless movie interviews. But there's a serious lack of in-depth coverage about your work around human trafficking. Even though you've been doing it for a while now, it's as if no one's really taking it seriously."

"You've nailed exactly how it is. My movies and my face sell magazines and move merchandise. But no one wants to know the uncomfortable truth about what really goes on in the States in terms of human trafficking. I think that's why my work in this area hasn't received much coverage. And that's why I really wanted to do *this* interview with *you*. I know that you'll do it justice."

Heat rose up Madison's spine. She hadn't expected Elodie to be familiar with her work, let alone be so full of praise for it. "I'll certainly try my best to help you change that. Shall we begin?"

"Go for it."

Elodie took a sip of her drink and licked her lips. Madison focused on staying professional despite the unassailable beauty sitting opposite her. "I'd like to start with your work with the government's Trafficking in Persons office. Tell me about what you do."

"My main focus is helping to build partnerships with NGOs, non-government organizations, and to try to help them with service provision for survivors. An important part of it is encouraging information sharing. If survivors and NGOs shared the information they have on the trafficking gangs, the law enforcement agencies would be able to work more effectively to shut them down. I'm also involved in trying to help educate people to recognize potential trafficking victims in their communities."

Elodie's passion for her work became clearer to Madison, but she had to wonder how one celebrity could make a difference to an international problem. "Tell me about recognizing those signs. What are the indicators that people should look out for in their neighborhood?"

"It's amazing what you miss if you're not really paying attention. There are simple things such as bars on the windows or barbed wire around the house, for example. Can your new neighbor come and go as they please, or do they have to ask permission from someone else in the house? Are they familiar with the rest of the community, or do they keep themselves separate? Are they able to have a conversation with you and look you in the eye? Do you see a lot of strangers visiting the house at all times of the day and night?" Elodie looked thoughtful for a moment. "It's strange that we're developing more and more ways to communicate, and yet we communicate less with those in closest proximity to us."

Madison nodded. "You're so right. So many of us seem to have our phones melded to our hands and never look up to see what's right in front of us. Who knows what interactions we miss out on?"

"Exactly. The instant messages, cellphones, social networking. People contact you from thousands of miles away and expect to connect with you immediately. If you don't answer the phone, they call back again and again. It doesn't seem to occur to them that you might be having a conversation with someone else who's actually in the same room with you. Like right now, there's nothing more important to me than this interview."

Madison stayed silent for a second. Elodie's rant had come from nowhere, but it was clearly something she felt passionate about. "Remind me never to call you more than once."

"I'd always answer if you were calling."

Elodie's words hung in the air, but Madison dismissed the flirtation and tried hard to ignore how hypnotizing her eyes and smile were. *Goddamn, you are gorgeous.* Madison would have to think of an excuse when the interview was over to call her. *Focus. I'm a professional, not a starstruck fan.*

"I'm really sorry to interrupt, but could I have your autograph? I'm such a huge fan! I love your movies! You're so fantastic!"

The intrusion startled Madison from her reverie.

"Thank you," Elodie said without missing a beat. "You're very kind."

One of Elodie's bodyguards quickly placed herself between Elodie and her fangirl.

"How could I not? You're so real no matter what you play. You're like the acting, speaking version of a chameleon."

Madison sighed. Fangirl ended every sentence with an almost visible exclamation mark.

Elodie laughed a little. "I'm sure you mean that as a compliment?"

"Of course! I just can't believe I'm meeting you. My sister is going to be soooo jealous. Would you sign…me?"

Elodie looked faintly amused. "Do you have a pen?"

"Of course!" Fangirl thrust a black Sharpie forward for Elodie and lifted her top to reveal a white bra straining to do its job.

"Your bra?" Madison laughed at what she supposed must be a usual request, given Elodie didn't seem fazed by it at all. Fangirl eyed Madison dismissively before returning her attention to Elodie. Fangirl sighed with obvious delight as Elodie signed her left breast. She handed the pen back.

"I'll never wash this again!"

The bodyguard took Fangirl by the shoulders and turned her away, gently but firmly.

Elodie looked back at Madison, her gaze probing. "I'm sorry about that."

Madison shrugged. "There's no need to apologize to me. But I don't know how you cope with your privacy being invaded constantly. It's like people think you're public property."

Elodie looked rueful. "It goes with the territory. I've put myself out there and cultivated a certain image."

"But even the sexiest woman on the planet is entitled to a private life."

A knowing little smile played on Elodie's lips. "You noticed?"

"It's hard not to." Madison never had been any good at flirting, though there was no way Elodie would be interested in her. There was really no need to worry about her lack of game. "Anyway, let's get back to the interview," Madison said.

Elodie smiled. "Would you be able to put the details for the national hotline at the end of the article?"

"I'm sure that'll be no problem. So was there a specific incident in your life that made you decide to use your celebrity to raise awareness of what's been labeled 'modern slavery?'"

"My awareness of the issue was really heightened when I was filming in Cuba for *Strapped.* I'd naively thought it was only an issue in other countries. I had no knowledge whatsoever that it was happening in the U.S. We're busy trying to tell China, India, and Mexico how to treat their people, but right here on American soil, people are being exploited for the financial gain of organized gangs. California's proximity to Mexico's border, our ports and airports, and our immigrant population, all make it too easy for those gangs to…to just *sell people.*"

Madison noticed something pass across Elodie's eyes and decided it was sadness. She clearly had a lot of empathy and compassion for human suffering. When she was preparing for the interview, Madison had a niggling fear that Elodie's volunteer work was simply a ruse to garner her more publicity to make her movies more successful. Madison liked to have her instincts proven correct, but this was one instance where she was strangely glad for them to fail. "Does your time in the military inform your work?"

"If you don't mind, I'd rather we didn't touch on that."

Elodie straightened her previously relaxed posture, and Madison could almost see her shut down. Elodie had never publicly spoken of her military service, and Madison wanted to know why. She'd push later. "I'll put some facts and figures in here about the extent of the problem in the States. If there's anything you can tell me or send me that I might not find out through my own research, that'd be really helpful. From what I've already been looking at, I think the stats will be shocking for some of your followers."

Elodie smiled disarmingly, and her bright white, perfect teeth made Madison wish she'd stayed in braces a little longer as a child.

"Followers? You make me sound like a preacher."

Madison held up her hands in apology. "I didn't mean it that way. Fans, if you prefer, though I did see that you were at number five and have over one hundred million fans on Instagram." Heat fired up her spine at the admission of her stalker-like behavior. Elodie flashed a killer smile that made her a little twitchy, and Madison was unable to hold her intense gaze.

"I'm told I'm the only actor in the top twenty. It seems egotistical to know that, but Paige, my agent, likes to keep me informed of these things."

Elodie's cheeks flushed a little, but Madison didn't think it could possibly be embarrassment. "Probably because your success means more money for her." She was glad to see Elodie nod. For all she knew, her agent might also be her best friend from high school, and she could've taken offense. "Singers seem to dominate that particular social network. It might be something to do with music being a more accessible medium than movies." Madison stopped herself from rambling off-topic and looked to Elodie to respond to her original point.

"I'd never thought of it that way. Maybe I should give up acting and become a singer if it'll raise the profile of my humanitarian work."

She laughed that easy laugh again. Elodie was so entirely different from her usual interviewee. She seemed so relaxed and at peace with herself. Her genuineness almost had Madison relaxed too. Almost.

"Well, my followers who'll be surprised are the people I'm trying to reach. Regular readers of this publication are already conscious of the issue. It's inevitable that some people will pick it up simply because I'm in it, but that's what me using my celebrity to raise awareness is all about. I have to reach the people who need educating about issues this close to home, instead of letting them live in a fantasy that America is the greatest country on earth and believing we don't have a care in the world."

"Do you think it's a problem of ignorance or unwillingness to consider that slavery could be happening in our country again?"

"That's a tough question to answer without causing offense to someone, somewhere."

Madison felt herself being drawn in as Elodie continued to speak. Not only was she incredibly beautiful and a brilliant actress, but she also had a hint of soft vulnerability Madison hadn't picked up on in previous interviews or appearances. She was intrigued and wanted to know more. She had no illusions that someone like Elodie might find her even remotely attractive, and Madison wasn't looking for a relationship anyway. But she'd very much be interested in a new friend.

Almost two hours later, Madison was sure she'd gotten enough for the detailed article she wanted. She also managed to get something she wasn't expecting: an open invitation to Elodie's library, which apparently housed several million dollars of first edition and rare books. It was an invite she couldn't wait to take up. "That's a perfect place to end, Elodie. Thank you so much for your time and your honesty." Madison had pressed on particularly sensitive topics for honest answers, and Elodie had been open, and even happy, to respond. The only topic Madison had been unable to get Elodie to elaborate on was her military service, which made it even more intriguing.

"Strangely enough, I didn't plan on being quite that honest and forthright."

Madison thought she saw a flash of vulnerability behind Elodie's sparkling eyes, but it was gone almost as quickly.

"Would you…stay for lunch with me?"

Madison frowned then dismissed Elodie's hesitation. "Thanks, but I can't. I have to follow up a potential whistleblowing on an organ trafficking organization. I had a meeting scheduled yesterday, but the informant didn't show up. I'm a little worried about him."

"Let me know if you need any help. It might be that my connections in the TIP office could come in useful for you."

Madison placed her Zoom in her shoulder bag and stood. "Thanks, but if the information this guy is promising turns out to be true, I might have to be careful who I trust."

Elodie touched Madison's hand. Static electricity made them both jump.

"Be careful, Madison. Those gangs don't mess around, and they usually have no regard for people who get in the way of their business."

She sounded like she was speaking from experience. That would have to be a topic for their next conversation. Her concern seemed gentle and honest, and a buzz of excitement ran through Madison. It was unusual to meet someone she had so much in common with, and they'd barely scratched the surface. Elodie was the kind of person she could envision having conversations that started at lunch and didn't end until way past midnight. She hadn't been this interested in a friend for a long time. "I appreciate that, thank you. I'll definitely call you for the library tour."

"I'm already looking forward to it."

"Me too." Madison walked away and had to work hard to control the overwhelming urge to look back repeatedly. She spotted Fangirl at a table close by and ignored the unpleasant look she threw Madison's way. There was nothing to be jealous of. She'd just been doing her job, and Elodie had gotten nowhere near *her* bra, though Madison would have to be practically dead not to find Elodie attractive. Still, there was a possibility of a new friendship, and God knows, Madison was lacking in that department. And if she were honest with herself, a friendship was about all she had the emotional capacity for right now. And who wouldn't want to hang out with one of Hollywood's most influential women?

Chapter Eight

Therese reclined, eyes closed, body completely relaxed, and inhaled deeply. She let the smoke sit in her mouth and seep down to her lungs, warming to the point of burning. She exhaled slowly, allowing the drug to course through her nostrils. The woman who sat astride her, naked but for a flimsy khaki tank top and the leather strap that secured her wrists behind her back, sucked in Therese's exhaled fumes. Linked by the dark gray silicone dildo strapped around Therese's hips, the pace of their sex was nonchalant and casual. The flickering flame of the nearby open fire cast a sensual light on their bodies, which, when Therese opened her eyes, she could fully appreciate. She slipped her free hand around the tied woman's body and pulled at the leather cord. The woman's chest tautened, and her eyes opened wide as her breath escaped her body in the way it only does during heightened pleasure.

"Therese."

"Shh," Therese said. "Not a word, Casheen." She flipped the joint away, wrapped her fingers around Casheen's slender neck, and squeezed softly. Another breath escaped, and Therese closed her teeth on Casheen's bottom lip, forbidding her to emit any more words. Her hips bucked against Therese as she forced her back, her body arching until her long, blond hair skimmed the wooden deck. Therese knew her lover well enough that in this position, with blood rushing to Casheen's head and her complete lack of control, her orgasm was imminent. She quickened her rhythm a little and could feel Casheen gripping onto the silicone shaft within her. Therese lifted her back up by her tank top, and their mouths clamped together as Casheen screamed her release.

Just at that most perfect moment, Nat wandered out onto the deck. Therese saw her nostrils flare. It would have been imperceptible to anyone else, but it was the same reaction she'd seen many times before, one that she did whether she was angry or horny.

"Peterson called to finalize some arrangements. He wants to get moving."

Nat's all-business tone didn't fool Therese. Casheen shifted slightly on the cock, and Therese placed her hands on her hips and pressed her down firmly. She expressed her requirement for Casheen to stay still with a look. "Tell me more," she said to Nat.

"Surely she shouldn't be hearing this."

Nat's disgust for Casheen was less than subtle. Casheen didn't care for Nat either. They'd always had a healthy dislike for each other borne from competition for Therese's attentions. She smiled and traced a casual line with her fingers from Casheen's neck, down between her breasts and to her exposed pussy. She pressed down on her clit, and her smile broadened when Casheen moaned and ground down on her cock.

"Casheen knows if she repeats a word of what she hears when she's around me, I'll keep her alive while I peel every inch of skin from her body with a serrated carving knife. So, go ahead. What did he have to say?"

"He says he's close to securing you San Nicolas. A band of Luiseño people claimed cultural affiliation to the tribe that was there until 1835, so they've halted the archeological digging. The Navy has decided to give it back to them rather than deal with another Native American embarrassment. The tribe are looking to make a quick buck as long as the new owner signs a contract not to excavate any further, so he's negotiated a price of five million. He needs to know if you're willing to pay that since it's slightly more than your original budget. If you are, he can have the sale finalized this week."

"Thanks for the political history lesson." Therese could see Nat wanted desperately to avert her eyes, but she knew full well that Therese demanded eye contact when she spoke to anyone. She didn't trust people who couldn't hold her gaze. She didn't trust people, period. "Tell him to go ahead. Transfer the money to his account now."

Casheen moved in slow circles on Therese's lap, but her attention had already switched to Nat. She was even sexier when she was made. "Since you're here." Therese beckoned Nat to come closer.

Nat's nostrils flared again as she approached them. When she was within reach, Therese pulled at her leather jacket and brought her down to kiss her. It was hard and aggressive, and Therese could feel her resentment. Nat's teeth bit down on her lip. If they were alone, it would have been foreplay. Given the company, Therese knew it was carefully measured antipathy. "Careful, girl." Therese's hand slipped from Nat's jacket onto her crotch, and she squeezed hard. "Open your jeans."

Nat's dark brown eyes flamed. It was a look Therese always enjoyed provoking. Saying nothing, she undid her belt and unbuttoned her jeans. Therese pushed her hand into Nat's jeans and slipped two fingers inside her. Despite her evident fury at being used at the same time as a rival, she still let out a throaty breath of arousal as Therese began to fuck her.

"When you've moved the money across and the deal's done, I want you to get Dawkes over there right away. I want the refurbishment started as soon as possible." Therese pushed in harder. "Do you understand?"

"Yes," Nat whispered.

"Yes, what?"

Nat grasped Therese's wrist as if to stop her, but Therese just jammed her fingers in brutally. Casheen was oblivious. She'd fallen back, and her hands were scratching at the deck as Therese thrust into her, her body arched with the flexibility of a Cirque du Soleil contortionist, with Therese's hand pushing down on her stomach. Therese pushed harder, and Nat released her wrist. "Yes, what?" There was no choice for her.

Nat exhaled deeply. "Yes, I understand."

Satisfied, Therese continued to fuck both women, intrigued to see if she could get both to come at the same time. Nat wrapped her fingers in Therese's hair. Therese synchronized the rhythm of her hips and hand and concentrated purely on how she felt inside them. It was during sex when she was at her most tumultuous, as beautifully chaotic as when she was killing or mutilating someone. Violence and sex were her two favorite pastimes.

She quickened her pace in response to the increasing volume of their moans. Nat teased Therese's nipple in the way she knew would help her orgasm. That, combined with the cock base pressing on her clit, drove her straight there. Nat was pushing her luck, trying to get Therese to come before they did, and she knew it. It was a question of control, which one of them had the strength of will to hold their release. Therese never lost this game, and she fucked her even harder. Nat surrendered, and she eased up, still grasping Therese's breast but no longer competing for supremacy.

Casheen pulled back up to ride Therese's cock hard and deep. She slid her hand down Nat's jeans and squeezed her ass. Nat clutched a handful of Casheen's long hair and kissed her, sucked and bit her tongue. Therese could see what she was doing, fucking her mouth, angry at her intrusion, but she allowed it. Casheen cried out as she came again, and Nat quickly followed, howling her orgasm like a banshee. Therese seized Nat by the hair and crushed her mouth to Nat's. She held on to her own orgasm a few moments longer before she bucked wildly and moaned into Nat's mouth. She closed her eyes and focused on the aftershock pulsating through her body, before pushing Casheen off her cock and pulling her fingers from Nat.

"You can go now."

Casheen looked wounded and wanting but gathered her clothes from the deck and left quietly. Nat smirked as she straightened her clothes.

"Have you heard anything from Reed?" Therese asked.

"I passed your message on. He knows what's at stake."

Therese bristled. "Don't give me attitude, Natasha. Even you're not irreplaceable."

Nat held her stare for a moment before looking at the floor. "I'm sorry. It's just…you know I don't—"

"*I* don't have the time or patience for your jealousies, you know that. Don't bring that bullshit to me. How close is he to identifying who the second package went to?"

"He says he had to back off for a little while. His supervisor was asking questions. Apparently, the package has had a little world tour, but he thinks it ended up in L.A. He's pretty certain he'll know with who by the end of the week."

"I don't need this, not when I'm so close to setting up the US clinic."

"We'll sort it out, Therese. I promise."

Therese clenched her jaw. "Don't make promises your talents may not be able to cash. It could be bad for your health." She looked down at her cock and the cum Cash had left all over it. "Right now, you can use your talents to clean me up. On your knees."

Nat grinned. Normal service had been resumed now that Casheen had gone. She knelt down and took Therese in her mouth.

Therese sighed deeply and ran her hand through Nat's hair. "Damn, you're good at this. Taking you off the streets was one of the best moves I ever made."

Nat looked up, her eyes watering as she held her gag reflex. Therese could feel her love. She just had no use for it.

Chapter Nine

When she left Elodie in the restaurant, Madison drove to the LAPD to chat with one of her contacts, Ash, in the hope that he'd be able to shed some light on Carlos Santiago. Best-case scenario was that he'd been arrested and was locked away somewhere. Unfortunately, she couldn't dismiss the very real possibility that Carlos had been discovered putting together the information Madison had asked for.

She waited by the roach coach outside the station, and it hadn't taken long before she'd given in and bought a tempting veggie burrito. Ash emerged from the building as she swallowed the last bite.

"Thanks for taking some time for me, Ash. I appreciate it."

"Anytime, Madison."

Madison smiled, glad that there was at least one remaining friendly face at the LAPD. The exposé she'd written on the misogyny rife in the department several years ago still meant she wasn't welcome inside the building. "Is it good news or bad?" She pointed at the manila folder he was holding.

"We should sit. Let me grab something to eat." He pointed to the dribble of green hot sauce that had escaped the confines of her tortilla. "I can see you've already eaten."

As Madison went to the nearest table, she avoided the blatant glares of the other officers and concentrated on the takeout coffee cup as if it were the most interesting thing in the world. She hated the confrontation her words invited. When challenging prejudices and fast-held beliefs, it was unavoidable, but she avoided engaging with the aftermath as much as possible. Madison had way too much aggressive history in her family to cope with it in her adult life. The moment someone raised their voice, her stomach dropped, and her entire body became tense. She'd prepared herself for battle so many times as a child that her capacity for it now was long diminished.

Ash dropped his folder onto the metal table, and she jumped a little.

"Nervous much? Too many bullets whizzed past your head in Afghanistan?" He shoved a taco into his mouth before he'd even sat.

"If only they'd just gone past my head." Madison reached under her tank strap to the spot just below her collarbone where the bullet had entered her body. It was barely half an inch above her body armor. "So should I be worried about Carlos or not?"

Ash tapped his finger on the folder. "Take a look. I'm figuring you're still not squeamish."

Madison took a deep breath. It was too late to fear the worst. Ash's flair for the dramatic simply confirmed her fears. She flipped open the folder and was faced with a close-up of a charred face. Flicking through the rest of the photographs simply provided more detail of two bodies, burned beyond recognition. She assumed one was Carlos. "Who's the other body?"

"His dad."

Madison raised her eyebrows, hoping for Ash to expand.

He wiped the corner of his mouth with a napkin, closed the folder, and leaned in closer. "What's your interest in this one, Mads?"

"He contacted me two weeks ago before I left for the Russian assignment. He said he was involved with one of the largest organ trafficking organizations in the country, and he wanted to provide me with information to close them down."

"An attack of conscience, huh?"

"Maybe. I asked him to get me some concrete evidence, details of those involved, photos, recent organ transactions, that kind of thing, and we agreed to meet yesterday. He didn't show. Now I know why."

Ash tilted his head slightly. "You can't blame yourself for this. Santiago was a bad man, and he didn't get out clean like he'd hoped."

I think I can safely blame myself. "I know that. The cliché about dying by the sword couldn't be more appropriate." The particularly graphic shot of Carlos's father and his wide-open throat pushed into her head. "Although I don't know what his father was doing there. Is there any evidence to suggest he was involved somehow?"

"No, he didn't have to have anything to do with it. These people, these gangs…if you cross them, they take out your whole family. There's no mercy."

"Do you have any leads on who he was working for?"

"Nothing solid, and certainly nothing we can act on. Now that you've said he was going to blow the whistle on an organ trafficking racket, it could be the gang we're calling the Hunters. They're pretty prolific and their leader is particularly vicious. The details are sketchy, but there's rumor that their leader is a woman, and she likes to skin people alive. It wouldn't be a stretch to connect her with this. I don't know that I believe it though. I think it's just smoke and mirrors to keep us off the scent."

Madison had already been hoping the Santiago lead would be her next big assignment, but with the added possibility that this gang could be led by a woman, it made the story even more appealing. She could see the front cover of *Time* magazine already. No doubt there'd be some notional comparison to Aileen Wuornos, still America's most notorious female serial killer after over thirty years. There was something about the double standard of how female murderers were treated compared to their male counterparts that irritated Madison. As if all women were supposed to be sensitive, compassionate, and incapable of such rage and aggression. And despite Ash's insistence that she wasn't to blame for Santiago's death, it was added motivation to investigate and bring the gang down.

"I've seen that look before, Madison. Surely you can't investigate this cold?"

"It wouldn't be cold." She smiled and tapped the folder on the table. "I've got you." Madison hoped she was convincing enough to make Ash see that he absolutely had to help her and feed her any and all information on this gang.

He shook his head. "I don't know about that. You're not exactly a favorite around this place." He glanced sideways toward some of his colleagues who'd been staring and blatantly gossiping about her throughout their conversation.

"We'd be helping each other out, Ash. If I could find out who this mysterious gang leader was *and* bring you enough evidence to take them down, we'd both win." She could see him contemplating the enticing potential of putting an end to the "Hunters."

"You'd need to be careful and more so than you usually are. I don't want to be pulling your charred corpse from your car."

Madison shook her head. "I'm not green, Ash. I don't take unnecessary risks. You might need to keep it quiet though. Santiago mentioned they had connections in the FBI, and it's not like the LAPD has the best reputation when it comes to corruption."

He mock-punched Madison on the shoulder. "Hey, some of my best friends are corrupt officers."

Ash's joke was lost in the darker, unmissable undertone beneath his words.

"Lucky for me, you're one of the good guys."

He leaned in a little closer and said quietly, "Some days it feels like there's not many of us left."

"Hang in there, Ash. The last thing this place needs is to lose great cops like you."

He smiled and nodded slowly. "Thanks, Mads. That means a lot coming from you. How is your dad?"

Madison's jaw tightened at the mention of her father, the decorated LAPD officer who was a legend here. He'd said her exposé was like a betrayal, but it was from him that she first learned the meaning of misogyny and how it could manifest. "He's fine. Enjoying retirement in Florida like a regular cliché." She had no idea how he was; she hadn't spoken to him for a long, long time. He'd apologized for what he put her through as a child, using the age-old excuses of "that's all I knew" and "that's how I was brought up too," but they didn't ring true so she chose to distance herself from a past that impacted far more on her present than she wished it would.

"Next time you speak to him, tell him I said hi. We could do with a few more of his kind around here."

"Of course." *Absolutely not.* She picked up her iPhone, flipped open Ash's folder again, and began to take photos. "Where did this happen?"

"It was in the back of the old garment factory in the South Figueroa Corridor. It was reclaimed by the city for development plans a while back, so it was empty. The perfect place for a sadistic barbecue."

She made a note of the location on her phone.

"If you have to go out there, don't go alone."

"It can't be that bad in the middle of the day, surely?" She pushed her phone into her bag, desperate to get going.

He shook his head, clearly frustrated. He'd known Madison a long time, and she thought he knew her better. She followed her leads wherever she needed to, and a dangerous neighborhood wasn't going to stop her. And besides, she was already engrossed with the possibilities of the investigation. She thought of the 2014 Pulitzer for Explanatory Journalism finalist and his exposé on a Mexican drug cartel. Something like this had the potential to win her a second accolade. And maybe it would prove the first one wasn't just due to Geva's involvement, another thing her therapist wanted her to recognize.

She pushed her chair back and stood. "Thanks, Ash. If you come across anything that might be useful, give me a call."

"I will. Just promise me you'll be careful. I don't know anywhere near enough about this gang as I'd like."

"Even more reason for me to follow it through." And she wasn't about to let Carlos's death be for nothing.

Chapter Ten

"What do you want?" Elodie looked across the table to Brad for his line.

"Is it done?" His Russian accent was damn near perfect.

"Yes." Elodie looked away.

"You did it precisely as instructed, yes?"

She was supposed to have murdered his rival after luring him to bed with another woman for a torrid threesome. She closed her eyes and shuddered at the thought. "Yes."

"How did he take it?"

"Why?"

"Do not answer a question with another, Elya. Answer me, how did he take it?"

Elodie smirked. "Like any other man, pitiful and weak."

Brad shook his head. "Do not push me, Elya. You are not indispensable either, yes?"

Elodie smiled and made her contempt obvious. "That's what I'm counting on."

"You are still very useful to me. Do not wish for a quick ending to all of this." Brad's laugh had a believably cruel edge.

Elodie sighed and drew on the emotional strain of the forced separation of mother and daughter. "I am no longer capable of that. I stopped wishing years ago when it became clear to me your word means nothing."

"And that's where I slap you," Brad said, dropping his accent and motioning to strike Elodie. "You may not think anything of your own life, but do not forget the life I hold in my other hand."

Al Fox jumped up from his seat and smacked the shoulder of his assistant director. "That was gold, people, absolute gold. I hope you extras are all watching this master class in magic."

Elodie smiled. "You flatter us, Al."

"Let him. Some of us need that kind of attention to get our best work."

Brad laughed. "Are you sure you want me to slap you for real? That'll be weird. I've never hit anyone before."

"What can I say? I like realism in a movie."

"I hope your last film didn't have too much realism in it," Lela Darvis, the actress playing Kiana, said.

She'd been sitting beside Brad, but she got up and came over to Elodie, close enough for her to smell Lela's perfume. Elodie clenched her jaw. "What do you think?"

"I hope you had a body double." Lela winked at Brad as he and Al walked away to attack the craft services table.

"Did you watch it?" Elodie asked.

"Maybe."

"Do you really think I need a body double?" Elodie resented any implication she wasn't in good enough shape or brave enough to show whatever was needed on set.

"I didn't say you needed a body double. I'm just hoping it was."

"Well, *did* you watch it?"

"Yeah, I watched it. Everyone's watched it. You had to if you wanted to be part of any conversation once it was released. It was all anyone was talking about."

"So do you think I used a body double?"

"I don't know. It's been a while. I didn't memorize your *every* contour." Lela smiled seductively. "But I think it was you."

Elodie winked. "It was me. If my name's on a movie, it's all me in the film." Elodie played along and didn't show her irritation.

"Relax, I was only kidding."

Elodie found Lela's attempt to placate her even more annoying.

"I read your interview with Madison Ford. You're really putting your heart and soul into that work."

Elodie was glad of the change of subject, and the mention of Madison's name made her smile. She was bummed Madison hadn't stayed for lunch, and she'd spent the rest of the day berating herself for the "I'm already looking forward to it" line. It was too cheesy, and Elodie didn't want Madison to think she was coming on to her. Not that she wouldn't if Madison seemed open to it, but there was something closed off about her that made Elodie think that wasn't an option.

"It's important to me. I saw a lot of ugliness in Afghanistan, and I didn't get to do anything about it other than shoot some terrorists from a mile away."

A nearby runner paused abruptly, probably in anticipation of some juicy gossip to peddle. Elodie wasn't comfortable sharing much of the details of her time in the Marine Corps. She was proud she'd served, but it was a part of her history she didn't like to talk about with civilians.

"Mr. Fox wanted me to let you know he'll be back shortly to continue the reading, Ms. Fontaine." The plain-looking runner had sidled up to them to deliver the message, rather than deliver it from a distance she couldn't hear anything.

"Thanks, Roxy." Elodie waited for the runner to slink off before turning back to Lela.

"Maybe you should get Madison to write one of her long features on you and your time in the army. She's a great writer, and she's easy on the eye if you like bigger girls. Not that you've ever limited yourself to a type."

"I'm done with that life, and there's nothing wrong with a fuller figure."

Lela *was* right about Elodie not having a type. Almost every woman had something appealing about them, even if the attraction was fleeting.

Lela raised her eyebrows. "Ah, so you *do* like her."

"What's not to like? She's blond, has amazing blue eyes, an off-the-scale intellect, and a Marilyn Monroe figure." Elodie grinned as she recalled seeing Madison for the first time at the restaurant. Every part of her had liked every part of Madison.

Lela punched her lightly on the shoulder. "Earth to Elodie. No prizes for guessing where you went. Are you seeing her again?"

"Maybe. We didn't make plans. She's working on a new investigation into an organ trafficking gang, so she may have not time."

"No time for Elodie Fontaine? Surely that can't be the case. Have you finally found someone immune to your charms?"

Elodie laughed. "That's such a clichéd phrase, Lela, even for you. I don't expect every woman to fall into my arms."

"You might not, but the rest of the world does."

"Can we just drop it and concentrate on this?"

Lela shrugged. "Sure. Maybe when we start filming, I could drop by your trailer at night?"

Elodie knew she didn't mean so they could rehearse lines. She thought of Madison but didn't really know why. They were getting to know each other and were just friends. Besides, movie-work sex meant nothing to her or other actors. It was just an easy and enjoyable way of taking the edge off after a long day of filming. She delivered a typical sex-dripping trademark Elodie Fontaine smile. "I guess you'll want to practice our sex scene."

"You did say you like realism in a movie."

The look in Lela's eyes was clearly an attempt to tease Elodie into offering to take her home and think nothing of blowing off the rest of the read-through. "Indeed I do."

"We probably shouldn't wait until the rehearsals begin. We could get a head start, in the name of method acting."

Elodie nodded. "Sure. Is tonight too early?"

"We could grab some food after this and head to my place."

Lela parted her legs a little so her thigh touched Elodie's hand. She responded with a gentle caress but stopped just short of the hem of Lela's skirt.

"That sounds great. I just need to make a call to make sure I'm free for the rest of the day." Elodie left the room and quickly found an unlocked and vacant office. She closed the door behind her and settled into the basic office chair as she dialed Madison.

"Hello, this is Madison."

"Hey, it's Elodie." *I have no idea why I'm calling you.* "Are you free tonight for your library tour?" She pinched the bridge of her nose. A library tour or no strings sex? What had possessed her to make this call?

"I would've loved to, but I've just arranged to meet the editor of *Time* magazine to discuss an organ trafficking feature."

"Is that something to do with the whistleblower who didn't show to your meeting?"

"Yeah. He was found dead in his car in South Figueroa."

"Jesus." Elodie rubbed the back of her neck. This was getting serious fast. Maybe her old buddy Ice would know something. They lived in such different worlds since they'd served together in Afghanistan and hadn't connected in a while. It was long overdue. "Doesn't that make your investigation impossible?"

"It makes it harder but not impossible."

There was a long pause. "Are you still there?"

"I am. It's just…I feel responsible for his death which makes it impossible for me *not* to investigate."

"Why do you feel that way?" Elodie asked. "Was it his gang that killed him?"

"The police think so, and it wasn't just him. They killed his father too. I'd asked him to get some information for me: details of previous clients, financial dealings, photographs of the gang. I think he might've been discovered trying to pull those things together, and that's why he was murdered. That makes it my fault."

Elodie could feel Madison's sadness almost as strongly as if she were in the room beside her. "You can't know that. His gang may have already known he was trying to get out, and no one gets out of these organized gangs alive. Do the police have any leads?"

"They've got nothing. As far as they're concerned, it's one more scumbag off the streets. I've got a friend there who's going to find out what he can, but they don't even know the leader. They don't know their name, what they look like, or if they're male or female."

"Would you let me help? I can make some inquiries at TIP, and I've got a good friend in the CIA who might know more or could find out. If no one else knows anything about this gang, I'd bet a million dollars she'll know all about it."

There was another long pause.

"Do you trust her? My contact said they had friends in the FBI keeping them off the radar."

Elodie nodded. Ice was chosen family; she'd trust her with anything and everything. "I trust her with my life. And if the CIA wants to know something, they don't let anyone stop them, least of all the FBI."

"Okay, if you don't mind, that sounds great. Maybe we could talk about it some more after my library tour?"

"Sure. Are you free tomorrow evening?"

"I am."

"Let me send my driver to pick you up at six. We can have something to eat." Elodie stopped, conscious she was dictating the evening. "If you want. Obviously, you don't have to."

"No. That sounds nice, but I'd rather drive myself. I don't want to be tempted to drink too much."

Elodie wasn't sure how to take Madison's words but decided not to ask. "No problem. I'll text you the directions."

"Excellent. See you tomorrow."

Thankfully, Madison ended the call before Elodie could say she was looking forward to it. She didn't want to make the same mistake twice. She left the office and went back to the reading room to find Lela back in her own seat. She turned around, her look questioning.

"I'm free," Elodie said, aware that she was strangely looking forward to tomorrow evening with Madison far more than tonight's promise of sex, which she had a niggling feeling she'd back out of. Christ, what was happening?

Chapter Eleven

"This is too much, Elodie. I can't accept it." Madison held a Patek Phillipe watch in her hand. It was a beautiful piece, solid platinum and encrusted with diamonds. Elodie was extravagant beyond comprehension.

"Why? It's just a thank you for doing the interview. You're going to help raise the profile of my work. I'm allowed to be grateful for that, aren't I?"

Madison huffed down the phone and placed the open box on the chaise longue, worried she'd drop it, break it, and wouldn't be able to return it. "There's gratitude, and then there's this."

"Come on," Elodie whispered. "You're not trying to tell me you don't like the watch now, are you? I don't believe that's possible. It's perfect for you."

Madison headed to the kitchen to get a drink. "It's beautiful. But what makes you think it's perfect for me?" She poured herself a glass of water. She wanted a coffee, but it was late, and eventually, she wanted to sleep.

"I know watches and I know women. It's the perfect weight, size, and shape for your wrist."

"Who knows the size of someone's wrist when they've only spent a couple of hours with them?"

"I watch people, especially people I'm interested in. I observe every detail and commit it to memory. I suppose it's something I picked up for acting."

"What's my shoe size then?" Madison poured a small glass of red wine.

"Six or seven."

"Hips?"

"Ah, tough one. You were wearing hipsters that can appear to add an inch. But if you're going to push me for an answer and not be offended if I get it slightly wrong, I'd have to say thirty-eight."

Madison recorked the bottle. It was hard to be offended when the answer was correct. "Right hand ring finger?"

"Four and a half."

"Left hand pinky?"

"I'm going with two and a half, but you probably don't even know that. You can't ask a question when *you* don't even have the answer."

Madison laughed as she wandered back into the living room. "Guilty as charged." She lay back on the chaise longue and looked at Elodie's impeccable face on the cover of the *HumanKind* magazine she hadn't been able to leave on the plane. "Look, it's a beautiful watch and a wonderful gesture, but I really can't accept it. Please. Just let me give it back to you."

"Fine."

She sounded grumpy about it, but Madison couldn't accept a gift that probably cost more than her apartment. "Thank you for understanding… What are you doing?" She should end the call before it escalated into something more serious, but she couldn't bring herself to do it. She loved that Elodie had called her after her meeting with *Time*. It made her feel special, and it was really nice to have someone to talk to.

"Learning lines and swimming laps."

Madison laughed. "Isn't your script getting wet?"

"I've had every page laminated and stuck to the bottom of the pool. It's fine," Elodie said.

Madison bit her lip and didn't respond. *She'd done what?*

Elodie's chuckle broke the silence. "I'm joking. God, you're easy. I've just gotten back from running lines with Lela Darvis."

Madison swallowed hard, reminding herself that she was talking to a new friend and that she should ignore the tiny stab of jealousy at the mention of another woman's name. Lela was Elodie's co-star. Of course they'd spend time together. "Thank God. You were just about to undo everything you'd said in the interview and become a true movie—"

"Diva? Like you expected?"

"I never said that."

"You didn't have to," Elodie said. "It's okay. I know I've got a certain image and reputation. Maybe when you come over to see my library, you can really start to get to know the real me."

"I'd like that," Madison said softly. There was a moment of comfortable silence before her phone beeped to announce another call. She looked at the screen to see it was Geva calling. She bit her lip. She wanted to keep talking to Elodie, but she hadn't spoken to Geva since they'd parted ways at Heathrow on her flight change. "I've got another call. We're still on for tomorrow?" Madison still couldn't quite believe she'd scored an invitation to view Elodie's rare book collection.

"Of course. You're sure you don't want my driver to pick you up?"

Madison gave a short laugh. "I'm sure." She really wouldn't trust herself if she didn't drive and ended up having a few drinks. How was she supposed to maintain her self-control and keep her hands to herself with her inhibitions loosened by alcohol?

"If you have any trouble finding my place, give me a call, and I'll come out to get you. And again, I'm really glad your meeting with *Time* went well."

"Thank you." Madison bit her tongue, unable to decide which act of thoughtfulness she should respond to, and how to do it appropriately. Like a friend would. "See you tomorrow then."

"You will," Elodie said and hung up.

Madison connected Geva and tried not to think too much about wishing that Geva *hadn't* called. "Hey, what're you up to?"

"Why are you being weird?" Geva asked.

"What are you talking about?" She couldn't be *that* obvious.

"You're all…giggly. What's going on?"

Madison patted a cushion down and got comfortable. This was going to take a while. Geva knew her too well to successfully hoodwink her. "I was on the phone with someone else when you called."

"Really? And they make you go all gooey?" Geva huffed. "Who are you, and what have you done with Madison?"

Madison chuckled. "Seriously, I sound different?" She couldn't hear it, but Geva wasn't usually wrong.

"You do. Is it anyone I know?"

"Depends on whether you know Elodie Fontaine, I suppose." Madison suppressed a smile, feeling a little like a giddy high school girl with a crush.

Geva whistled into the phone. "It can't be follow-up interview stuff at this time of night."

Madison tucked her feet under her butt and sat up. "It wasn't. She was calling to see how the *Time* meeting went about the organ trafficking piece."

"Oh, right. How's that going? Did you meet up with your

whistleblower?"

"Unfortunately not." Madison quickly told Geva the story so far and about her plans to meet up with one of the clients Carlos had named in the file.

"Be careful, and I don't just mean with this investigation. I know you're not looking for a relationship, but is a sex-addicted movie star your speed either?"

"That's such bullshit double standards." Madison put her water on the side table and stood. She paced the living room, instantly irritated. "How is it okay to label a woman enjoying her youth and vitality as a sex-addict and just accept that 'guys will be guys' when they go sleeping around with anyone and everyone?" Madison convinced herself that her indignation came from her strong belief in the right for women to enjoy sex just as much as men, and not from any need to defend her new friend.

"Whoa, okay. Let me rephrase." Geva cleared her throat. "Are you happy being one of a long line of women? You're kind of a serial monogamist."

Madison sighed. She couldn't argue with that. "I'm just seeing if we can be friends, that's all."

"And you *don't* want to have sex with her?" Geva asked, clearly not believing that was possible.

"Like you said, I'm not looking for a relationship, but she's a very interesting woman, and she wants us to be friends."

"Huh, is that all she wants?"

Madison went back to the chaise longue and looked at the crazy-expensive watch again. It still seemed way too grand a gesture to thank her for the interview, but Elodie lived in an extravagant world. To her, this might be the equivalent of buying someone a meal. "Well, she did send me a watch." Elodie described it in detail.

"Jesus Christ," Geva said. "Now I really wish I'd done the photography for the article." Geva sighed. "Please be careful. I don't see how you couldn't fall in love with her if you start spending a lot of time together."

"We'll probably hardly see each other in reality, Geva. I've got a meeting with Dom coming up, and it's bound to be a job that'll take me away from home again." As soon as she said the words, Madison was hoping it wouldn't turn out to be a premonition. She wanted to be around Elodie. She wanted this friendship to work. "I don't want to get hurt. After

I met her…" Madison shook her head. "She wasn't what I expected. She's someone I could fall for, and I can't begin to consider that she'd ever feel the same. She can have anyone, anytime, and she's not about to settle down with one woman. Why would she?"

"You're frightened you can't tame the lion, so you don't even want to try?"

Madison closed the watch box and sank back down to the chair. "There doesn't seem like much point."

"I understand that, I really do. And I've got my reservations because of her reputation. But you deserve to be happy. What if the person you'd least expect to fit the bill turned out to be *your* person? Wouldn't you have fun finding out?"

"No doubt." Madison had already woken, wet and aroused, from a sex dream on the night of their interview. She was certain they'd have the best sex of her life. But then it would be over. "But I don't want to put myself through that. I'm sure she'd get bored pretty quick."

"Maybe. Maybe not," Geva said. "I guess you're not one to gamble with your feelings."

Madison shook her head. Geva knew her family history and how hard it was for her to trust or be her true self with someone. Trying that with Elodie didn't seem like the best idea. A friendship was safe. It would be fulfilling intellectually. The possibility of a lasting friendship was better than a short and wildly sexual fling.

If she kept telling herself that, maybe she could ignore the parts of her that wanted to roll the dice and find out.

Chapter Twelve

This meeting was the last piece of the jigsaw for Therese's new medical facility off the L.A. coast. Transplant tourism was getting too risky. The U.S. government's Decade of Delivery was beginning to pay off, and countries all over the world were trying to get their status improved on the *Trafficking in Persons* report. Therese had thought her operation would be safe in Cuba, given its history with the States, but even they'd become unhappy with their tier-three classification. You just couldn't rely on old enemies anymore.

She needed to figure out a way to ensure her operation had longevity before the situation in Cuba became untenable. She had to find a way to stay ahead of her competitors, and this was it. A custom facility on American soil. The beauty of Cuba, however, lay in the ready supply of desperate, poverty-stricken people ready to sell any part of their bodies they could live without…and some they couldn't. And although there were desperate Americans and illegal immigrants, it was too risky a business plan. No, Therese needed something different. She thought the Chinese had the right idea, using the organs of executed prisoners, but that method wasn't readily transferable in the States. Not enough criminals made it to death row, and even then, the average time before their sentence was carried out was more than a decade because of appeals, petitions and all the things a democratic country should have. Political dragging of feet, an underfunded defense system, and the state fighting litigation battles around the legality of lethal injection all got in the way of Therese's business.

What she needed was an entrepreneurial prison warden, and she'd found that in Todd Wilson, CEO of California Collective, the largest private prison portfolio holder in the country. He was a far-right Republican who believed criminals were the scum of the earth, and spending U.S. tax dollars keeping them alive in cozy prisons all over the country was a misguided liberal concept. For a relatively small fee per body, Wilson was more than prepared, happy even, to provide Therese with a steady stream of healthy organ donors to order. He already had the prison infrastructure in place. He'd established a fight-to-the-death betting ring in six of the prisons his company had won private contracts for. Criminals were being murdered by other criminals. It was a win-win situation, and there was always an unerring stream of new criminals entering the system at any given time. The medical intake would have to be a little more stringent to establish a database for Therese to choose her donors, and the selection process for her clients would be slightly more mysterious, but the principle was bulletproof.

"Ms. Hunt, it's a pleasure to finally meet you." Todd Wilson bowed his head slightly.

He didn't offer his hand. Therese assumed Nat had briefed him on her dislike for the formal ritual.

"It certainly seems to have been a long time in the making, Todd. Please, call me Therese."

"Natasha tells me you have acquired your location and that your facility is being refurbished. That's great news for us."

Therese smiled at his presumptive use of the term "us" but let it slide. She would have to set aside some of her personal prejudices if this relationship was going to work. Thus far, she had made a deliberate choice to avoid close working partnerships with men. While they were eminently easier to control and manipulate than women, she found them abhorrent and unpleasant to be around. Sometimes, even just the *smell* of them was nauseating. Carlos Santiago had been an unusual exception to her rule, and that had eventually bitten her on the ass. "It is. The work will be completed by the end of the month. The Navy left behind a facility that was almost perfect for what we need. It's so pristine that I suspect it may have been a human testing lab. The barracks require the most upgrading, but I've employed the right people to make sure the schedule is met." Therese was beyond eager to get her new facility up and running as fast as possible. Right now, she was reliant on foreign contractors and at the mercy of the corrupt officials within the Cuban government, and they could be ousted at any moment. This endeavor would be under her complete control: U.S. medical staff, fewer palms to grease, no borders to negotiate. As soon as it was operational, Therese's profits had the potential to increase by five hundred percent, the kind of projection that pleased her enormously. Clients who had balked at the necessity to travel to a Third World country and who were suspicious that the care they would receive wouldn't be up to scratch, would now view her as the only option if they wanted to avoid the risk of being caught by the authorities. This way, her island would just be seen as an exclusive getaway. It would cripple her competition and make her the most prolific organ trafficker in the country.

"I've been impressed with your outfit thus far. You seem to be running a very smooth operation. I think we're going to have a very profitable and long-running business relationship."

"I'm glad you see it that way. You're operating a very neat venture across your prisons."

Todd preened in response to her compliment. He straightened his tie, sat up a little stiffer in his expensive-looking leather chair, and smiled, clearly pleased with himself.

"Then you enjoyed the tour of this particular prison?"

"Yeah. Yeah, I did. I'm looking forward to watching your fight club."

Todd nodded vigorously. "I promise it's worth the wait. Dodge is unbeaten in six fights. I think he's made out of marble. Lucky for us, there's always someone who thinks they're bigger and better than anyone else."

Therese appreciated the sentiment. It was the same in her line of work. There was always a bigger dog in the next yard. That's why she made sure her crew outnumbered any challengers and why she'd cultivated a particularly vicious reputation. It helped that she thoroughly enjoyed maintaining it. "Do your guards ever fight?"

"Sometimes. For obvious reasons, those bouts aren't to the death. Criminals are disposable, guards not so much." He laughed again.

Therese was beginning to get the picture that Wilson amused himself far more than he ever amused anyone around him. "How do you get your inmates to volunteer themselves? Surely they don't all have death wishes?"

"The privileges that come with fighting are enough to tempt them. We have a special cell for the winner, practically a studio apartment. It has everything they miss in the outside world. It's amazing what people will put themselves through for a chance of home comforts."

"And do you ever have to *encourage* them to volunteer?" Therese wanted to understand exactly how Wilson's set-up worked. She couldn't believe all the inmates would be dumb enough to risk their lives for a brief stay in a pimped-up cell.

"You have to understand, Therese, everyone here is here for good. They know there's no real chance of parole. They're lifers, and this is the end of the line for them. That's why I've got them, in here and in the other five prisons. These are inmates the system has washed their hands of. Family and friends have deserted the majority of them, and I certainly don't allow any of that prison pen pal nonsense. The life of a champion in here is as good as it's ever going to get for them."

"So you're sure you'll be able to cope with demand on top of your fight club deaths?"

"I'm positive. Our population could do with thinning down. Looking at the numbers Natasha projected, we'd be able to cope with three or four times what you need."

"Plenty of room for expansion, that's good to know. Our facility should put other suppliers out of business, and that'll mean an increase in the market share for us."

"That's something I can cope with, be sure of that."

He pushed his chair from under the desk and stood. He was an unimpressive height, something she saw as more of a failure in men than women. Her own stature often meant she was able to tower over most women and a good percentage of the men she came across. Height was intimidating, and it was another weapon in her arsenal she always used to full effect.

"Shall we go and watch the fight?"

Therese smiled. "Sure. There's nothing like watching someone die to make you feel more alive."

Chapter Thirteen

Madison pulled into the long driveway of Elodie's house and took a deep breath to calm the confusing but undeniable butterflies in her stomach. Though she'd spent the day combing through the thick package that had arrived that morning from the now dead Carlos, the thought of tonight hadn't been far from the forefront of her mind. Elodie opened the oversized wooden door, and the butterflies turned to hummingbirds. She was dressed in low-rise faded jeans and a deep V-neck shirt with a wing design that stretched across her breasts perfectly. Madison concentrated hard on trying to park in a reasonable fashion, rather than staring at her new movie star friend. *Friend.* She climbed out her car and picked up the watch box, hoping that returning this unbelievably generous gift wasn't going to be awkward.

"I'm glad you could make it," Elodie said as Madison walked across the drive to the front door.

"Thanks for inviting me..." Madison held the gift in two hands and offered it to Elodie. "But could we get this over with? I love it, I really do. And you're right, it would be perfect for me, though I didn't actually try it." Madison glanced away. She *had* held it to her wrist, but she'd been too terrified she would drop or break it to put it on properly. "It's too much. Getting to see your books is thank you enough, honestly."

Elodie took the box and smiled. "No problem. I don't want to make you feel uncomfortable." She put it on a side table in the hallway and ushered Madison into her home. "I've just taken delivery of a new addition for the library. I think you'll like it."

Relieved that was dealt with so easily, Madison relaxed her shoulders and sighed. "I love books. If I was homeless and could only choose one thing to keep with me, it would be my antiquarian book collection. I can't wait to see what you've got—what books you've got." *Breathe and get a grip.* Madison couldn't fathom why she was acting like a girl with a high school crush when all she was doing was meeting a new friend.

Elodie smiled genuinely, and Madison began to relax. She'd met royalty before and not been this off-kilter. She followed Elodie into an open hallway that led into several large rooms. In the center was a double-wide steel staircase, and at the top, there were floor to ceiling windows to a view Madison couldn't see.

"Would you like a drink? It's killer hot tonight."

Elodie's eyes sparkled. It was little wonder that women couldn't resist falling into her arms. She reminded herself once again she wasn't looking for anything other than friendship. "Do you have any herbal tea?"

"I probably have a few varieties. Do you want to come to the kitchen and choose something?"

"Sure." Madison followed a few steps behind and guiltily checked out Elodie's ass. "So tell me about your new acquisition." Madison sat on a bar stool beside the marble breakfast bar while Elodie searched through the many cupboards, making Madison wonder if she ever really came into her own kitchen.

"It's *The Federalist*, the essays of—"

"Some of the greatest political thinkers from the time our Constitution was being ratified."

Elodie nodded. "Impressive. It's over two hundred and thirty years old."

"Jesus, that's got to be worth some money." Madison wanted to pull back the comment immediately, not wanting to seem crass with her new friend who probably earned more in a day filming than she could in a year of reporting.

"My dealer got it for me for one point four million, but it's worth it, don't you think?"

Elodie offered her three varieties, and Madison pointed to the middle one with little contemplation. "Absolutely. I'd sell my soul for books."

"Then I probably shouldn't tell you that my gym door's propped open with *The First Folio*, and when my bedroom needs a little fresh air, a fifteenth century copy of *The Canterbury Tales* does the trick."

Madison gasped. "They do *not!*" Madison felt her cheeks flush as she realized Elodie was joking.

"No, they don't, but you're very easy to tease."

Elodie smiled widely and continued to pour the iced tea. The crackle of the ice cubes as the hot liquid hit them resonated with Madison. She was the ice and Elodie the heat. Madison's anxiety began to diminish as she became inexplicably more comfortable with every passing moment. It was an unfamiliar but very nice place to be.

"How's your investigation going? Is *Time* going to commission you for the feature?"

Madison was impressed Elodie not only remembered what she was doing, but even the name of the magazine she'd met with. It wasn't like she'd expected Elodie to be self-absorbed as much as she didn't think other people really listened to her ramblings. She knew they read her words, but actually listening to her in person was something she was again unfamiliar with. "Yes, they are. They're even more excited about it after I let them know what was delivered to me this morning." Madison recalled the UPS guy who'd dropped off the mysterious package. He'd said the sender had been very particular about the package going on a laborious journey around the world before being delivered to Madison.

"Let's sit outside, and you can tell me about it."

This time, Elodie motioned Madison to go before her, so her chance of ogling her some more disappeared. *Why am I disappointed?* She ventured in the pointed direction, and the kitchen opened up onto a large decking area and infinity pool. Madison settled into a cushioned hanging egg chair overlooking the water's edge, and Elodie sat close but opposite her on a lounge chair.

"UPS delivered a package that had been around the world in thirty days, more or less. It'd been to England, China, India, and Italy before it reached me. It's from Carlos, my would-be whistleblower."

"The dead one?" Elodie sipped on her soda.

"Yeah, the dead one. Thankfully, he sent this package out before they got to him. It's got everything I need to follow up on. I even have the name and a few photos of the leader and her right-hand woman."

"Sorry, that was blunt. You're not still blaming yourself for his death, are you?"

Yes. "No. I've thought about it logically, and I know that was the risk he was taking in his line of work." *But he was getting out, and I asked him for information he wasn't leaving with.* "There are rumors that the gang is led by a sadistic woman, but the police had dismissed them as nonsense designed to throw them off track."

"But the rumors are right?"

Elodie stretched back in her chair. Madison could see the outline of her stomach muscles through her shirt and her lithe biceps strained against its short sleeves.

"Yep. Her name's Therese Hunt. She's five-nine with a similar build to you, only a little bigger."

Elodie tensed her muscles in response, and Madison laughed.

"What? Why are you laughing?"

"Nothing."

"Liar." Elodie sat forward in her chair. "Spill. What made you laugh?"

My therapist says to try connecting with people. Honestly. "You did." Madison could feel herself blushing.

"I flexed, didn't I? That's what made you laugh." She pulled up the sleeve on her right arm and tensed again, making Madison giggle more. "I can't help it. I can't have you thinking someone's in better shape than me."

Madison pondered her phrasing. *Why do you care?* "I didn't say she was in better shape. I said she was bigger."

"Ah, you see, this is one of the pitfalls of having an actress for a friend. You'll find my vanity is off the scale. I have to be better than *every*one in *every*thing."

"Is that an actress thing or a you thing?"

Elodie smiled and looked away briefly, almost shyly. "Are you a journalist or a shrink?"

"I've had enough therapy to be able to pop psychoanalyze a little." Madison was confident she could admit to that and not be judged. Everyone in Hollywood was getting therapy for something.

"I've always been the same, so I guess it's a me thing." She looked contemplative for a moment before grinning widely. "Anyway, you were describing the villain of the piece?"

"She's got dark, evil looking eyes and short black hair. And she likes to skin people alive. Carlos sent the names of some of the people who'd crossed her over the past few years. My cop contact, Ash, gave me a quick rundown of how they died. She definitely enjoys her work. And her right-hand woman is model-like beautiful."

"The kind of woman you like?"

"Oh God, no. Way too femme for me." Madison saw something in Elodie's eyes, but she wasn't sure what it meant. Was Elodie happy she didn't like femmes?

"Good. I mean great. Not that it matters what women you like." She shook her head and blew out an exasperated breath. "So now that you know more about the gang than the authorities, what are you going to do with the information?"

"I've given Ash a copy of the papers Carlos sent me. He alluded to Therese, the ringleader, having a connection in the FBI so he's being careful about how he investigates and who he trusts. In the meantime, I'm going to follow up on some of the client names." Madison sipped her iced tea to find it was peach flavor, her favorite. She took a moment to look out over the pool and onto the Hollywood hills. It was a peaceful spot and felt like hundreds of miles from the fanfare of L.A. A certain degree of envy kicked in. What might it be like to spend her downtime in such a beautiful location?

"Are you okay?"

Madison slipped back into the conversation. "Sorry?"

"I asked if you were okay. You seemed distracted."

Madison smiled, slightly puzzled as to how Elodie had managed to see her inner musings. "I was thinking about how lovely it must be to live here. It's so tranquil compared to the city, to life generally."

"I got lucky when I bought this place. That's what I was aiming for, a slice of serenity in an otherwise chaordic existence. I'm glad you like it. You're welcome to drop by any time."

Elodie looked away briefly again, and Madison saw that same vulnerability. She figured it must be hard for Elodie to make real friends, people who wanted to get to know her as a person, rather than Elodie, the movie star. She knew she'd be unable to cope with that kind of uncertainty. "Thanks. I'd like that."

A brief silence followed, but it was a comfortable one. As she spent more time in Elodie's company, her comfort level increased. She was also realizing how guarded and closed down she must usually be, which was exactly what her therapist kept telling her.

"I know you're a seasoned player, but aren't you a little concerned that Therese might figure out Carlos was in contact with you?"

"I'm not worried about that." Madison grinned. "My new best friend is an ex-Marine."

"Are you asking me to protect you?"

"Only if you think I need protection." Madison played along with the mild flirtation.

"If your foray into Afghanistan is anything to go by, the answer to that is obvious."

"Really? What do you know about my time over there?" It intrigued Madison that Elodie would know anything about her past assignments.

"I know you were shot." She pointed to Madison's shoulder. "Let me see it."

"Why?"

"I want to see if you got preferential treatment, and if they fix journalists up better than soldiers."

"What will you show me in return? Do you have any war wounds?" Madison's pulse quickened. She wasn't good at flirting, and it seemed ridiculous to be doing it with the world's sexiest woman, even if she was gay.

"I do, but I remember a movie where the characters comparing scars end up in bed together."

"Given that we're just friends, we should be safe, don't you think?" Madison's words contradicted her feelings. She wasn't sure she could trust herself to keep her hands off Elodie's perfect body if she began to undress to show her scars, and she didn't want to ruin the growing friendship by Elodie feeling uncomfortable by having to reject her.

"Okay then." Elodie stood and pulled up her shirt.

Madison let out a gasp at the sight of Elodie's physique. Her lightly muscled stomach and tanned skin would've been enough to stir Madison's interest, but when she saw the anchor, globe, and eagle tattoo adorning the left side of her torso, her interest piqued between her legs. On the other side of Elodie's body was a six-inch scar Madison assumed was from a knife wound. "That beats mine, and that's a beautiful tattoo. You cover it up for your movies." Madison had seen several of the movies where Elodie had been semi or fully naked, and she'd never seen that tattoo.

"Yeah, I do. I had it done when I served. I'd never have it removed, but it's not for anyone else's consumption."

She released the hem of her shirt, and Madison tried hard to hide her disappointment. "My turn." She pushed the material of her tank to the side and looked away as Elodie moved in closer to inspect it. She jumped slightly when Elodie touched her skin.

"Nice."

Madison missed the warmth of Elodie's fingers as soon as she moved them. "You win. Yours is bigger than mine. How'd you get it?"

"That's a story for another time. Back to your investigation. You remember the friend I was telling you about in the CIA who served with me? I've reached out, and I'm waiting for her to get back to me. I could ask her to make some discreet inquiries if that's okay with you?"

"Of course. You told me you trusted her with your life, so I'll assume it's okay for me to trust her with mine too."

Elodie laughed with an obvious confidence. "Therese wouldn't stand a chance if she tried to get near you with both of us around."

Madison smiled, very much enamored with the thought of two Marines on her personal protection detail. Elodie was quite the package: beauty, strength, and intellect. *The library*. Madison remembered why she was there. "Now I've seen you half naked, are you going to show me your books too?"

"Ah, I don't know. That's a bit bold, Ms. Ford. Millions of people have seen me naked but hardly anyone has seen my book collection."

"Forgive my presumptuous nature," Madison said, trying hard to keep a straight face. "If it pleases thee, might I visit your antiquarian library?"

Elodie made an exaggerated nod. "Why, of course, madam. I'd be honored to show you my timeworn texts."

Madison could get used to being around Elodie. She was so normal away from the cameras and public scrutiny. And this kind of friendly flirting was a lot of fun.

Chapter Fourteen

The evening traffic was even worse than usual, and it did little to ease Elodie's mind. Talking her situation over with Ice was lethal. Their shared gung-ho attitude to life didn't seem applicable to this situation. The last thing she wanted to do was scare Madison off, but there was an inescapable feeling that she had to pursue. She had to knock hard on that door and hope to God that Madison would be willing to open it.

Elodie pulled into the space outside Madison's apartment. She picked up the bouquet of African rainbow roses from the passenger seat and got out of her car. The entry door buzzed open before she reached for the intercom, and she smiled. *She's watching me.* Madison stood at the top of the first flight of stairs in her doorway. She looked stunning in a pretty summer dress and heels. Her long, blond hair draped over her shoulders and caressed the top of her breasts. Elodie wanted to press her against the wall and bite down hard.

"You bought me flowers?"

"Of course not, because *this* isn't a date. I bought them for your apartment instead. I heard it needed to be gayed up a bit."

Madison smiled and her eyes brightened. Elodie had a desire to make her laugh with every sentence. She jogged to the top of the stairs and gave Madison the bouquet, who placed it inside and locked the door.

"You think I'm not gay enough? I've had that accusation my entire life."

"Oh baby, you're plenty gay, and anybody that's even half looking can see that."

Madison looked happy at her comment but shook her head. "Then nobody's been looking much because I've never been hit on in a bar. Ever."

Elodie offered her arm. Madison took it and they began to walk down the stairs.

"How about this? After we've had dinner, I'll take you to a new superclub that's just opened. I'll leave you at the bar and then I'll come back and try my best lines on you."

Madison huffed. "Looking the way *you* do, you don't need lines."

"I haven't for a while, so it'll be fun to see if I remember how."

Madison giggled but she didn't say no. Not wanting to push too far too soon, Elodie opened the front door into the humid evening heat. Her phone buzzed, and she checked the alert. "Traffic is getting worse. I have reservations, and I don't like to be late."

Madison followed her and pulled the door closed behind them. "I'm sure they'd hold the table for you."

"I'm sure they would," Elodie said. "But I don't think my time is any more precious than anyone else's, so I don't like to keep people waiting." She opened the passenger door and indicated for Madison to get in. She looked contemplative, and Elodie hoped she was reconsidering her insistence that this *not* be a date.

Madison looked up and down the street. "No bodyguards today?"

Elodie frowned then remembered she'd had two with her at Madison's interview. "Oh no, I don't really have them except for big events. The women you saw at the restaurant were in training, and I was just doing Paige a favor."

"I see." Madison gestured to Elodie's car. "That's a nice ride."

"You know cars?" Somehow Elodie didn't think Madison was a gearhead, but maybe she'd misjudged her.

Madison laughed as if the question were incredulous. "Oh God, no. It just looks pretty." She climbed in and slowly lowered herself into the seat.

"It's the same car James Bond drives."

Madison smiled as she looked up at Elodie with devastatingly beautiful eyes. She willed herself to breathe.

"Is that important?" Madison asked.

"It is if you like 007."

"I'd like 007 if she were a strong, hot woman."

Elodie closed the door. "I might have some interesting news for you on that front." She ran her fingers over the hood as she came around to the driver's seat, thinking of how she'd come across this particular car on the way back from an Amnesty International event for Romani children in the Czech Republic. It'd been harrowing, so the visit to the Aston factory in England had been a welcome distraction. Elodie's stay at the Langham's Infinity Suite had been made even more pleasurable by one of Aston's cute technicians. Her customer service had been so exceptional that ordering a bespoke Aston was the least she could do. The image of how Madison might look naked on the hood of the car with Elodie's fingers deep inside her invaded her thoughts.

"Where'd you go?" Madison asked as Elodie joined her.

Caught in the act of thinking about another woman and then Madison made Elodie feel instantly guilty. "Uh, nowhere. Why?"

"It looked like you were having filthy thoughts."

Elodie frowned. "How do you know what that looks like?"

"You're way too easy to read, El. A nice memory or wishful thinking?"

Madison's tone was teasing, and Elodie couldn't get a handle on it. Was she interested or not? She liked that Madison was paying enough attention to read her face. "Since this isn't a date, you probably don't want to know what I was thinking, but…" She told Madison the story of the car but left out the cute technician.

A little color flushed to Madison's cheeks, and she couldn't hold Elodie's gaze. Elodie smiled, satisfied that Madison wasn't completely immune to her charm.

"What's your interesting news about Bond?"

Elodie grinned at Madison's clumsy change of topic. "It's Jules French's next planned project. A reboot of the entire 007 series with me starring as the legendary secret agent."

"Really? That'll be worth watching, and far better than the misogynistic catalogue of Bond films before it. Is there any chance they'll make Bond gay?"

"I won't be Bond exactly. The character would get the number but not the name. We don't need Bond to be a woman; we just need more movies with strong, female protagonists." She wiggled her eyebrows. "You wouldn't mind seeing me on IMAX doing lots of girls, Bond-style?"

"As a friend, I'd worry about STDs, but other than that, why would I mind?"

Elodie didn't answer but she *did* want Madison to mind.

They drove a little way in a comfortable silence before engaging in some small talk.

"You're one of the most well-known faces in the world. How can you wander into any restaurant and club without being bothered?"

"We're in L.A. Celebrities are everywhere. But things have changed a little since JD Sawyer's death. There are fewer paparazzi and more respectful, professional photographers trying to earn a living." A heavy sadness fell over her unexpectedly.

"Were you close?" Madison placed her hand on Elodie's, apparently sensing her melancholy.

She liked the feel of Madison's soft, small hand on hers. It was so petite compared to her own. "He was the first great actor I worked with. He was a little like a cuddly grandpa to everyone on set." The unusual burn of tears stung the back of her eyes, and she blinked them away, hoping Madison hadn't noticed. Her hand remained for a few moments more before she pulled it back. "It's sad that it took something like that to change things so dramatically. I enjoy my freedom, but it came at a high cost."

"That's very often the case."

There was hurt in Madison's voice, and Elodie berated herself. She was bemoaning celebrity status to a woman who'd seen multiple genocides and tragedies all over the world without the hardcore training she'd received as a Marine. Elodie had worked hard to disconnect herself from her own military past and in doing so, had softened. Until she'd established her work with the TIP office, the lives of others far less fortunate than her was only a distant memory. Her daily life was rubbing shoulders with people whose only worry was how fat they looked in their most recent movie. "I'm sorry, that was insensitive of me. You must've seen your fair share of heartbreak." Elodie sensed a degree of consideration before Madison responded, almost as if she was censoring herself before she spoke. She couldn't shake an awareness that Madison was harboring so much pain and fear, and maybe it was that keeping her from wanting to engage with Elodie beyond a friendship. Who'd hurt Madison for her to be this cautious? It had to be something more than a particularly hard breakup. Everyone had bad breakups and got over them eventually. Whatever it was seemed to run deeper and more historic.

"No more than you, and not quite as up close and personal, I expect."

"We all have our own experiences to bear. Some worse than others." Elodie didn't want to push, but if she could assure her she was safe, maybe then she'd allow herself to open up. Maybe then she could feel what Elodie was feeling: a growing sense of needing to find out what this might be.

Madison looked at her. Her unasked questions were practically visible. *How can I make you trust me?* Elodie pulled into the parking lot of the restaurant, got out, and jogged around to Madison's side to open her door.

"My, aren't you chivalrous?"

Elodie smiled widely. "Only when I'm in the presence of a lady." She was rewarded with a smile that set Elodie's heart racing. *You're even more beautiful when you smile.* Madison was nowhere near ready for those kind of lines. Except they weren't lines designed to get Madison into her bed. They were simply truths. Elodie offered her arm, and Madison hooked hers through without comment. They walked into the restaurant and were seated with minimum fuss.

"When do you go to Russia?"

"Huh?" Elodie was caught off guard as she looked through the menu for something without garlic on the off-chance Madison might acquiesce to a good night kiss when she dropped her home.

"Aren't you filming parts of your new movie in Russia?"

"Ah, sorry, yes. We might not be. There's a lot of anti-gay sentiment over there so Jules is reconsidering filming there. He doesn't want to fund a government that persecutes the LGBTQ community, given that he's part of it and so are most of his actors."

Madison looked relieved. "I'm glad. I was there on my last assignment following a group of vile extremists hunting and torturing trans people. I was kicked out of the country by their military police. It'd be an understatement to say it was an unpleasant experience."

Elodie clenched her jaw. "Did they threaten you?"

"They did more than threaten my MacBook. They smashed it into pieces and said it'd be a shame if I found myself in a similar accident. It'll be a while before I'm welcome back into that country...especially if they read the article I've written about them."

"I've read a lot of your articles. Given what you cover, I wouldn't expect you're welcome back in many of the places you write about."

Madison laughed ruefully. She straightened in her chair and clasped her hands together. "You're probably right. It's *Requiem* they've adapted, right?"

"It is. Do you know it?"

"I do. I like his work." Madison tapped her finger on the table. "Are you playing Elya?"

Elodie smiled. Madison's guess smacked of an understanding she shouldn't rightly have, but Elodie liked it nonetheless. "Playing Kiana would've been too easy. The—"

"Audience would side with her immediately, and that's not enough of a challenge for you?" Madison smiled when Elodie nodded. "You were brave to sign up with FlatLine."

Madison sounded businesslike, but Elodie felt there was a deeper interest. Before she could answer, they were interrupted for their orders. When their waiter had gone, Elodie picked up the thread. "I like French's vision. I think he's the brave one. His approach is idealistic, but at the same time, business-oriented and efficient. I think he'll make it work."

"Have you signed up for the Bond franchise too?"

"Not yet. I want to complete a project with him and be sure he's what I think and hope he is. It's not until a movie is out that you can be sure it's what it was supposed to be." She thought of some of her early movies that had ended up being disastrous. "There's so much they can do in editing and post-production that the message you thought you'd captured can be lost. I imagine it's the same for you as a writer. Until you see your words in print, you can't be sure they're exactly how you wrote them."

"I'd never thought of it that way, but you're right. I've read about bit part actors having their scenes removed, but I didn't think it would apply to the stars of the movies. Has that happened to you? I have to ask, which movies?"

"I can't possibly answer in case you write an exposé on Hollywood and you name and shame the people involved." Elodie grinned, but she was already hoping that their interview would turn out as positive as she'd expected.

"On that basis, it might be best if we don't talk about anything other than the weather."

"That might not make for a very interesting friendship. Maybe this isn't such a good idea after all."

Madison shook her head and laughed. "Maybe it isn't, but I haven't enjoyed someone's company this much for a long time. If I promise not to record all our conversations to further my career, would you trust me enough to give it a try?"

"If an honest friendship is what you're offering, I'll take it." *Even though I want more than that.*

Madison extended her hand across the table. "Deal?"

Elodie shook it gently, and then bent her head to kiss her knuckles.

"Deal, m'lady." She was sure she saw something in Madison's eyes as she pulled her hand back that gave Elodie a glimmer of hope. Then again, maybe she just wanted to see something there. The waiter brought their food to the table and disturbed the moment, though Elodie wasn't sure what she would've said even if he hadn't. Madison had made it clear she was only looking for friendship, and Elodie wanted to respect that, but there was something about her that made her want so much more. Settling for friendship had to be better than losing her altogether if she pushed too hard for something Madison didn't want.

"Where'd you go?" Madison asked as she scooped quinoa onto her fork.

"Nowhere."

Madison rolled her eyes and harrumphed. "That might work for most people, but I see a look in your eyes when you're not being completely honest. I think you're too used to Hollywood types who ask the questions but aren't really interested in the answers."

She looked so serious it made Elodie smile. *Do you even know how beautiful you are?*

Madison touched Elodie's hand gently. "I'm interested."

Elodie tried to smile though she was already imagining Ice's reaction when she told her that she hadn't made a move. *You're not interested enough.*

Chapter Fifteen

Madison arrived at the offices of Stones and Chase fifteen minutes before her appointment. She stepped out of the elevator and walked toward the petite receptionist behind the glass fronted desk area.

"Can I help you?" Her smile was saccharine sweet false, and lipstick bled onto her overly whitened teeth.

Madison smiled as genuinely as she could manage. "I have a meeting with Patrick Powell at eleven thirty."

"Can I take your name, please?"

"Of course. My name is Meghan Jacks."

She glanced at the computer screen on her desk and clicked her mouse a few times before nodding. "Ah yes, there you are. If you'd like to take a seat, Mr. Powell's assistant will come get you shortly."

Madison thanked her and took the seat farthest away from the desk. She opened her handbag, made sure her Zoom recorder was positioned in the specially designed side pocket below the zipper, and set it going. She'd closed it back up as a young man in a half-decent suit sidled up to her.

"Mrs. Jacks? Would you like to follow me?"

He waited for Madison to rise before walking in the opposite direction to where he'd come from. She followed him into a small glass-walled room and sat in one of the comfortable-looking fabric chairs.

"Mr. Powell will be with you in a moment. Would you like something to drink, Mrs. Jacks?"

"I'd love a soy latte."

"Certainly."

He retreated from the room but was back quicker than Madison expected. He placed her latte in front of her and a black Americano close by.

"Thank you."

He nodded, smiled, and left once again. The overweight man she recognized from the firm's website as Powell entered moments later.

"Mrs. Jacks, it's good to meet you."

She shook his extended hand. It was clammy and limp. *Why doesn't anyone shake hands properly anymore?* He sat opposite her, placed his iPad on the table, and leaned forward conspiratorially.

"So. Tell me all about this cheating husband of yours, and I'll work out how we can take him to the cleaners for you."

Madison moved slightly closer to him. "It's not my husband I need to talk to you about, Mr. Powell."

"Patrick, you must call me Patrick. But I'm a little confused. Did my assistant make a mistake when he took your information?"

Madison shook her head. "No, he didn't. But if I told him what I really needed to speak to you about, I'm not sure you would've seen me."

Powell tilted his head and pushed his chair back a little, a suspicious look on his chubby face. Madison placed her hand on his knee. "Don't worry. I still need your help, Patrick. And I'm more than happy to pay whatever you need to make the introduction." She took her hand away, picked up her latte, and waited for him to digest her words.

"Sorry, Mrs. Jacks, I don't understand what you need from me."

"I need an introduction to a very special organization." Madison looked over his shoulder deliberately to indicate her discomfort with the level of visibility afforded by the glass box they were in.

"Would you like more privacy?"

Clever boy. "Yes…if you wouldn't mind. This is a very delicate situation."

He pressed a button on the central panel in the table, and the clear glass became frosted.

Madison adopted a relaxed expression. "Thank you so much. That's much better. You simply don't know who might be able to lip read. This isn't a discussion I approach lightly, Patrick. It's taken me many hours of deliberation to get to this point." Madison liked that Powell looked so confused. She briefly thought of Elodie and wondered what she'd make of her little masquerade. *Maybe she could give me some tips.*

"Perhaps you could give me a little more information, Meghan."

His use of her first name indicated his suspicions had abated somewhat.

"It's my sister. She needs some very specific help, and she can't get it…legitimately."

"Are we talking tax breaks? We're a very discreet firm. I have a colleague who'd be much better qualified for that particular requirement."

"No, it's not that." *He's hooked. Out with it.* "She needs a kidney, preferably two." Madison took a sip of her coffee and watched Powell's reaction. His body became tense again, and his eyes shifted from left to right as if he were a kid caught stealing from the cookie jar.

"I…I don't understand why you think I might be able to help you, Meghan. I'm a divorce attorney."

"Yes, I know that. But I've also been told you were in a similar position not so long ago. I was told you were able to find your way out of that predicament quite creatively and not using regular channels of healthcare."

Powell cleared his throat and shifted his weight in his chair. "Who told you these things?"

Madison put her finger to her lips briefly. "I'm as discreet as your firm, Patrick. I'd never reveal who told me. I wouldn't want to put anyone in danger of prosecution, especially when they're helping me save my sister's life."

Powell looked ponderous. She needed him to care about her situation. Carlos's file said he was racist and had insisted on a white American match donor. It had caused them some serious sourcing problems.

"I know I'm putting you in an awful situation, Patrick, and I'm so sorry to have to do this. You're my sister's last hope. She was beaten by her Black neighbor, and he almost killed her. I just can't stand to think that…that kind of person will be responsible for my sister's death." The vile words were like acid in her mouth, but she had Powell caught on her metaphorical line.

He nodded more emphatically. "I understand. And the man who did this to her, what's happened to him?"

"He's more or less gotten away with it because the police don't want to look racist by prosecuting him. It's so ridiculous."

"Let me take your details."

"Your assistant already has them."

"No, Meghan. When I leave this office, the story will be that we're not the law firm for you, so I don't want to be seen digging out your contact details. Give them to me directly now. That'll be safer."

"Oh, Patrick, I can't thank you enough. I could tell the moment I saw you, you'd be willing to help us. You have such kind eyes."

He had shark eyes, dark and empty.

"Absolutely, Meghan. We have to stick together."

She swallowed her nausea at his disgusting prejudice. "You couldn't be more right," she said, with a whisper of conspiratorial camaraderie.

He took his cell from the inside pocket of his jacket, played around with it for a moment, and handed it to her. "Type your number in there. I'll speak to Therese's assistant, Natasha, and get back to you as soon as I can. I know these things are time sensitive. In the meantime, I'll pray for your sister."

Racist but religious. He obviously ignored the love thy neighbor sentiment. She typed in the number to the burner cell she'd purchased yesterday and handed his phone back. "Was your surgery a complete success?"

"Yes, it was. There were no complications at all. Therese runs an extremely smooth business. I had my concerns regarding traveling to South America, but I believe she's setting up on an island off the coast somewhere, so you really don't have anything to worry about."

Madison sighed deeply. "That makes me feel a lot better. I did wonder about the hygiene of it all, you know. Please tell them I'll pay whatever it takes. There's no amount that's too big." Madison stood and picked up her bag. Powell held out his hand, and she was loath to shake it again. "Thank you so much for your time, Patrick. I'm forever indebted to you."

He opened the door and accompanied her to the elevator. She stepped in and as the doors began to close, Powell stopped them.

"Perhaps when this is over and your sister is safe, we could share a drink."

Madison nodded and gave him the best sexy smile she could. "I'd like that." *About as much as I'd like to run a marathon naked in the Antarctic.* The doors slid to a close, and she exhaled deeply. She looked at her hands. She was shaking slightly and not from the caffeine, but from the familiar rush of adrenaline when she was on the investigative trail. Her thoughts drifted to Elodie and when she might see her again.

As she reached into her bag to stop the Zoom recording, her cell began to ring. Something inside her jumped a little when she saw it was Elodie calling.

"Hey you."

Elodie's voice was so breathy and seductive, she could probably make a woman come just by speaking to her. Madison echoed Elodie's greeting.

"Do you have any plans tonight?"

"Other than rustling up a sad stir fry for one, not really." The elevator doors opened, and Madison headed for the exit.

"Excellent, so I can take you to dinner?"

The hot L.A. air hit her as soon as she was outside, but that wasn't what took her breath away. "*Take* me to dinner? In what capacity?"

Elodie's easy and gentle laugh made Madison tingle a little.

"'In what capacity?' Is that how you always respond when someone asks you on a date?"

"A date?"

"For someone so eloquent, you seem strangely lost for words."

Madison smiled, and she regained some composure. "I'd like to come to dinner with you, but let's not call it a date. That's not what it should be."

"What should it be?" Elodie sounded puzzled.

"Dinner with a good friend. Someone who's turning into a really good friend, and I want one of those far more than I want a short-term lover." There was a pause, and Madison gave Elodie enough time to come back with a smart remark, but there was none. She was doing the right thing. She'd much rather have Elodie in her life for the long haul than have some short fling that was over before it even began. She felt a connection to Elodie, something she'd never felt with anyone, and she didn't want to ruin it. She could only ever disappoint someone like her.

"There's a great new Thai place in WeHo. I could pick you up at eight. Not a date, just a time."

"Smartass."

"Nice ass."

Madison let out an exasperated sigh. "I'll see you later then."

"Sure thing, *friend*."

Elodie had hung up before Madison could respond. "Friend." She couldn't possibly deny Elodie was everything she could want in a woman. But she didn't want a relationship. She didn't want a partner. She didn't want Elodie.

Something deep inside disagreed completely.

Chapter Sixteen

Brad dipped his fingers into the chalk sack hanging on the left side of his harness, and Elodie laughed. "You're such a pussy, you don't need chalk on this boulder. How're your hands ever going to get ready for the real thing?"

"I need to keep my hands nice and delicate. Not all of us want calloused, construction worker's hands like yours, thank you very much."

Elodie slapped Brad on his Lycra-covered ass. "Be careful with that kind of comment, I'll be holding your life in these hands when you're climbing the walls. You'll be thankful for them soon enough."

"Race you to the top?" Brad shoved Elodie, leaving a chalky white handprint on her shoulder.

She dusted if off and smiled. "You're always such a sore loser. I don't like making you cry."

"Maybe I've been practicing since we last played here. I've had a hell of a lot of free time since I came out."

Elodie shook her head at the apparent double standards of their industry, but sometimes, an actor just fell out of favor. She wasn't about to voice that theory. "That's all going to change after this movie. Jules seems like the kind of guy who likes working with the same actors, and he said you had to be the Italian for this movie. He loves you." Elodie jumped onto the boulder, leaving Brad to ponder her words.

"Hey, you didn't say go," he yelled and scrambled to catch her.

"I told you, I'm not racing you. It's like beating my kid brother." She increased her pace, moving quickly from hold to hold, and was atop the twenty-foot artificial rock before Brad was barely halfway. She scanned the huge gym as she waited for him to join her. As usual, the owner had sectioned off over half the walls for Elodie's personal use so she could exercise in peace. She usually told him to let a few pretty climbers in but today, she'd asked him for total privacy. Her thoughts were all about Madison, and she didn't want to be distracted by anyone else. Brad had whined and given her his best pouty face, so she'd said he could tell Dylan the type of guys he'd like to see stretched taut scaling the gym walls. She could see at least three of them already.

When Brad finally joined her, he was breathing hard, and veins were popping in his arms and shoulders.

"I can't wait to start filming." Brad tried to shake the lactic acid build-up from his solid forearms.

Elodie wrinkled her nose. Filming meant leaving the country. Leaving the country meant no more time with Madison.

Brad narrowed his eyes. "What's up? I thought you couldn't wait to get started either."

She waved her hand and tried to focus on the climb. She'd wanted to clear her head and concentrate on challenging her body.

Brad smiled broadly. "I've missed this. I've missed you."

"You know what I'm like, Brad. I need space from everyone after a movie, and we were in each other's pockets for almost a year this time."

"I know. It's just been lonely without you around. Boys are good for fucking, but I'm still waiting to meet the guy who can interest me beyond the bedroom. Or the pool. Or the restroom."

Brad wiggled his eyebrows before his attention drifted to a guy climbing a nearby wall.

"I always had the same problem." Elodie stopped, debating whether she should discuss what was going on with her and Madison. She wasn't sure she wanted to speak to anyone about it until she got a handle on it herself. She and Brad had always shared a similar perspective on their bedfellows and had often come to each other for more meaningful conversation. Brad had once joked that in another lifetime, they could have ended up as man and wife. "Do you want to do a rope climb?" Elodie asked.

Brad, already cruising the cute guy in a white tank and cargo shorts, had obviously missed the past tense statement. "Sure, but pick one close enough to that guy so he can watch me, but not so close he can hear me struggling. And make me look good; don't choose some Mount Everest-type climb."

"Follow me." She scooted down the boulder with practiced ease, pausing to stretch her body out on the overhang, holding on with her right hand.

"I said make me look good, not show everyone how amazing *you* are."

Brad eventually came alongside her and tried the same move. It wasn't long before his arm started to shake. "He can't see me let go first, Dee, do me a solid."

Elodie sighed and dropped elegantly to the soft mats below. "Hold it for a little longer, he's still watching… Okay, you're good to go."

Brad dropped to the mat and leaned against the inside wall of the boulder, out of sight. He massaged his forearms and shoulders. "How do you make that look so easy?"

"Practice, Bradley, practice. Are we moving closer or are you cruising from afar?"

"Like I said, close enough for him to watch, far enough so he doesn't hear my cursing."

"Do you want to lead?"

"You're the rope gun, Dee. See how I'm learning the lingo? You know I'd love to, but you also know I'm not good enough yet."

"I'm suitably impressed. I'll choose an easy one. No overhangs, just a five point zero. C'mon, you can do it." She tilted her head toward Brad's admirer. "It'll impress him."

Elodie pulled Brad toward a climb in view of his imminent conquest.

"How are things with you anyway?" he asked while he struggled to create a figure eight in the rope end. "I haven't read much about your latest sexploits in the Huffington Post recently, apart from the fake *wish* and tells. Are you finally getting tired of the endless line of willing women?"

She'd usually dismiss such a ridiculous notion with a pithy comment, but when she didn't respond immediately, he adopted a worried expression.

"You're okay, aren't you? No health scares you should be telling me about?"

"I'm fine." She took the rope, tied the knot, and handed it back to him.

"Then what's going on? You've been uncharacteristically chaste, according to the tab-rags."

Elodie considered her response. Brad was the closest thing she had to a best friend apart from Ice, and she was usually too busy saving the world to be bothered with trivial things like personal relationships. Elodie had reached out to Ice about the organ trafficking gang, but she hadn't responded yet. But her attraction to Madison was one of the very things she should be discussing with Brad, a friend who was here right now. "I'm kind of dating-not-dating someone. Well, we've had one date-non-date, and she's seen my library."

Brad's eyes widened. "First, whoa, you let someone see your library? And second, what the hell is 'dating-not-dating?'"

"Excuse me, but aren't you Brad Carlton?"

The guy Brad had been admiring had bravely sidled up to them. Dressed in a tight white tank and baggy cargo shorts, he looked like he'd just walked off a porn shoot for gay jocks.

"I am." Brad dropped the rope and smiled.

"I'm such a huge fan, of your movies and you. You coming out is making a big difference to lots of gay men." He touched Brad's arm and lingered on his bicep.

Brad put his hand on his chest. "Do you really think so?"

"Of course. You're Brad fucking Carlton! You're an all-American action hero. You're living proof that we're not all little pop tarts with tiny bodies and whiny voices." He touched Brad's chest. "I mean, look at you; you're like Captain America."

"I did test for that part, but—"

"You were too muscular?"

Elodie turned away and stifled a laugh. The guy was blatant, but she liked that about young gay guys. If they wanted someone, they just went for it. Women were far less obvious. Sure, they were more brazen now that she was famous, but they still had a degree of emotional vulnerability that a lot of gay guys seemed to be missing. She shrugged. She couldn't base her whole world view of a section of society based on her observations in the fishbowl that was Hollywood.

"I loved you both in *Bought and Sold*. I can't believe I've gotten to meet my favorite two actors today. I've always been a huge fan of yours, Ms. Fontaine. You've been an inspiration to gay kids the world over your whole career."

Elodie politely thanked him, though he sounded like he was presenting a GLAAD media award for lifetime achievement.

Brad looked at her with his puppy dog eyes. "Dee…"

She held up her hand. "I can amuse myself traversing."

"It's been great to see you. Can we do this again next week?"

Elodie laughed. "We'll have to see when the read through schedule is finalized. We won't have as much free time when that starts."

"You're working together again?" the guy asked before Brad could speak. "That's exciting."

Elodie held her fingers to her lips and winked. She hugged Brad then watched them leave. They'd be in bed all day, no doubt. She hadn't had sex with anyone since meeting Madison for that damn interview, and she hadn't done this much masturbating since she hit puberty. Brad was right, the real kiss and tells had dried up so dramatically that the rags only had wish and tells to print. She didn't fear for her reputation as much as her sanity. Sex had always been her way of releasing any sort of tension. Now she was tense *because* she didn't want to fuck just anybody.

How was she supposed to relieve *that* kind of tension? She grabbed a volume on the wall and began her ascent. It wasn't sex, but a free climb would get her adrenaline pumping.

And she needed something, anything to get her mind off Madison, who seemed set on a "just friends" scenario for them despite the obvious chemistry. Ice would probably say that Elodie had been captivated by the novelty of being turned down and this was only about the chase. Most times, she'd be right, but there was something about Madison that seemed very much like she was worth the chase. And even if she did catch her, Elodie had a sneaking suspicion that she wouldn't be in any hurry to let Madison go.

Chapter Seventeen

Madison woke to the sound of her phone ringing. *Elodie*. She hesitated for all of two seconds before snatching it from her bedside table and answering it. "I wasn't expecting to hear from you so soon."

"Sorry, I don't have the latest copy of the *Friends Protocol* book," Elodie said. "Just talk to me. I want to know more about you."

Madison rubbed the sleep from her eyes, got up, and headed for the kitchen. She needed coffee to handle a conversation like this. "I don't know what I can tell you that'd interest you."

"Anything you've got to say is interesting."

"You're so smooth." Madison chuckled. "What do you want to know?"

"Tell me about your family."

Madison took a deep breath. This wasn't the conversation she'd envisaged when she answered the phone. And this wasn't the kind of stuff she spoke about to, well, *anyone* other than her therapist. "Now that's a complicated place to start."

"I like complicated. Simple is boring. Do you have brothers or sisters?"

"I had a twin sister called Safia." *Why am I telling her things I haven't even told my best friend?*

"Past tense?"

"Past sums it up perfectly. She did something I could never forgive her for." Madison switched her Gaggia on and took milk from the fridge. "And now she's dead. As is my mom. And my father may as well be."

"I'm sorry," Elodie said quietly. "There's no mention of a sister on Google."

"You've been googling me?" *That* was unexpected. "Are you a stalker?"

Elodie laughed, and the sound warmed Madison inside.

"I'm an interested party."

Madison poured her coffee and headed back to bed. "If you've been googling me, why all the questions?"

"Clearly, the Google gremlins don't have all the answers on you. Can I ask what happened with your twin?"

Madison took her first sip of coffee. It wasn't enough to steel her for this conversation, but it'd have to do. She considered shutting Elodie down, but something about her made Madison want to keep talking too. "The short version is that she managed to get my best friend and her family driven out of town when we were twelve."

There was a silence on Elodie's side. "That *is* a short version. More, please."

"Tell me something about you first," Madison said.

"You got plenty of my story for your magazine. I want to know about you. Are you more than just a Pulitzer-prize winning journalist, or are you as shallow as you took me for? Tell me about your evil twin sister."

Madison couldn't help but smile at her teasing. "I don't know that she was evil, just misguided."

"I need to have all the information so I can make up my own mind."

Madison paused to take a sip of coffee. Conversations like this led to a deeper understanding of each other. For Madison, deeper understanding and undeniable compatibility inevitably led to the bedroom. She didn't want to end up as just another conquest for Elodie. "She was jealous of my best friend, Jordyn. We spent all our time together, and Safia had it in her head that we should be joined at the hip. The problem with that was that I never liked her all that much. We were very different people. She was my twin only in looks. Anyway, Jordyn was from India. You could probably say she was my first crush."

"You knew you were gay in school?" Elodie asked.

"I guess that was my first real inkling. What about you?"

"I started to figure it out when I was about eight. Nice try; get back to the story."

Madison could still picture Jordyn in her mind. She swallowed down the rise of emotion in her throat that might otherwise be followed by tears. "Before we moved to L.A., we lived in Perle, a tiny town in the middle of nowhere. Racism was rife, and Jordyn's family was struggling to fit in. Safia stole a laptop from school and put it in Jordyn's locker—"

"I have to play devil's advocate here and ask how you knew for sure it was Safia who did the stealing?"

Madison shook her head. "Jordyn wasn't capable of something like that, but Safia was a thief, plain and simple. If she wanted something, she would just take it. That, and she told me she'd done it."

"No ambiguity then."

"None." Madison remembered her being so matter-of-fact about it, like it was nothing.

"How do we get from a stolen laptop to her whole family being driven from their home?"

Madison puffed her pillow and snuggled under her comforter. So she was doing this then. "I'm getting there, have some patience. You *did* want the long version."

"My deepest apologies for interrupting, your highness. Pray, continue."

Madison grinned at Elodie's impressive Shakespearean accent and imagined her bowing as she spoke. "So, the laptop was found, due to a not-so-anonymous tip-off from my lovely sister. Jordyn's parents were called in, as were the police. A scandal ensued, and our backwater townsfolk ostracized the family even more. It got out of hand and Jordyn's father was badly beaten by some of the town's assholes. My father knew Safia had taken the laptop, and he kept it to himself for fear of ruining the family name. He let innocent people suffer just to protect his daughter's reputation. Jordyn and her family moved out of town in a hurry, and she didn't leave any new details. She probably didn't know where they'd end up. I couldn't forgive my father or Safia for what happened. Soon after, Safia died in a car accident with one of her friends, and we left because my father couldn't handle staying in the town where his baby girl had died. We headed to L.A., and he got a job with the LAPD." Madison stopped, emotion choking her. She often wondered if he took his grief out on her, wishing she'd been the one to die instead of his favorite. Madison touched her face and found her cheeks wet with tears.

"Are you okay?"

Elodie's gentle tone comforted her, but Madison wished she was there with her arms wrapped around her. She wanted to feel Elodie's strength, bury her face in her chest, and sob until she was dry and empty. She hadn't told that story to anyone. Not Geva. Not to a partner. She'd kept it buried deep inside and yet, here she was in bed pouring it out to a relative stranger. *She doesn't feel like a stranger.* Something about Elodie made her want to open up in a way she'd never done, to anyone. Somehow, she made her feel safe. "Yeah, I'm fine. Why?" She held the phone away from her as she made an attempt to snuffle the tears away.

"It…it felt like you were sad." Elodie sounded hesitant.

Madison grabbed a tissue and dried her tears. "I've never told that story to anyone. It took me a little by surprise."

"I'm sorry. I shouldn't have pushed."

Madison sighed. "It's okay. You probably weren't expecting all this tragedy and sorrow when you asked for some history at nine in the morning."

"I wasn't, but I prefer this to small talk," Elodie said. "How about we lay off the heavy stuff, and I'll try to ignore the fact that your father was a cop and *still* did what he did. Let's talk about Princeton, my little childhood prodigy."

"You really have been stalking me, haven't you?" Madison ignored the possessive reference. She kind of liked it.

"It's a habit. I have to be careful who I let into my inner sphere. My agent says I have to watch out for gold diggers, and crazies, and people who want to paw me, but I'd still hope to be pawed by you."

Madison nearly choked on her coffee. "I'm not that kind of girl."

"Maybe you are, and you just don't know it yet."

"I'm pushing forty, you think I don't know myself by now?" Madison asked.

"I learn new things about myself all the time. You think you're a finished article?"

Madison frowned. She hadn't expected to be having such a deep conversation so early in the morning *and* before her second cup of coffee. "What do you mean by that?"

"If you're done learning, about yourself or the world you're living in, is there any point in carrying on?"

"I didn't say I'm done learning about the world or other people." And Madison definitely wanted to carry on despite the horrors of the world. "I'm learning new things about you every time we speak. I just meant I think I should pretty much know myself by now."

"What have you learned about me today?"

"I've learned that you're a crazy early morning person and a Grade A stalker."

Elodie laughed hard. "That seems ironic—"

"When it's the stars who're usually stalked?"

"Yeah," Elodie said. "But at least you know it's not for nefarious purposes."

"Do I?"

"You do. Otherwise, you wouldn't have taken this call. Like you said, you're nearing forty, so you're probably a decent enough judge of character by now to know a serial killer when you meet one."

Madison blew out a long breath. "I don't know about that. Serial killers tend to be exceptionally charming people. Look at the love letters Manson got right up to his death."

"So you find me charming?"

Madison had fallen into that trap way too easily. "Are you saying you *are* a serial killer?"

"I asked my question first. You're charmed?"

Madison laughed. "Isn't everyone?"

"I'm not interested in everyone. I'm interested in you. But I'll take that as a yes. And no, I'm not a serial killer. But then, I would say that even if I was, wouldn't I?"

"All the more reason never to visit you at your mansion again, if you're not to be trusted."

Elodie made a noise on the other end of the line. "You were about to tell me about Princeton."

No. Madison was still thinking about Elodie's comment about hoping to be pawed by her. "What do you want to know that you haven't found out on Google?"

"Are you an actual genius in the real sense, not the Apple Genius Bar sense?"

Madison considered her answer. She was conscious there were a lot of secrets coming out. Not so much secrets, as untold stories. Things she'd put to the back of her mind. It was history she'd not shared with anyone. This was another one, and they'd barely been on the phone for twenty minutes. "I thought you wanted to keep it light. My mom died as soon as I left for Princeton."

"You're a screenplay waiting to be written."

"Everybody has a history." Madison swallowed hard. She shouldn't have allowed herself to be pried open quite this easily.

"Not one as interesting as yours," Elodie said. "I don't think you've let anyone really know you since…well, ever."

Madison frowned. This was getting way too deep and personal. Elodie was unerringly close to the truth. Suddenly, it stopped being fun, and it was time to shut it down. "This has been fun, as usual, but I've got my editor coming for a lunch meeting. I have to go." Madison didn't want to sound too abrupt, but she didn't want Elodie knowing she'd hit a nerve.

"Really? That's an early lunch."

Madison cursed her lack of composure under pressure. "It's a breakfast meeting that will inevitably bleed into a lunch meeting. She always has lots to tell me; she's a gossip." Madison stopped before she said anymore, realizing she was embellishing too much.

"Okay. Have fun."

Elodie didn't sound at all convinced. *I'm just being paranoid.* "Her edits usually aren't fun, but if she has any dirt on your fellow thespians, I'll be sure to let you know later." Madison snapped her teeth shut, immediately regretting both the assumption and invitation.

"Then I'll call you later."

Elodie didn't miss a beat, or make a big deal out of it, but Madison knew she'd have that smug smile only she could pull off and still look sexy. She ended the call before Madison could say anything more.

Madison threw her head back and sighed loudly. At some point, she was going to have to make a decision about where she was willing to let this go. With every conversation, she got to know Elodie a little bit more. And the more she knew, the more she liked her. Now she was letting Elodie know her, almost without her own consent, and they were getting into dangerous territory. The point of no return was beginning to loom large.

Chapter Eighteen

"Patrick Powell called us earlier today. He said a woman came to see him at his office and knew all about his operation."

Therese looked at Nat. "Who the fuck is Patrick Powell?"

"He had a kidney op about six months ago. Paid over the asking price to have a white donor because he's a racist cunt."

Nat's sweet description recalled the client to Therese's mind. "Ah yes, I remember that little fuck. He was an attorney with a big law firm in L.A., wasn't he?"

"That's him."

"He was a cock. I remember hoping that he'd die on the table."

Nat laughed. "But the remaining seven hundred thousand was a bigger pull."

"Of course." Therese smiled. "What does he want?"

"He says a woman came into his office this morning wanting your contact details because her sister was sick and needed two kidneys. She offered to pay him a fee to introduce her to you."

Therese narrowed her eyes. "Did Santiago's package contain Powell's details?"

Nat nodded. "It did. He was one of the five clients whose information was compromised."

Therese stretched out her hands then clenched her fists. "And they're all L.A. based, yes?"

"Yeah."

"Call Reed right now. I want to know where that second package was sent, and I want to know now. Someone out there is starting to lift rocks, and I don't like not knowing my enemy."

***

Nat had been convincing when she called Powell to discuss the possibilities of helping the woman who'd come to his office that morning. He knew the importance of Therese's operation being kept secret and obviously thought nothing of the remote spot in East L.A. where she'd arranged for him to meet them. As they waited for his arrival, his lack of punctuality irritated Therese and forced her to consider the more creative ways she might end his life. She despised being made to wait for anything or anyone. Waiting for people was a particular bug bear, as if their time was more important. It'd be a waste of time to teach him some manners since he'd soon be dead, but his disrespect would make killing him even more pleasurable.

She saw the nose of his Jaguar pull into the chop shop. Such an old man's car. And it wasn't American. Her crew would be more than happy to tear it into pieces after she'd finished with him. He pulled up, and Nat opened the car door for him. Therese saw his lascivious smile and the way he looked her up and down. She imagined cutting his mouth open and chopping off his lips for that disrespect. Nat belonged to her, and he knew that.

"Thank you for taking this meeting," he said as he walked around to the front of his car.

Six words from his mouth, and he was already sickening her. Nat activated the door, and its corrugated iron rattled aggressively before it hit the ground with a metallic thud. Powell looked at the shutters, and Therese saw a hint of fear in his eyes when he turned back to her.

"I know that I broke your protocol in contacting you, but I think this constitutes a medical emergency, even though it's not my own."

She clamped her teeth together and clenched her jaw. She didn't give a rent boy's ass about his opinion. "Tell me more about the woman who came to you."

"Her name is Meghan—"

"I don't care what her fucking name is. Describe her to me." Therese closed in on him, and he backed away until the back of his knees touched the hood of his car. Nat stood to his left, blocking his path back to the safety of his seat.

"She was average height, about five foot five, I should think. And she had a curvaceous, sensual figure. Her hair was long and blond, and her eyes were a beautiful blue."

"Did you call us because of a medical emergency or because you have a hard-on for the woman?" She watched Powell's brow furrow as he began to understand he'd misjudged the reason for Therese's willingness to meet.

"I'm a married man."

Therese laughed. "That means nothing. You don't think I know all about your philandering?" She addressed Nat. "I love that word. Philandering. So British. Like your car." She pushed him in the chest. He lost balance and fell against the hood of his car. "Given that you're so racist, it surprises me you'd buy a foreign car. Or does your prejudice only extend to skin color?"

Powell steadied himself and placed his hands on the hood in an effort to appear casual. He didn't fool Therese. He was terrified and rightly so.

"I'm sorry to have upset you, Ms. Hunt. I thought you'd appreciate the opportunity to make some money. She's prepared to pay more because she's so desperate—"

"And I expect she offered to pay you too?"

He didn't need to speak. His eyes answered her question.

Therese shook her head. "Men. You're so easily manipulated, it's pathetic. Did she give you contact details?"

"Yes. Yes, she did."

He moved to take something from the inner breast pocket of his jacket, but Therese caught hold of his wrist. "Allow me." She released his hand, took the lapels of his jacket, and pulled it over his shoulders to his elbows. Nat reached over him, pulled out his cell, and handed it to Therese. "Code?"

"419031."

She tapped in the code and quickly found Meghan's contact details. "Let's see who this mysterious Meghan is, shall we?"

It rang three times before someone answered. "Patrick?"

Therese recognized the accent as local. "I hear your sister needs our help?"

"Therese?"

Therese pressed mute. "Did you give her my name?"

Powell nodded. Therese lifted her chin toward Nat and watched her drive her fist into the side of Powell's head, knocking him unconscious.

"I meet all my prospective clients. Where and when can I meet your sister, Meghan?"

"She's very ill in the hospital. She couldn't possibly meet you…but I can."

Therese smiled. *This woman has some mettle.* "If I decide to give you what you need, we'll have to move your sister to my facility, or is she too ill for that?"

"If you can help us, I'll move my sister anywhere you want her."

Therese bit her lip, already excited for the potential hunt. Nat dragged Powell across the concrete floor to the hydraulic station used for chemical dipping to strip cars of their paint. She snaked the chain under his right arm, behind his neck, and back under his left arm, before snapping the carabiner into a link to tightly connect the loop.

"Do you know the South Coast Plaza?"

"I do."

"Meet me at Marché Modern tomorrow at one p.m. There'll be a reservation in your name. We'll discuss your sister's needs in more detail then. I'll need to know her blood type and medical history. If you're not bringing your sister, make sure you come alone. I can't risk exposure in my line of work. I'm sure you understand."

Nat looked at her, obviously puzzled, before she opened the ground level hatch doors on the dipping station.

"I do, and I will. I look forward to meeting you, Therese, and thank you so much for being willing to meet me."

"It'll be my pleasure, Meghan." *And eventually, your pain.*

"Is it possible to speak to Patrick please?"

"I'm afraid not, Meghan. He's just about to take a bath." Therese ended the call without further conversation and threw the phone into the vat of acid Nat had revealed. Therese smiled as she felt the familiar rush of imminent satisfaction. This method of killing was a new one, and she wondered how it would compare to the intimacy of a knife. She hoped he would stay alive as he was submerged to his shoulders. She needed to see the excruciating pain of the acid eating him from the outside in.

"You know it's a trap. There'll be cops all over the mall ready to take you down."

"I'm not stupid, Nat. Of course I won't be going, but Reed will. Call him again and give him the details." She nodded toward Powell. "Wake him up. Let's show him what happens to loose lips."

Chapter Nineteen

"That's beautiful, people. I want to work on every fucking movie with actors like you. Why can't I do that? Is that too much to ask?" Al Fox was yelling, but it made everyone around him smile. "Elodie, you are delicious. I want to cry my fucking heart out every time I hear you speak. Oh, the pain, the wanting, the conflict. I love it. You're nailing this to the wall and saying, 'Give me a fucking Oscar.' Rory, you are a beautiful man. What is this bitch thinking not allowing you access to her fucking cunt? She should be throwing down the red carpet and guiding you in with runway lights. Let's call it a day, people. All this brilliance has made me hungry. See you all tomorrow."

Al left the room and everyone but Lela drifted off to their evenings.

"Your director has a very interesting turn of phrase."

Elodie recognized the voice, turned toward it, and laughed. "That's rich, coming from someone with a mouth like yours." She embraced the woman hard. "Thanks for coming to the set, Ice."

"Fuck that. Anything for you, babe."

"Are you going to introduce us?" Lela asked.

Elodie knew from Lela's tone that her interest was sexual. Ice stood out in this environment, and Lela had a thing for tall, dark strangers. Unlike Elodie, who'd reduced her musculature when she came out of the Marines, Ice had maintained hers, and she was stocky and muscular in a way that meant business. She scared the shit out of Elodie's bodyguards, and they weren't exactly meek. She'd shown up in her civvies, her off-duty uniform of fucked-up jeans and a battered leather jacket. Her long, dark hair fell around her shoulders, and it softened her dark eyes somewhat. She was exactly Lela's type. Breathing.

Ice held out her hand, and Elodie saw the look of excitement and surprise when Lela saw the gun on Ice's hip.

"I'm Ice, Elodie's buddy from her days in the Corps."

"Well, I bet you've got some fabulous stories. Care to share them with me some time?"

"Maybe. If you share your movie stories with me."

Ice was still holding Lela's hand, and Elodie coughed indiscreetly. Ice raised her eyebrows.

"There'll be no story sharing, thank you."

"We could all go out and share," Lela said.

Elodie and Ice laughed at her thinly veiled invitation for a threesome.

"It's been a long time since we *shared*, Dee."

Ice smiled mischievously, and Elodie recalled the many instances they'd cruised and scored together. There wasn't much they hadn't shared in their previous life, but Elodie wasn't interested in picking up where they'd left off. Her concern at the moment was very much centered around Madison and her investigation. "Not tonight, Ice. I need to talk to you about something." Elodie was glad the other actors had left the room. All she had to do now was get rid of Lela, who'd made it clear that, even though they hadn't slept together the other night, she was available whenever Elodie was interested. But after the time she'd spent with Madison, she found her thoughts turning more to her than further meaningless encounters with anyone.

Ice pulled out her card and handed it to Lela. "I'm in town for a few weeks. Feel free to call me some time."

Lela took the card and caressed Ice's fingers as she did. "Is it true the Marines have the filthiest minds of all our armed services?"

Ice smirked. "Call me, and you'll find out."

"I'll call you. You can count on that." Lela picked up her bag and headed to the door, while Ice unashamedly watched her ass.

"You're a dirty dog." Elodie punched Ice's shoulder. "Isn't old age doing anything to calm you down?"

"What's that phrase about stones and glass houses?"

"How's work?" Elodie wasn't interested in revisiting her recent sexual conquests tonight.

"Dee, you know I appreciate the thought, babe, but if I tell you that, I'll have to kill you. What's up with you? What do you need? Let's start with that."

Ice's blunt approach to conversation differed vastly from anyone else in Elodie's circle. She had no use for idle chat. She had important shit to do, and never enough time to do it.

"Let's go to my place. This isn't something I want to talk about where people might overhear."

Ice adopted a more serious expression. "Okay. I'll follow you."

"Thanks, buddy."

On the drive home, Elodie found herself thinking about last night with Madison. Being in her company was so easy. After she'd given Madison the tour of her library, they'd ordered some Thai food and talked for hours about their careers, interests, and eventually their love lives. Madison was reticent in sharing details of her own, making it clear that there was a past she wasn't prepared to divulge. Yet.

As she parked her Aston Martin between her Audi R8 Spyder and BMW i9, she wished she'd made a move as they'd parted on her doorstep. The goodbyes had been said, but Madison had briefly paused and Elodie couldn't decide whether or not to lean in for a kiss. The moment passed quickly, and Madison hurried to her car.

Elodie couldn't deny Madison was attractive, and her intellect made her even more so. She got out of the car and resolved to invite Madison on a date. She wanted to make it clear that she was interested in something more than the growing friendship to see how Madison reacted. If she declined, Elodie was sure they could still remain friends.

Ice pulled up in her black pickup truck and jumped out onto the graveled yard. She grabbed Elodie by the shoulder and pulled her toward the house.

"Come on, hotshot movie star. Time to feed me while you tell me all your troubles."

Once inside, Elodie instructed her chef to rustle up a stir fry for her and a burger and fries for Ice. They downed a couple of beers and chatted about a few past missions before the chef served them and left for the night. Now that they were properly alone, Elodie could talk about Madison. "I've got a friend."

Ice's eyes narrowed. "Fuck off. Other than me, you don't do friends, Dee. Has someone finally gotten through to you?"

Ice was one of the only people on the planet who spoke to Elodie so brusquely. It was the thing she appreciated most about her and treasured about their friendship. It was real. "What're you talking about?"

"You know I fucking love you, but you don't connect with people. They think you do, but you don't, and it's a rare fucking thing for you to call someone a friend with that tone of voice. Cut the shit and fill me in.

You know I'm a busy woman, babe."

Elodie smiled, but she was uncomfortable. It seemed Madison had gotten under her skin more than she cared to admit.

Ice took another mouthful of her burger. "This is the best burger I've ever had. Maybe I should've followed you into this business rather than continue to serve our country." She took a long swallow of her beer. "Let's start with the basics. What's her name?"

Elodie didn't bother to challenge why Ice would assume her friend was female. "Madison Ford. She's a—"

"World-renowned journalist. I know who Madison fucking Ford is, babe. She's a cutie. What's the problem? Don't tell me she's immune to your come-fuck-me eyes."

"It's nothing like that." *But it might be*. "She received a package from a whistleblower in an organ trafficking gang. Lots of the information checks out, but the guy's been found dead. He sent the same package to the FBI. There's been nothing about it in the news, and no one at TIP has heard anything. The whistleblower said the gang had insiders at the FBI, and Madison doesn't know who to trust. I'm worried about her, Ice. I think she might be in over her head, and you're the only person I trust to help."

"I can make some inquiries. But I've got a feeling that's not all you want me to do. What else do you need?"

"You're on vacation, aren't you?"

Ice wasn't a patient woman. "You know I am. What've you got in mind?"

"I want you to keep an eye on her. I'll pay you, whatever you want. And I know you've always wanted to stay at the Chateau Marmont. You have a thing for Belushi."

"I don't have a *thing* for Belushi. He was a misogynistic prick."

Unperturbed, Elodie continued with her bribe. "Well, Salma Hayek then. I can arrange for you to sleep in the same bed she did."

"Fuck it, Dee, you know I owe you. And if this Ford woman means this much to you, I'd be happy to help you out."

Elodie leaned forward and put her hand on Ice's knee. Ice slipped her hand around Elodie's neck and kissed her forehead. "I told you you'd never have to repay me for that," Elodie said gently.

"Still. I owe you my life. I always will until I get to save your ass."

They disengaged, the moment of vulnerability fleeting. Marines weren't prone to being particularly emotional.

"I'm already staying with my brother and his wife. They'd be all kinds of pissed if I bailed on them. Maybe you could just introduce me to Salma instead. That way, I can get her into my bed for real."

"You got it." Elodie fell silent. She felt a need to talk about Madison. She could count on one hand the number of real friends she had, but it was easy to imagine Madison adding to that number. But Elodie's feelings for her went beyond friendship. They'd chatted for hours the night before, and there was an undeniable connection, but Elodie could practically feel herself being metaphorically held at arm's length. If she could talk to anyone about her, it was Ice. She was candid and honest. She had a real-world understanding of relationships, something you didn't customarily experience in Hollywood, where everyone was out for something with anyone they could get their claws into. With a Master's in psychology and the kind of work experience she'd had in places you didn't want to know about with people you didn't think existed, Ice understood people. Elodie needed her take on the situation.

"What else?"

Four years living three feet apart had synched the two of them more than they cared to admit. Ice was family. "I need your help," Elodie said. "I think I'm even asking for your advice."

"Are you hot for your journalist?"

Elodie smiled at Ice's intrinsic knowledge of her. "Not exactly. Well, sort of. Maybe. I don't know."

"Wow, she's got you so you don't know which fucking way is up. She cast a spell on you?"

"It feels like it. If I'm honest, she's all I can think about. It's all I can do to stop myself from inundating her with gifts and flowers. I'm sure she can feel something too, but it's like she's shut that part of herself down, and I don't know why. She just wants to be friends, but I think there's more. There's got to be more." Elodie surprised herself with her verbalized stream of consciousness. Madison had gotten in deep without Elodie truly realizing.

"Are you convincing you or me?"

"I'm not trying to convince anyone. I don't know where I'm going with it. We're connected. There's something there, and I know it. She knows it. She just won't let it happen."

"What do you expect, babe? You're one of the most famous women on the planet, and your fucking is as eminent as any role you've played. Let's be frank here, you're great for a sex-laden weekend, but any woman'd be stupid to fall in love with you and think they could be the one you settle down with and adopt five cute orphan babies. You've never had a serious relationship in your life, and that includes your fucking parents. You wouldn't know what love was if it smacked you in the face with a wet pussy."

"Jesus Christ, your mouth is disgusting. And sugar coat it for me a little, why don't you?"

"That's not what I do for you, babe."

"What if she *is* someone I could have a serious relationship with?"

"You've got to convince her that's a possibility…if you've even convinced yourself. You've gotta be sure this isn't just about the chase, babe. You're not used to people saying no to you. Are you absolutely certain that's not what this is about?"

Elodie shifted in her seat and straightened her T-shirt like it'd help her find the answer. "No, it's not. This feels real in a way nothing has before."

"Wanting it doesn't make it so, babe. Do you feel it? In here?" Ice shoved Elodie square in the chest, and she rocked back in her chair with the force.

"Easy, Ice. I'm not one of your informants. I'll push back."

Ice laughed. "Don't make me kick your ass just because you need someone to take your sexual frustration out on."

"It's too early to be talking about here." Elodie pressed her fingers to her own heart. "But I do need to explore it further. There's something pulling me closer, and I won't let that go. I have to see it through, even if it does turn out to be a spectacular failure."

"I know. No regrets."

It had been their motto when they'd served together, and it was as appropriate now as it ever had been. She didn't know what the future held or if there even was a future for her and Madison, but she had to know. "No regrets."

Chapter Twenty

"She's not going to show at the restaurant, Madison."

"Hello to you, too." She thought Ash would be more optimistic about the opportunity to snare Therese Hunt.

"Uh, yeah, hi. But anyway, Hunt won't be showing at the restaurant, and neither will you."

Madison didn't like his matter-of-fact tone or where the conversation was heading. Everything had been set up perfectly, and she'd handled her surprise phone call with Therese well enough. She didn't seem to suspect anything, though the bath reference was slightly strange since all evidence pointed to Therese being gay. Why would she be anywhere near a slime bag like Powell when he was getting naked?

"What are you talking about? Says who?"

Ash motioned to the comfortable-looking sofa in the corner of the coffeeshop. It was one of Madison's favorite places, and she frequented it so much that the waitress, Joni, placed her regular soy latte on the table just as she sat down.

Ash huffed. "I'd like straight black coffee, please."

It was clear from Joni's expression that Ash's request was unusual… and unwanted. "Certainly, sir."

"He's a cop," she said, as if that explained everything.

Joni rolled her eyes. "Apology accepted."

Madison chuckled then turned her attention back to Ash. "You were saying why I won't be meeting with Therese."

Ash took off his light jacket, threw it onto the back of the sofa, and sat beside Madison. "Around six forty-five last night, Powell's PA said Powell headed to a meeting that he didn't give him details of. At seven fourteen, his cell records show him making a phone call to your burner cell. A few minutes later, the signal was lost and now it's going straight to voice mail. His PA hasn't been able to get hold of him since, and he didn't show at the office this morning. The tracker signal on his car is lost. The front desk at his apartment building says he didn't come home last night, and his wife says he always comes home even when he's been fucking around. I think it's safe to say Hunt is on to you and Powell is dead."

Madison sipped her latte and took a moment to let Ash's information dump settle. "Maybe she'll show up to see who I am."

"You want to be bait?"

"You'd be there, wouldn't you? I'd be safe."

Ash shook his head. "Didn't your daddy tell you that's just something cops say? 'We promise we'll keep you safe.' But we can't really make that kind of promise. Not really. We can't fully control the outcome of a live situation like that. So no, you probably wouldn't be safe."

Hard to hear what Daddy says when he's burst your eardrums with his fist. "Thanks for being honest." Disappointment sank into the pit of her stomach like bad coffee. Surely this couldn't be the end of the story for her? She'd never ducked out on an assignment, and she had a contract with *Time* magazine to honor. She couldn't let them down. She hated to let anyone down. That was something she had learned at her father's hand. "So, what's next?"

"You need to toss that burner cell and be careful. The last thing you want is for a woman like her to be on the hunt for you. Pun intended. And don't go after any more of the people on her client list, as much for their sake as well as yours. I'll shake a few of them down and see what they're willing to tell me. If I tell them she's already killed Powell because he talked, maybe they'll be prepared to cut a deal with me, and we see what other information they can give us."

"I'll come with you."

Ash shook his head. "No, you won't. I can't have a journalist spooking them out."

"Then we don't tell them I'm a journalist," Madison said but pulled herself back from an all-out plea.

"You're asking a police officer to lie? Something that simple could get any case we bring against her thrown out of court."

"But you're not going as an official police officer, Ash. You still don't know who you can trust in your own station. But you know you can trust me."

Ash leaned back in his seat and looked toward the counter in anticipation of his coffee. "Your dad would kill me if I let anything happen to you."

How he'd managed to keep his lack of affection for his own daughter a secret from so many people was beyond her. "Nothing will happen to me. I'll be fine."

Joni placed Ash's coffee in front of him, and he took a big swallow of the dark nectar.

"No. I don't think so. I've got some leave coming up in a couple of weeks. I'll pick it up then. You should just steer clear of it all."

Madison gave him her best sad smile. "Okay, but you have to tell me everything. I need this story." *And I'm going to get it by myself. Like always.* She wouldn't go to the restaurant meeting. That'd be suicide without Ash. But she would follow up on the other four donor recipients that were in Carlos's file. She just wouldn't ask for an introduction this time. She'd have to come up with a different story instead. *One that doesn't lead to another murder*. No matter how much death she saw, it didn't get easier. There was no desensitization. Each loss of life was as hard for her as the first one. If anything, these were worse than in a war zone because she knew she was responsible for them. She was trying hard to convince herself it was for the greater good, and that the people dying weren't the "good guys." It wasn't working so well.

"I'll give you whatever I can, Mads. Always. Just promise me you'll let it lie for a few weeks. She's got nothing to trace to you right now, and I want to keep it that way."

"Of course I will," she said, with her fingers crossed under the table. "My agent's been bugging me for a meeting about a celebrity biography. I'll busy myself with that and let *Time* know the story is on hold for a while. I'm sure they'll understand."

"Good." Ash finished his coffee in another long slurp. "I have to go." He stood and pulled on his jacket. "I'll be in touch."

"Thanks."

She waited for him to leave before she took her leather satchel and carefully placed it on the table. She opened it, withdrew Carlos's folder, and turned it to the next person on the list of Therese's clients, Christine Hinds. Madison tapped the number into her phone.

"Hi, this is Christine. Leave a message and I'll get back to you."

She had an easy SoCal lilt to her voice that sounded melodic. Under other circumstances, it might've appealed to Madison, but all she could think about was the fact that Christine Hinds had stolen someone's life to continue living their own. A privilege of the rich. She flicked through her contacts and dialed Elodie. Their non-date date night had been the most fun and most relaxed she'd been for a long time. Maybe ever. Elodie had made it clear she was interested in more than friendship but hadn't pressured her at all. For the life of her, she had no idea why the "world's most beautiful human" would find her remotely attractive.

Maybe she was tired of skinny, silicone-sexy Barbie doll types. And who was she to argue? They could have some fun, Elodie would probably tire of her quickly, and they could go back to being friends. Madison was emotionally unavailable, and Elodie was far too sexual to settle with one person. It was possibly the best hookup she could stumble across. Neither of them were relationship material, and Madison had needs that extended beyond the abilities of her bedside battery-operated companions.

"Hey you, I've been hoping you'd call."

Madison's pussy throbbed in response to Elodie's low and seductive voice. Now that she'd made the decision, there was really no point in waiting any longer. "Really? Why?"

"I like talking to you. Where are you?"

"I'm in my happy place. It's a coffee-slash-bookshop near the Grand Canal. It's been here nearly three decades, and they make the most amazing lattes." She cradled her cell in her neck and took a sip from the oversized mug she needed two hands to pick up.

"Drop me your location and let me try one then."

"You should just take my word for it. This is a nice, peaceful place. It wouldn't do well with the whole Elodie Fontaine hoopla descending on it."

"I told you, it's easier now. I can go anywhere I need to go, anytime. Not harassed."

"What if I harassed you?" Madison surprised herself with the line and wished she could drag it back before Elodie heard it. The silence from the other end of the phone did nothing to make her wish otherwise.

"How about you grab a skinny chai latte for me and bring it over to my house?"

Oh my. Elodie's voice was sexy enough already, but she dropped it a few octaves lower, and her intent was obvious. "Is that a good idea?" Madison asked.

"I've thought so since I met you, but you've been playing hard to get.

Don't change your mind now."

"I'm leaving right now."

"I'll be waiting."

Madison ended the call and ordered the drink for Elodie. What the hell had she just done?

Chapter Twenty-One

Elodie was waiting in the doorway as Madison pulled up the long gravel driveway in her CR-V. Her lack of pretention was yet another thing for Elodie to like about her. Madison could probably afford some showy, eye-catching gleam machine, but instead, she preferred to blend into the crowd and go virtually unnoticed. Some of the things Madison had said indicated her nagging self-doubt, so perhaps that's what made her choose such a common car in the pursuit of anonymity. Either way, it made her all the more endearing.

Madison swung the door open and had to use it to climb down to the ground. Her diminutive stature and the height of the SUV sidestep made a simple exit effectively impossible. Elodie would've laughed if it weren't for the unfamiliar apprehension that threatened to pull her heart into her stomach.

Madison walked toward her quickly and with obvious purpose. She didn't say a word, just wrapped her arms around Elodie and held her. She felt a wave of what she could only describe as safety sweep over her. She was usually the one doing the holding, however briefly that might be. She couldn't rightly recall the last time anyone had held her, truly held her, in their arms. The last person to hold her that way had been her father, before he lost himself in drink following her mother's betrayal. She hadn't ever considered that her lack of interest in real intimacy might have come from the issues her parents had. She buried her face into Madison's neck to push that intrusive thought away, and she inhaled her feminine scent in deeply, finding it both comforting and arousing.

Elodie finally pulled herself out of the embrace. "Hey you."

"Let's go inside. You feel cold."

Elodie was still dressed in her morning workout clothes. Instead of getting dressed for her imminent company, she'd spent the last half hour zipping from room to room trying to prepare for Madison's visit. Madison's touch on her bare shoulder made her shiver, but it wasn't from the cold.

"Can I get you a drink?"

Madison looked at Elodie and smiled. "I'll take a tea. Where's your kitchen?"

Madison kicked off her sneakers to reveal bare feet. Elodie noted her toe rings and instantly thought her feet looked sexy peering from the baggy bottoms of her well-worn jeans. It gave her an unexpected beach-bum girl kind of style. "This way."

When they got to the kitchen, Madison took Elodie's hand and guided her to one of the stools by the kitchen bar. "You take a seat. I'll make us both tea since I dropped your chai all over the sidewalk in my rush to get here."

"Are you secretly British?" Elodie made an attempt to take away from the anticipation that hung in the air and gave her a natural smile, so different from her trademark smile. She couldn't see herself, but she could feel the difference.

Madison laughed. "No, I just hear it's customary to drink tea in…these kinds of circumstances."

"Oh? And what kind of circumstance is this?" Elodie rose from the chair only for Madison to put her hands on her shoulders and gently press her back down to the seat.

She placed her fingers to Elodie's lips. "Just for once, let someone else take control."

Elodie looked away, unable to bear Madison's strong scrutiny. Every word that came from her mouth was like she'd opened up Elodie's head and pulled out her hidden, inner truth. There was literally no hiding place. At least when they were on the phone, she could conceal her body language, her expressions. Although Madison had proved able to divine so much more than her words should ever reveal, even without being face-to-face. "Fine. The green tea is on the counter next to the coffee machine."

Madison smiled at her Gaggia. She muttered something about matching tattoos that Elodie didn't quite catch. "Sorry, what was that about tattoos?"

"We have the same coffee machine," Madison said. "It's a bit of a cliché, like matching tattoos…"

Her cheeks colored slightly, making Elodie smile. She rested her feet on the side struts of the breakfast bar chair and sighed loud enough to distract Madison from her tea making.

Madison motioned to her position. "Are your legs open wide enough there, cowboy?"

Elodie laughed gently but didn't move. She'd never adhered to the societal model that prescribed girls should keep their thighs tightly clamped together to maintain a more feminine appearance. She was far more comfortable in clothes that allowed her body to position itself where it damn well liked, and she only made begrudging exceptions when she was necessarily sheathed in an elegant Dior or Versace.

"You should concentrate on making our tea." Elodie's iPad buzzed to signal an incoming message, and she cursed herself for not switching it off.

I've been following your girl. Imagine my fucking surprise when she ends up at your place. I'm not watching you two have sex. Txt me when she leaves, and I'll pick her up again. So far, nothing unusual.

Elodie smiled, turned it off, and returned her attention to Madison. She watched her move quietly around the kitchen, finding spoons, mugs, and honey. It felt so normal and natural. She couldn't stop herself from thinking that she'd like to watch her putter around her kitchen every day and let herself drift into a daydream where she was watching Madison making them dinner. They were talking about Elodie's day at rehearsals, Madison's latest feature piece. It seemed idyllic. Perfect, even.

"Hey, where'd you go?" Madison stood in front of her, mugs of steaming tea in her delicate hands.

"Who said I went anywhere?" Elodie was genuinely puzzled by Madison's seemingly intrinsic knowledge of her.

"I could see it in your eyes. Where'd you go?" She set the mugs on the counter and placed her warm hands on Elodie's naked thighs.

"I was thinking about your story." She wasn't about to tell her she was picturing domestic bliss.

"Okay." Madison didn't sound convinced. "What about my story?" She pulled out a chair and sat down.

Elodie missed the feel of her hands instantly. "I'm worried about you. Ice tells me this Therese Hunt is a big deal in the organ trafficking business and that she's a bit too fond of wreaking her revenge on people. And the guy you went to see *undercover*? Ice says he's disappeared and is presumed dead. It's likely she knows who you are. I don't want anything bad to happen to you."

Madison took Elodie's hand and clasped it between her own. They felt soft and her grip was gentle. Despite her very real concern for Madison's well-being, Elodie wanted Madison's hands all over her body. She wanted to be held just as Madison had held her at the door, but she wanted more than anything to be naked against her. She was craving the warmth and solace she instinctively knew she would find in Madison's arms. The all-enveloping feeling of safety in her presence was infinitely comforting.

"You're worrying about nothing. I was supposed to be meeting her, but Ash has warned me off, saying it's too dangerous. He's going to check out the rest of the clients when he's on vacation. I'm leaving it alone until then."

"I don't know why, but I think you're lying to me. I don't think you're the kind of person that lets anyone tell them to back off from a story." Elodie felt the unfamiliar burn of tears behind her eyes, and her nose buzzed uncomfortably. The thought of losing Madison already hurt more than she cared to contemplate, and they hadn't even slept together. *How can our connection be this strong so soon?* Madison stood and wrapped her arms around Elodie. She felt the swell of Madison's breasts against her face and sensed she was home. She wrapped her arms around Madison's waist and drew her in even closer. She wanted to burrow beneath her skin, because even being held this close wasn't close enough.

She pulled away slightly and tentatively kissed Madison's collarbone. Madison placed her hand beneath Elodie's chin and tilted her head so their eyes locked. There was no anger or judgment in her eyes. All Elodie saw was understanding and a desire that matched her own.

Madison kissed her, and the intensity made Elodie sag on her stool. So she hadn't romanticized it beyond reality. Madison slipped her hands over Elodie's shoulders and traced the naked muscles on her back. Their lips parted, and they simply looked at each other.

"Take me to bed," Madison whispered.

Elodie stood, took Madison's hand in hers, and headed to the master bedroom. It seemed to take an impossibly long time, in which Elodie prayed Madison wouldn't come to her senses and change her mind. For once, Elodie felt something akin to nerves. She'd bedded hundreds of women, and she'd never doubted herself. *It's never been this important before.* As she guided Madison through her mansion, all she could think about was not letting her down or disappointing her. All she wanted was to be good enough. Madison had finally decided to let whatever this was take its course, but now Elodie was suddenly plagued with self-doubt. Despite having had sex with countless women, only now did she comprehend that she'd never made love before. Did she even know how? And when had that become what she wanted?

Madison stopped, tugged on Elodie's arm, and turned her around. She took Elodie's face in her hands and kissed her again, deep and hard. "I want *you*, Els, not your reputation."

Elodie tried to hide her bewilderment. Was this connection so enigmatic that they didn't need words to communicate? Eager to push such transcendental thoughts to the back of her head, she pushed Madison against the wall and kissed her with an almost vicious desire. Madison responded and twisted her hand in Elodie's hair. The pure, animalistic drive to consume Madison thrummed within her. Her pulse pounded and her pussy throbbed. She wanted Madison so badly it was painful. Her body ached for her touch, for the caress of this woman who had appeared in her life and enthralled her so completely.

They stumbled the last few feet to Elodie's bedroom. She picked her up, and Madison wrapped her legs around Elodie's waist, their mouths never losing contact. Elodie tried to stop thinking and concentrated on the feel of Madison's body against hers. She knelt on the bed and gently laid Madison on the cloud-like comforter. She took the hem of Madison's tee and pulled it over her head before quickly tossing it aside. Her breath caught in her throat as she took in the beauty of Madison's breasts. She reached around and uncoupled her silken bra and trailed her fingers along her shoulders and arms as she took the straps down. She bent over and took Madison's nipple in her mouth, moaning when Madison called out her name. It exploded in the air and showered Elodie with the passion of a thousand orgasms. Plenty of women had called out her name in the past, but none had made it sound so exquisite, so unequivocally vital, as if she needed it to continue breathing.

Madison grasped at Elodie's tight tank and ripped through the flimsy material, exposing Elodie's breasts.

She laughed and looked a smidge sheepish. "Oops."

Elodie grinned wickedly and discarded what was left of her tank. "Who knew you were so brutal?"

They fell together again, kissing with ferocity as they tore at each other's clothes. Elodie was desperate for the feel of Madison's naked flesh against her own. She pressed her body firmly against Madison's and took the time to look into Madison's eyes. Desire and wanting reflected back to her. "You're so beautiful."

Madison shook her head almost imperceptibly. "Thank you."

Elodie frowned. "You don't believe me?" How could Madison doubt the authenticity of her words?

"I believe *you* think I'm beautiful."

Elodie leaned into her, kissing and nibbling at her neck, trying hard not to tear at her skin with the ferocious intensity she wanted to. Elodie worked her way down Madison's body, reining in her impatient craving to taste her, to drive right through her. She kissed the soft, yielding flesh of her curved stomach and reveled in its perfect disparity, both to her own muscle-hardened stomach and the skeletal nothingness of so many of the women she'd slept with.

Elodie peeled off Madison's jeans and tossed them aside. She caressed the soft give of Madison's thighs with her lips, her breath dancing lightly on her wet lips as she passed from left to right.

Madison twisted her hand in Elodie's hair. "Please. Suck me off."

Elodie wanted to deny her, deny herself. She wanted to kiss every inch of Madison's skin from the tops of her thighs down to the toe-rings on her tiny feet. But she couldn't hold herself back. She yearned to discover how Madison tasted and how she'd respond to her tongue. She slipped farther along the bed and parted Madison's thighs deliberately slowly. She tongued her wet opening, where she could see the copious pooling of Madison's juices. Madison moaned loudly and whispered Elodie's name again. Just as before, it sounded beatific, each syllable so sensual.

Elodie worked two fingers inside her as she clamped her mouth around Madison's engorged clit. Madison cried out quietly while Elodie licked and sucked. She started gently, but the harder she sucked, the louder Madison's cries became, so she happily obliged, all the time keeping a firm rhythm with her fingers. She hadn't been there long when she felt the natural rise of Madison's hips, and she pressed Elodie's face harder to her core. She convulsed beneath her, shouting out to God as she came.

"Fuck me. Fuck me hard."

All self-doubts had faded as they'd hit the bed, as their kisses became as familiar as if they'd been doing it their whole lives. She pulled away from Madison's soft, wet lips, got onto her knees, and thrust her fingers deeper and harder.

"Give me more."

Madison's throaty, hoarse instruction made Elodie throb harder. She guided a third finger inside her slowly, before resuming the steady, solid pace Madison was responding to. She grabbed urgently at Madison's breast, pinched and flicked her hardened nipple. The noises Madison was making drove Elodie insane. The hungry, desirous look in her eyes and the way her body moved in response to Elodie's touch excited her like never before. She'd always loved to make women come; she loved the utter abandonment of pretense and the inevitable release of their sexual energy. A woman was at her most honest as she orgasmed, which was probably why Elodie liked it so much. The constant façade of Hollywood and life was wiped away in that instance.

But the look in Madison's eyes was on a whole different level. This connection was like an invisible element binding them together. *What was this intensity?* Madison lifted her ass from the bed and forced herself further onto Elodie's fingers. Her moans became louder, and she shouted out yet more expletives. The pace of her hips meeting Elodie's rhythm quickened, and her whole body shook violently. Her muscles clamped down hard, keeping Elodie exactly where she wanted her.

"Now."

Somehow, Elodie knew exactly what Madison needed. She powered her fingers in as deep as they would go.

"Oh my GOD!"

Madison bucked so wildly beneath her that she struggled to stay inside, but there was no way she was coming out yet. Madison stilled, opened her eyes, and focused on Elodie. Her expression was a finer reward than another Best Actor Oscar.

"Baby…"

Elodie slowly picked up her rhythm again and fixed her mouth around Madison's breast.

"Oh fuck…"

She pumped her arm, and the faster she went, the more Madison's chest heaved. Elodie grinned. Madison was connected to her sexuality so acutely, another indication that they were a damn fine match. This felt so right, easy, and natural, like they'd been doing it for years, that Elodie might be inclined to revisit her generalized dismissal of all things spiritual. *Something* had brought them together.

Madison came again, screaming out her name. Elodie paused to enjoy Madison's body. She looked so relaxed and satisfied, her natural voluptuous curves rising and falling in semi-exhaustion. She was so wonderfully real, completely different from the women Elodie usually fucked. But she wasn't certain this was just fucking.

Elodie leaned over, kissed her vehemently, and began to work her fingers inside her again.

Madison clamped her hand around Elodie's wrist. "Your turn, handsome."

Madison slowly extracted Elodie's fingers with a breathy gasp. She sat up and kissed Elodie hard as she guided her onto her back. She undid the rope tie on Elodie's shorts and pulled at the waistband. Elodie lifted her hips obligingly so Madison could pull them off, though they got caught around her feet. There was an awkwardness in disrobing that sometimes stunted the spontaneity of a sexual moment, but Elodie just looked at Madison and they laughed. Madison's laughter soon dissolved into a growl when she registered Elodie wasn't wearing any underwear. She lay down beside her and traced her fingers around the light ridges on Elodie's stomach. She followed the central line between her rib cage up to her breasts, before squeezing her nipple between her index and middle finger. Elodie took a sharp intake of breath, and Madison raked her nails from Elodie's shoulder, over her bicep and down, pausing momentarily to caress the snake tattoo on her forearm. As she reached Elodie's palm, she pushed her hips toward Madison.

Madison smiled when she saw the effect she was having on Elodie. "You like my nails?"

"They seem to have found a direct connection to my happy parts, yeah." The feeling surprised Elodie. She was a giver, always had been, and when women did try to give back, she soon grew impatient with their efforts and would flip them back over to receive again. It wasn't that she didn't enjoy receiving, it was just that she'd much rather be the one dishing out the pleasure, and she took enough satisfaction from that herself.

Madison drew another line from Elodie's palm, across her stomach, and down her thighs to her feet. When Madison's nails scraped the underside of her feet, Elodie squealed and kicked out, unable to control herself.

Madison laughed lightly. "Sensitive much?"

"Apparently."

Madison gripped Elodie's ankle with her right hand and sketched the lines of a windy river on the arch of her foot. Elodie twisted, and writhed, and grabbed a pillow to bite down on to control the involuntarily jerking of her foot. Her reaction seemed to make Madison do it more, until she lifted Elodie's foot to her mouth and her tongue followed a similar path. "Jesus, babe, you're gonna make me come if you keep on doing that."

Madison stopped. "And that would be a problem why?"

She grinned and returned to Elodie's foot to suck on each toe, watching how she reacted, like she wanted to learn everything that aroused her. Madison snaked her left hand along Elodie's thigh and came to rest between her legs. She pushed two fingers inside her and let out a lusty sigh.

"Oh fuck, you feel good." Madison released Elodie's foot and knelt between her thighs.

She pressed her palm to Elodie's and interlocked their fingers, fitting together like two perfect puzzle pieces.

"I should warn you, Mads, no one's ever made me come from fucking me." She didn't like to declare such a thing, but she didn't want to disappoint Madison, particularly given how quickly she'd orgasmed. She also didn't want to fake it, as she'd occasionally done before. She wanted this to be honest and real in a way she'd never needed.

"That sounds like a challenge. Unless you don't like being fucked?"

"It's not a challenge. I don't think I'm built that way, and women tend to get bored if they don't see a payoff. I'm a big fan of Freud's immature orgasms, though."

"So, do you like being penetrated, or do you prefer just to have your clit enjoyed?"

"It feels good, yeah. I guess not many people have been bothered to do it enough. People expect orgasms or they think they've failed."

"Well, I'm bothered enough, and I'll have plenty of fun trying even if I do fail."

Madison moved her fingers inside Elodie, and she let out a sigh. She bowed her head and drew her tongue over Elodie's nipples, before pulling one into her mouth and sucking on it hard. Elodie moved under Madison's hand. Whatever she was doing, it felt damn good, and Elodie was in no hurry for it to stop. Madison shuffled down the bed and lowered her face to Elodie's wet core. She tongued her clit lightly before drawing the whole hood into her mouth. She pulled her fingers out and Elodie moaned, hating their absence instantly, and she raised her hips from the bed, trying to follow them. Madison pressed her hand, slick with Elodie's juices, onto her stomach and forced her back down. Their other hands still entwined, Elodie squeezed petulantly, bemoaning the vacuum Madison had created.

"I want you to focus on my mouth." She pressed her lips back where Elodie needed them and centered her efforts.

"I hope you've got stamina, because I can take a while." When someone else was down there trying to make her come, she'd never been able to orgasm just with the feel of someone's mouth on her. She always accompanied their efforts with a graphic video playing in her head. They were lucky if they even featured in it, though they never knew.

"Els, will you just relax and let me enjoy you?"

Elodie wanted more than anything to do that. She wanted to be present entirely in this moment. She wanted Madison to be the first woman to make her come by stimulus alone and just by enjoying the fact that it was Madison between her thighs. She relaxed back onto the bed and stuffed the pillow under her head so she could get a good look at Madison. Her long hair, so soft and silken, cascaded over Elodie's thighs and stomach. It was the same vision she'd been having since they'd met, and it was even better than she'd fantasized it would be. It didn't take long for Madison to figure out exactly what she liked, and the intensity built rapidly. Elodie placed her free hand on Madison's head and pulled her in closer. Madison moaned and carried on, her hips rising and grinding onto the mattress as if she might come just from sucking Elodie off.

"Oh…God…that's…so…fucking good." She sank back into the pillow as she felt her climax rise. The throb developed into something altogether different, like her ass was weightless and rising from the bed. She tried not to let her pussy contract, knowing that if she did, she'd tip her over the edge into the orgasm, and she wanted this to last for as long as possible. She took one last look at Madison, whose stared right back at her, looking as high as she felt, and it was all she needed. She cried out with primal passion, riding Madison's face as she surfed the shuddering orgasm to shore.

When Elodie raised her head from the pillow after fully enjoying the post-orgasm aftermath, Madison was looking suitably pleased with herself. Elodie could see her juices covering her chin. Madison lowered her head again, but Elodie tried to wriggle free. "Babe, I take time to recharge."

"So *you* say." Madison had clearly impressed herself with the relative speed in which she'd made Elodie come.

"Hold me?" An undeniable vulnerability came over her, as if she'd been completely laid open. The honesty she sought in other women when she fucked them had claimed her too. Somehow, Madison had managed to reach beyond all her bullshit and pull out the real Elodie, a self she'd long forgotten existed, and a self perhaps even she wasn't familiar with. She lay, still and perfectly at peace on Madison's chest, and released a long, deep sigh.

"That's a big sigh. Are you okay?"

"I'm perfect, gorgeous. I'm just relaxed." Elodie didn't want to expand and scare Madison with the full extent of the torrent of emotions and thoughts whirring around her mind. She was agonizingly aware that her beautifully crafted barrier had been breached. Madison had scaled its impossibly high walls with the athleticism of a ninja and in less time than it had taken the sex sweat to bead on their bodies. She had crawled under Elodie's skin, and though that should've been irritating, it felt symbiotic. Elodie felt completeness in herself and an absolute absorption in another, in Madison. Inextricably linked with a pure physicality and undeniable energy, their sex had matched their impassioned conversations, and Elodie had to come to terms with the fact that she was truly enchanted with Madison.

"If this is going to work, Els, you have to start sharing what's really going on in that beautiful brain of yours."

Elodie smiled, though once again slightly disconcerted with Madison's unerring perception of her stream of consciousness. "So you'll be back?" Elodie surprised herself with the question, but she had to know whether this was going to be a one-time thing.

"Do you really need to ask?"

Chapter Twenty-Two

FBI Special Agent John Reed scurried up the steps of the Walt Disney concert hall with a thick padded brown envelope clutched in his right hand. Therese sat in the garden and waited; he'd think he was safe meeting in a public place. Nat had said he was suitably anxious after her last conversation with him. She'd explained that his prominent position within the agency was no deterrent for Therese. Criminal, innocent, or lawman, she didn't discriminate. He thought she was a crazy bitch. She'd seen it in his eyes when he'd witnessed Therese take her time to creatively dispatch a spy from another trafficking gang. Crazy was unpredictable and volatile. Crazy didn't care for consequences, and nor did she. The knowledge of her disregard for the law made people pliable and responsive to her demands. Reed was no different.

She headed back to the outdoor stage and paused at the Lillian Disney fountain. She didn't much care for public art. It all seemed so condescending, the so-called creatives of the world trying to bring great art to the attention of the ignorant masses. Or rather, what they thought was great art. But she did have a particular fondness for this one: a massive rose made from eight thousand broken tiles and two hundred smashed vases. She liked the idea of destroying something that was already beautiful to make something else even more so. And she enjoyed the occasional sharp feeling of the rose's curves beneath her fingers as she caressed its oversized petals, threatening to make you bleed if you touched it just the wrong way. Since its creation, Therese had considered it a tribute to herself.

Reed was already at the stage with Nat when Therese made it back. A selection of happy-snappy tourists milled around, trying to capture the perfect Facebook cover photo of the Gehry architecture. They wouldn't have been so impressed if it'd ended up being made of stone, as was originally planned.

Reed stood as she approached and smiled widely. He was clearly pleased with himself, but the fresh sweat stains on his Oxford button-down shirt evidenced his true level of discomfort.

"You've discovered who Santiago sent a second package to, yes?"

He sat and tapped his hand against the package. "It took a lot of grunt work, but yes, I have."

"It's good that you finally came through. Just in time." Therese hadn't really planned to kill Reed. He was useful and had proved his worth a few times over with details about planned FBI raids. She wasn't interested in grooming another FBI schmuck as her mole. It took time and money, neither of which she liked to waste.

"I'm in no hurry to become another victim of your inhumane interest in theatrical carnage," he said.

Therese raised her eyebrow, appreciating his use of language. "That sounds like a tag line. Maybe I should have that on my business cards."

Nat laughed. "I'll get right on that."

"Do I have a problem?" Therese returned to the reason for their meeting.

Reed took a breath, and his eyes darted around the crowd. "Well, there's not a simple answer to that question, I'm afraid."

Therese shot him a warning look. "You should be. Explain."

"Have you heard of Madison Ford?"

"No. Should I know her?"

"She's quite a famous print journalist. She recently won a Pulitzer for a fascinating article on a female to male transition. And she's done a lot of reporting from war and conflict zones."

It was bad enough when Reed said the word "journalist." When he added that she'd won one of the most sought-after awards in journalism, the situation worsened. "I'm going to assume that this isn't your idea of a joke."

He scoffed and shook his head. "Of course not. I know what's at stake here."

"Show me what you have." Therese would have to devise a solid plan. Journalists like Madison Ford weren't easily corrupted, no matter how much money they were offered.

Reed opened up the thick envelope and pulled out photos of an attractive, blond-haired woman with a full figure, exactly as Powell had described her. Therese liked the look of her, and she didn't miss Nat's appreciative expression. One of the worst things about living in L.A.

was the seemingly infinite number of skeletal women parading around, obsessed with sculpting their bodies to fit the nonsensical Hollywood ideal conceived to satisfy the unrealistic notion of male-defined perfection.

"What do you know about her?" Therese wondered how long it would take to break her, to find out what she knew and who she had passed it onto. It'd be a shame to kill her, but Therese had to look after her interests. She was too close to making the offshore facility happen to be thwarted. This journalist was pretty, but she was a threat, so she had to die.

"She was born in Baldwin Park, California. Her father was a highly decorated cop, her mother a waitress, and she's their only child. Her mother was ill a lot while she was growing up, and there's some indication that the father was abusive to both of them, but no charges were ever filed. She left for Princeton on a scholarship when she was just sixteen and her mother died shortly after. She travels the world extensively with her journalism and hasn't settled down. She's had a few relationships, mostly with women, but nothing that lasted, so there's no husband, wife, or children angle to exploit. Her only friends seem to be the people she works with when their paths cross. And since she hasn't really spoken to her father in over two decades, there's not much point snatching him."

Therese rolled her neck. Loners were harder to threaten than people with family and loved ones. "Bad things happen to journalists all the time. Where is she right now?"

"Well, that's the good news. She's here in L.A., and as far as I can tell, she's not on an assignment. Though she did just finish a very interesting piece on Elodie Fontaine."

"Really? Nat, get me a copy of whatever magazine that's in." Therese was temporarily distracted by thoughts of the goddess movie star and all the wonderful things she could do to her. Nat grinned, and Therese could practically see the same thoughts race through her mind. She couldn't decide if it'd be more fun to fuck her alone or double-team her with Nat. She'd spend some time thinking about that more in bed tonight.

"She's already been in touch with us," Reed said. "They put her through to me, and I've been stalling her, but she's not given anything up. She seems a little suspicious, so I assume the package from Santiago included detail about your connections with the Bureau. I'm hoping that's all it is. I was under the impression my assistance was very much on a need-to-know basis, with only you and Nat being those people? That *is* what we agreed."

Therese put her hand on Reed's shoulder and squeezed firmly on a pressure point. He sank slightly toward the steps and grunted quietly. "Worried for yourself, *Special* Agent?" She released him and saw animosity flash across his eyes.

He massaged his shoulder. "I'm worried for all of us. But you have the most to lose, so I know you'll handle it."

Therese leaned back and let her jacket fall open so that he'd see the knives in her specially made shoulder holster. "Don't test me, Reed. I'd just as soon slice your neck open right here and watch your blood trickle down to the stage for your lack of respect."

Reed held up his hands and lowered his eyes. "I didn't mean anything by that. It wasn't a challenge."

"Then you should be more careful with your words." Therese sat up and pulled her jacket closed. "You know I don't need much of an excuse to exercise my second amendment right."

"I'm sorry." He smoothed imaginary creases from his cargo pants.

"You've outstayed your welcome, Reed." Nat motioned for him to get up.

"Leave the package." Therese placed her hand on the envelope. "We'll be in touch if we need anything else from you."

"Of course. Ladies." He all but doffed his cap and trotted down the stairs with his tail between his legs. He looked back and offered a small wave before disappearing around the corner of the building.

"What's the plan, Therese? This woman's pretty high profile."

"We snatch her and take her to the island. Find out what she knows and if she's been talking to anyone else. I have to take her down before she does any real damage. Reed can only stall her for so long before she goes above him."

Nat wrinkled her nose and looked uncertain. "We need to be careful. She's moving in Hollywood circles, and people don't just disappear in Hollywood."

"Sure they do. They disappear all the time, and they die all the time. Overdoses, car accidents, home invasions." Therese counted the ways on her fingers. "Tail her and figure out the best time to snatch her. You need to do it fast. I have to know she's the end of this problem."

Nat nodded. "I'll get her if that's what you want. I won't let you fall at the final hurdle because of some journalist on the hunt for another Pulitzer."

"And I value your concern, Nat. You know I do. But I'm not making the same mistake I made with Santiago. We grab her and we find out what she knows. *Then* we kill her." She took a handful of Nat's hair and pulled her in close, brushing their lips together. "You know we'll have some fun while we're doing it," she whispered.

Chapter Twenty-Three

Madison awoke with Elodie wrapped in her arms, something that she expected was unusual for both of them. She was lying on Elodie's chest but felt the urge to ask if she could hold her. Elodie took what seemed like an inordinate amount of time before answering.

"I'm normally the one who does all the holding," she said. "I don't remember the last time anyone held me."

"Better get used to it." She wanted to pull the words back as soon as they left her mouth. It was too presumptuous, too forward. Though she couldn't help but hope that this wouldn't be one of only a few encounters, she hadn't planned on saying it out loud. The last thing she wanted to do was pressure her. Wordless, Elodie snuggled in so they could spoon, and Madison held her tight. She was a perfect fit, and it was a moment Madison wanted to last.

"You're willing to brave it and stick around, then?" Elodie asked.

Madison ran her fingers over Elodie's upper arm. "If that's what you really want."

"What do you mean?"

Madison let out a short laugh. "You're a gorgeous movie star, and I'm a frumpy hobbit. You'll tire of me soon enough, but I would like to see how long it lasts before the magic wears off."

Elodie shuffled her butt into Madison's crotch but didn't turn around. "Wow, that's some pretty heavy self-loathing, beautiful. That's not what I see." She smiled and kissed Madison's fingers. "How long do you *want* it to last?"

Madison was grateful they weren't having the conversation face-to-face. It was easier to talk to Elodie's back than settle on her gaze in case she saw something devastating. Though their conversations had been honest before, communication somehow seemed an awful lot harder now they'd had sex. She was going to have to drink more to have any chance of being as open as she wanted Elodie to be. "Maybe let's just sleep for now." It was a cop-out, but suddenly she was on a merry-go-round, and her usually sharp view of the world was fuzzy and out of focus. She didn't want to start exploring deeper feelings when she knew Elodie would eventually lose interest. *Just like everyone else.*

Elodie's breathing slowed and she relaxed in Madison's arms. She wanted to put it into words how good that felt, but they failed her. Sometimes, even for a writer, words just weren't enough. Madison drifted off, utterly exhausted, and they remained locked together like that until she was woken by the ache of her numb arm beneath Elodie's body.

Madison gently moved the wisp of hair that had fallen over Elodie's eye. She didn't want to wake her yet, but she *did* want to look into her beautiful eyes again and know everything Elodie felt. She wanted the old cliché about the eyes being the window to the soul to be true. She wanted to understand her, to know her thoughts and dreams, to share everything, as scary as that seemed. As she watched the slow rise and fall of her chest and the tiny movements of her body as Elodie dreamt, Madison could almost feel herself slipping deeper into the pit she'd had every intention of avoiding. Elodie would have to be the one to call this just sex between friends because after what they'd just shared in this bed, Madison definitely couldn't.

Now, as she was looking at her and waiting for her to wake up, there was an unfamiliar ache in the pit of her stomach, a wondering if she'd made the right decision to pull on the one-armed bandit and try for the jackpot.

"Hey there, gorgeous, have you been awake long? You should've woken me."

Madison's breath caught as Elodie had opened her eyes and she got to look into them again. It was then she was overcome with that feeling of wanting to stare into those eyes forever. She cautioned herself. *There is no forever.* "I was just enjoying looking at you. You really are the most beautiful woman in the world." Madison saw a flash of something, a hidden insecurity, pass briefly across Elodie's face.

"It's all smoke and mirrors, babe."

"Funny, I don't see any of either at the moment. I'm sure I did see a tiny chink in that otherwise impervious armor of yours just now."

Elodie looked away briefly. "What of it? I know you're not expecting me to be more than human. You already know me better than people who've known me for years. Witchcraft, I tell you." Elodie accented the last few words old crone style, almost negating the seriousness of her words. "Though you have me hoping that you turn out to be a white witch."

Madison giggled. "You're under my spell, then? It worked?"

"It certainly looks like it. I've never…wanted anyone like I want you."

Madison smiled and traced her fingers across Elodie's chest, before flicking her nipple playfully. "I'm glad that's not already past tense."

Elodie grasped Madison's wrist, flipped her over, and climbed on top of her. She pressed the heat of her center against Madison's stomach.

"You captivate me, little one. Cheesy and almost unbelievably fast, I realize, but absolutely true. I hope you're not already thinking we're past tense."

"Hey, get your own lines." Madison wriggled beneath Elodie's weight, but she had her pinned.

"I don't have to now that I have such an esteemed writer in my bed. No longer do my words have to be substandard and colorless."

Elodie's melodrama made Madison laugh. "Hardly," she said. "You don't need me to write your lines. You're smoother than I could ever be."

"You don't give yourself enough credit for your influence, lady." Elodie kissed Madison's nose. "You have no idea how powerful your words are."

"Tell me." Madison couldn't help fishing for compliments. She felt intensely vulnerable and with good reason. But she'd decided to run with this, and no matter the outcome, it would be an experience. She'd spent years studying people rather than becoming intimate with them, believing herself unworthy of their love and trying to figure out why. She was going to let herself simply be and see what happened. A broken heart healed eventually.

"You're sure you want to know? It might freak you out." Elodie released her grip and leaned back.

Madison rested her hands on Elodie's thighs and squeezed gently. "I'm not sure I could be any more freaked out than I already am. Yesterday, I had a great new friend. Today, I seem to have a lover."

"You need to relax, Mads. I want you, and you want me. It's simple enough if you just let it be."

Madison smiled and nodded. *If only it were.* "You were saying how powerful my words are…"

"You're the reason I got involved with the organ trafficking work."

Madison frowned, unsure she'd heard right. "Really?"

"Really." Elodie climbed off and lay on her back beside her Madison. She stared at the ceiling. "I've followed your writing for a while, particularly after you and your photographer friend won the Pulitzer for your feature on Troy. But your article on organ trafficking in the States woke me up."

Madison snuggled into Elodie's arms and laid her head on her chest. She followed the outline of her abs with her nails, drawing a passionate sigh from Elodie. "What do you mean by that?"

"I was at the height of my career—"

"You still are."

Elodie smiled and kissed Madison's fingers. "You're sweet, but anyway, I was banking the same amount of money as the top male actors, which was a first in Hollywood. I was on fire, and everyone wanted a piece of me, either on screen or between the sheets." She paused and stole a quick look at Madison, as if to gauge her reaction.

Madison laughed. "You can't be worried about what I think of your sex life?"

"Maybe," Elodie said, sounding a little shy.

"Don't. I couldn't and won't be trying to compete with your past." Madison would be shoving all invading thoughts of Elodie's bedroom antics to the deepest recesses of her mind. If she allowed them time in her conscious thoughts, she wouldn't be able to get past them, and this would already be doomed. "Carry on."

"I was hedonistic in the extreme. Anything I wanted, I could have. Any woman I wanted, I could have. People were bending over backward to make sure I was happy."

She smirked, and Madison thought she'd probably recalled an image of some woman actually bending over backward in some sexual scenario or another. "And back to the present moment, please."

"It was everything I thought I'd ever wanted. I had more money than I could ever spend. I had the house, the cars, the acting parts. I thought I was finally happy. Someone had left a copy of *Time* in my dressing room one day, and I ended up being late on set because I couldn't put it down once I started your article. It made everything seem so extravagant and insignificant at the same time. I realized I could be one of the people you were writing about. My liver could've failed me, and I could get a replacement like I was ordering a book from Amazon. I knew my agent would be the one making the call before I even thought about the consequences to another human being. It was a 'wake up and smell the putrefying flesh' moment." Elodie took Madison's hand in hers and stroked gentle patterns across her skin. "At first, I figured I couldn't do anything about it, apart from maybe stop living so decadently, although I couldn't figure out how that would help anyone else. But I talked to Ice about it, and she put me in touch with the TIP office. They practically snapped my hand off and got me involved with the 'Decade of Delivery.' I started trekking all over the world, meeting real people in dire situations, and I never looked back. You, your words, did that for me, and I'll always be grateful." She laced her fingers with Madison's and looked directly into her eyes. "You have to know, I haven't planned this, but I can't deny that I've had a thing for you since you came onto my radar."

Madison had listened intently to Elodie's pseudo-confession, but she struggled to believe it. She could barely believe this movie star had followed her work for so long; that was praise enough, but to admit to having a crush on her was astonishing. Elodie could have any woman on the planet, but she wanted Madison. She valued her work, and while past relationships had more or less supported her writing, they didn't understand it like Elodie seemed to. They never grasped its importance like she wanted, like she needed, them to.

Was this the whole package that was the mainstay of Hollywood movie endings? Had Madison somehow stumbled on the mythical magic of the Utopian relationship she'd never thought to search for? But how long could it last? They operated in such different spheres. Elodie, like the others, was sure to find that the rigors of Madison's work—the long hours, the constant travel, the inherent dangers—were too much to bear in the long run. Only time would tell…if she allowed it to run its course. "I don't know what to say. I'm speechless. And honored. I've always written in the hope that I can make a difference, but to know that I was instrumental in your decision to take the path you've taken, that's mind-blowing. When I think of the difference you've been able to make, raising the nation's consciousness about so many issues… and not just America, but worldwide. It's hard to take in that I had a little to do with that."

"You didn't have a little to do with it. It was all you." Elodie ran her fingers through Madison's hair slowly. "It was your words that changed my direction. I can still be extravagant with my money, but I guess I'm finding a balance. I'll spend half a million on a car, but—"

"Auction it for charity six months after buying it?" Madison had read many such accounts of Elodie's generosity.

"How did you know that?"

"You're not the only one who can use Google, you know?" Madison buried her face under the comforter.

Elodie pulled it from Madison's face and stroked her cheek softly. "But if my agent had her way, I would never have gotten involved. She's not so happy with fifteen percent of volunteer work."

Madison laughed, but she was still in a sort of shock. She had more to say, but she'd probably end up having to write it down and email Elodie. Her thoughts and emotions were always clearer with her fingers on a keyboard. Right now, she just had to show how she felt. Madison lifted her head and kissed Elodie with all the emotion she couldn't put into words.

Elodie responded, breathless. "If I'd known that telling you that would have gotten you this horny for me, I would've told you when we first met."

Madison replied with another kiss. Sometimes actions really were more powerful than words.

Chapter Twenty-Four

After finally managing to pull herself away from Elodie with the promise of returning in the evening, she headed off to meet her agent. She'd called Dom to cancel, but he was adamant he had the proverbial offer she couldn't refuse. That much-needed break was looking ever more distant. She'd been just as busy in L.A. as she ever was in New York.

She didn't much enjoy driving, particularly in L.A., where the traffic took the term to a whole new level. The lost hours sitting at a standstill in a never-ending march of cars gave her the opportunity to watch the people in the cars around her and wonder about their lives. She'd been doing that for a while now, and she'd noticed the same car behind her for miles, despite its driver having plenty of opportunities to pass. It was a black Escalade with darkened windows. The windshield was tinted so she couldn't make out how many people were in it, but she found it unsettling, like she was being followed. She took the turn off Santa Monica Boulevard onto Melrose. It was a diversion from her WeHo destination, but she wanted to see if the mystery truck followed.

The Esplanade took the same exit and followed her winding route until she swung into the parking lot of Soho House for her meeting. The truck continued past her. She tried to catch the plate details but didn't manage it. She'd been careful with Powell, and she'd ditched the burner cell, just as Ash had insisted. There was no other way for Therese to have found her. *Was there?*

Dom greeted her at the front desk with his trademark bear hug, but it did nothing to quell her absolute sense of anxiety.

"Hello, stranger."

Dom's crisp English accent was as strong as ever, despite his constant exposure to the Californian burr. Madison had a good ear for phonological variations, but she hadn't guessed Dom's correctly even though he'd given her three attempts, a challenge when they'd first met. If she'd guessed correctly, she was free to choose whether or not he'd become her agent. If she couldn't, she had no choice but to accept that he was the man to guide her career as she became more in demand. The very suggestion of the game was enough to secure her as his client, but her epic and unexpected fail sealed the deal. His Yorkshire accent had been polished by his eclectic education. "Have you missed me that much?" she asked.

Before she'd met with Elodie, Madison had made sure Dom knew how irritated she was being used to pay off a favor. She wanted him to know that asking her to do the Elodie Fontaine interview was quite the imposition and that it didn't suit her reputation. Now, she wanted to return his hug with ferocious gratitude. However things turned out, whether Elodie ended up being her friend or partner, Madison was enjoying being in her orbit.

"Force of habit, girlie. I'm used to you being away for far longer."

Dom was the only guy she'd let get away with that kind of endearment and only because he was practically family. One of the beautiful people came around from the front desk and pressed for the elevator. Madison had never quite decided if she liked this place or not. It was incredibly pretentious, but she could see its appeal for Hollywood's movers and shakers with actors able to come there without being bothered by adoring fans. Given that they weren't alone, Dom made small talk on the trip to the rooftop garden. Despite the fact that this was a member's club, and known worldwide for its discreet patrons and staff, Dom was always reluctant to share any of his business with anyone but his client.

The maître d' showed them to Dom's usual table before disappearing with their drinks order. Madison placed her satchel in the seat beside her before settling in her chair. She checked the Find My Friend app and was glad to see Elodie was still at her mansion. She liked that Elodie wanted to know where she was and that she could check in on Elodie in return. It wasn't a trust issue; it was comforting to know Elodie was that interested, and that she wanted her to feel safe as well. And even though Elodie had joked about being able to find Madison's body if any of the dangerous assignments she undertook went wrong, it did make her feel a little safer knowing someone was looking out for her, that someone cared enough to have her back. "Maybe I'm coming around to the idea that L.A. isn't that bad, after all." *Now there's a sentence I never thought I'd say.*

He raised his eyebrows in surprise. "If you've finally been Californicated, that may make this offer easier to sell to you."

Madison wrinkled her nose. "Sounds nasty. Have you trademarked that phrase?"

"Maybe I should, so don't steal it in the meantime, girlie."

"What's this offer that couldn't wait a few days? I'm supposed to be busy doing nothing for a few weeks." Madison thought of Elodie. She wasn't far from nothing, but she would definitely keep Madison busy.

"Okay, so Troy Donovan wants you to write his biography."

Madison's intrigue rose a fraction. "Really? Isn't he a little too young for a biography?"

"I think you'll agree he's already lived quite the life. The popularity of your feature vouches for the hungry readership out there wanting to know more. It's still one of the *L.A. Times*' most viewed articles. It's a good new direction for you, girlie, and you're his first choice."

"First choice? He has a list?" Madison tried not to be indignant, quickly challenging her uncharacteristic egotism. It wasn't like she had a *New York Times* best-selling pedigree or had published a book at all. She was lucky she was on such a list, let alone top billing.

"There's always a list, girlie, don't fret. In Hollywood, your favorite is very rarely available, unless you're prepared to wait, and there's a distinct lack of patience in this town. The point is, and the thing you should be concentrating on, is *you* are his first choice. He says you understand him, and he's comfortable with you. It's a six-figure deal, and it adds another string to your bow." He nudged her gently. "And it would mean no war zones for a while."

She appreciated his care for her safety. Dom was clearly excited at the prospect, and Madison didn't think it was just because he'd get a hefty ten percent agent's fee from both parties. However, she couldn't quiet the nagging at the back of her mind that a second successive celebrity piece might be perceived as her joining the dark side. Would she lose the respect she'd worked so hard to earn?

"My two favorite clients collaborating on a project that has the potential to influence and change lives. I'm in agent heaven. Say you'll make it so."

Taking on projects that could influence and change lives were two of the reasons she'd taken this career path. Madison had *written* books before. She had around five in her virtual bottom drawer that were all stuck around the thirty-thousand-word mark, where she always got bored, or disillusioned, or began to question her ability. So, she knew what it took to write a novel but not to actually finish it. Journalism was a different beast altogether, but a memoir was a little closer to her wheelhouse. "What exactly would it involve?"

"A lot of one-on-one meetings. He says he has notes, journal entries, and ideas, but he trusts you to do whatever it is you need to get the job done."

"I'd need three-hundred-sixty-degree access with no boundaries. And no censorship. If this is a story that needs telling, it has to be warts and all. I won't be involved in some fluffy rainbows and unicorns account of his trans journey. He has to be one hundred percent honest with me about everything. Kids going through this have to know the bad, the ugly, and the painful."

"He said you'd say that, and he said go back and listen to the New York part of his interview with you."

Madison recalled that his truth was beautifully brutal. He gave her everything she asked for that night and more. They'd both ended up in floods of tears and a sea of vodka.

"He wants to make the extended book version of your Pulitzer feature, with a photo-journal, if you will. So he wants Geva Doyle involved too, but I'm having real trouble tracking her down. She's a friend of yours. Do you have any idea where she is right now?"

"She's in China with the pandas, but I can get in touch with her. I think she'll be interested." After the Russian assignment, maybe Geva would appreciate a break on non-volatile soil too.

"You two are his dream team. Say you'll do it?" Dom pulled out a sizeable chunk of printed papers and placed it before Madison on the table.

The contract had her name on it. "Isn't that a little presumptuous?" She thumbed through it nonchalantly with no intention of signing it just yet.

He looked smug but pleasantly so. He was one of the few agents who was actually likeable.

"You know I'm a big believer in being prepared. My lawyer drew it up a few days ago. I was almost certain you'd go for it. You need a challenge, Madison. You don't need a few weeks' break. You'd be bored within three days, if that. I know you. If your fingers aren't dancing daintily across a keyboard, all is not well in your world. If you're happy in Hell A for a little while, this is the perfect solution. You can indulge your newfound Californication without worrying about bombs or militia."

Madison felt a little mercurial about the change in direction. She'd had a career path in mind since she'd started with serious journalism, and yet here she was, fresh from writing one of the best-selling print celebrity pieces in a decade, seriously considering writing a biography. *Who am I?* "I need to meet with him before I sign anything. Who else is on his list for the photographer?"

"Terra Gibson. And he said you'd say that too, so he's joining us." Dom checked his watch. "He should be here any minute now."

He'd barely finished the sentence when Madison spotted Troy emerging from the elevator. He was wearing a white tee and black jeans, and Madison noticed how much more muscular he'd gotten since the feature. Geva had taken shots of him at the gym and pool as he'd worked hard to rid himself of the feminine curves he'd inherited from his beautiful mother. He told Madison he wanted the perfect male form: the six-pack, the V-shape upper body, and biceps strong enough to hold a woman with her legs wrapped around him. The last part resonated with Madison. It was one of her fantasies to be fucked standing up by a dildo-toting woman with big muscles. After this morning, she was already wondering if Elodie was strong enough, or if she would even wear a cock. What her hands were capable of was magic enough. Madison hadn't had that many orgasms in a month, let alone one morning.

"It's so good to see you again, Madison," Troy said and held out his hand. "Thanks for taking this meeting with me."

Madison took his hand, and he pulled her into a gentle hug. His chest felt rock solid against her soft breasts, quite the difference from their last hug in New York. Troy had probably thought she wouldn't meet him because of his clumsy attempt to seduce her that night. He'd mistaken Madison's empathy for something else and made a move. She was stunned at first, the vodka and the deep discussion about gender identity had muddled her brain, and she wasn't sure at that exact moment who she saw him as. His lips were soft, his touch on her breasts practiced, and it had felt like the touch of a woman. In that, he already had a big advantage on most guys. Realization had kicked in, and she'd pushed him away firmly, before they had a calm conversation about desire, love, and identity. They'd spoken briefly on occasion since, but they'd never talked again about that night. He seemed nervous about how she might receive him now.

"It's good to see you too, and I'm always interested in talking about new projects, Troy." Madison didn't want to make him any more uncomfortable than he already was, so she didn't say that Dom had hoodwinked her into meeting him.

"And are you still interested?" Troy asked, his hope apparent.

Madison could hear and see how important this was to him and began to feel privileged that he'd chosen her to help him tell his story. "I am, yes. But I have a few questions."

Troy grinned. "Color me surprised. Shoot."

The waitress brought Troy's drink and their refills. She lingered as she handed Troy his beer and their fingers touched. Madison smiled when the girl blushed slightly. She wondered if the girl knew Troy's history. In the limelight, could he ever be free of it? "What are you doing this for? It seems a little early for a biography." For now, Madison held the blunt question she had in mind: *Is this just for a quick payday?*

"I'm seeing it more as a memoir than a biography. I want to tell people about my journey into manhood, now that I feel like it's complete. Now that I'm accepted."

Madison recalled his agony over his reflection in the mirror, pre-top surgery. "Do you accept yourself now?"

He took a slug of beer before answering. "I believe I do, yes. It's been a long trek, but I think I'm there… So does my therapist."

They all laughed.

"That's unusual," Dom said. "It's not like a Hollywood psychiatrist to deny themselves a lifetime of paychecks."

"He hasn't," Troy said." He still wants to see me, and I want to see him. I've got issues beyond my gender, just like any actor."

Madison had always appreciated Troy's sense of humor. He was grateful for where he'd gotten to in life but was still very aware he was a work in progress. "And you believe America's accepted you?"

"For the most part, I do. And not just America, but Europe. And England especially."

"That's not the experience Brad Carlton had when he came out. How does your situation reconcile with a Hollywood that sees fit to cancel contracts on the basis of sexuality?"

"I can't comment on that. Maybe it's more about his relationship with Hollywood than his relationships with other men that's faltered his career."

Madison decided to probe hard to make sure he was ready for the challenge ahead. Memoir was a particularly difficult pursuit, and the words hardly ever came forth without being accompanied by tears. "You think you're different? Special in some way?"

"No, I didn't say that." Troy ran his fingers along his bottle. "I do think Elodie Fontaine did the groundwork in many ways, and I'd love to emulate her success. She was always out, and she made the world love her regardless. They never saw her as queer first. They see their beloved movie star, they see her as a great actress, and now they see her doing amazing humanitarian work. Her sexuality and her sex life are almost a side note. Or at least they would be if she weren't so promiscuous."

Heat raced up her spine at the mention of Elodie, then she stiffened, uncomfortable to be reminded of Elodie's prolific reputation and what Madison was trying hard not to compete with.

"I think this book could educate people: parents of trans kids, the kids themselves, and anyone who wants to understand what being trans means."

"Do you not think you might be preaching to the converted?" Madison asked. "The people who will want to read your book are the ones who already support you and all trans people. How are you going to educate the ones who wouldn't dream of picking your book up off the shelf?" Madison was being argumentative, but she had to be sure Troy was doing this for the right reasons. She wanted to do it, and she was excited at the thought of working with Geva again, but it was a huge commitment and a big career move. It had to be perfect.

Troy took a long pull on his beer. "I have to take this one step at a time. The ones I'm most concerned about are people like me. If I can help just one trans guy on his journey, if I can make it better in any way and show that you can make it and all the pain and suffering is worthwhile, I'll be happy." He laid his hands on the table and stretched his fingers out. "This isn't a vanity project, Madison. You can be sure of that."

"Is it all about AFAB for you, or are you aiming it all trans people?" Madison asked.

"That's what I know from experience, sure, and I can't begin to know what it's like the other way around, but the journey is similar. We're all just trying to find our authentic selves."

Dom coughed. "So, Madison, are you green-lighting this project or no? I think you're a match made in heaven."

"Maybe you could give us a minute, Dom?" Troy said.

"Of course. I'll grab a quick puff of fresh air." He picked up his Camel Lights and headed for the smoking area.

When he was out of earshot, Troy took Madison's hands in his. "I wanted to say that I'm sorry again about what happened in New York. I was drunk, and you'd been exceptionally kind to me. I took your kindness for something sexual, and I'm so sorry for that. You'd been nothing but completely professional, and I disrespected that. Will you forgive me and work on my book with me? It has to be you, Madison, you and Geva. It wouldn't feel right any other way."

She appreciated his words, as rehearsed as they sounded. It made up her mind to go ahead and give it a try. With a subject that was close to her heart, it wasn't the fluffy celebrity hole she didn't want to be sucked into. It had deeper resonance, and she wanted to be a part of it. "We talked about this when it happened. There's nothing to forgive. You were vulnerable and needing something…something I could never give you, but something. I'd love to work with you again."

"You won't believe how glad I am to hear that. Thank you so much." He released her hands and finished his beer.

Madison sipped at her peach iced tea. "When do you want to get started?"

"Yesterday? Last week? Whenever you're ready. I'm filming a pilot for a TV series so I'm in L.A. all the time. Does that suit you? Dom said you were staying in the city for a while."

"Did he?" Madison shook her head. "I don't suppose he also told you that I was taking a break from work?"

"I wouldn't have listened even if he had," Troy said. "But I'll delay starting the project if you need a couple of weeks. If we can get Geva on board, I could start with some photos while you enjoy some downtime?"

It was sweet of him to offer, but he was desperate to start and clearly hoping she wouldn't accept his offer. "No, it's fine. I don't think I'm programmed to take vacation time." Though she might otherwise easily end up spending the next month or so in Elodie's bed, existing on nothing but sex and pizza, with nothing to do but wait around for more of the same until she came home from rehearsals. It'd be good to have something else to concentrate on. She wanted to maintain her sense of self through her work, because falling into Elodie's bubble was a very real possibility.

"Have you signed the contract, Madison, or are you still grilling our brave hero?"

Dom's return to the table was well timed. She wanted to get back to Elodie but didn't want to leave Troy alone. She thumbed through to the first section with a bright pink Post-it note. Dom offered her a pen, but she waved it away and retrieved the one she carried with her everywhere.

"That's a beauty. Is that a Caran D'Ache?"

Troy's interest reminded her he had a collection of rare and antique pens, from ones used by presidents to one of Hemingway's.

"Good spot," she said. "It was a gift to myself after I won the Pulitzer."

Troy raised his eyebrows. "Quite the gift. Is that platinum casing?"

Madison flushed. It was the most extravagant item she'd ever bought herself, and it still made her feel guilty to recall how much money she'd spent on it. "It is." She signed her name in the requisite places as Dom and Troy exchanged friendly, mocking "oohs."

Dom raised his glass. "A toast to my two favorite clients and the beginning of a very exciting project."

They clinked glasses and sipped their respective drinks.

"I hate to cut this celebration short, but that's exactly what I have to do." Madison pushed the contract toward Dom.

"You'll call Geva?" Troy asked as she stood.

"Of course. I'll get back to Dom as soon as I get hold of her. She'll probably want to meet you again, and she might take some convincing." Their Russian assignment might've given Geva the desire for something easier though, just as it seemed to have done for Madison. "This is a far cry from her usual assignments, but you might be in luck."

The men stood and took turns to hug Madison goodbye.

"It'll be good to have you in L.A., girlie," Dom whispered in her ear.

Madison smiled. The Troy project would be amazing, but so was the opportunity to stay in town to spend more time with Elodie. She wanted to enjoy what they had for as long as it lasted.

Chapter Twenty-Five

"This isn't a woman you play around with, Dee. She runs an organ trafficking gang worth millions, and they're not going to be gentle if they find out Madison is writing an exposé about their operation. If they know about the package she received and come after her, it will get real messy, real quick. Does she even realize who these people are? Every fucking government agency wants a piece of Therese Hunt, but no one has been able to prove anything yet, and every time they think they've got someone to talk, that person ends up in pieces or baked in a car."

Ice paced the kitchen floor, making Elodie nervous. It was something Ice did when she was on high alert or irritated. Right now, it seemed like she was both. "She's not really told me any more than I passed on to you. I know she's been working with a cop friend, and even he's warned her off doing anything else. He's worried for her safety after the Powell guy disappeared."

"Who's this cop? She trusts him why?"

"Ash Coleman, he's an LAPD lieutenant. I think he knew her father." Though, from what Madison had told Elodie about her father, he certainly wasn't someone to be trusted.

"That name sounds familiar. We knew a Coleman back in the military, and he was a real badass. Even gave us a run for our money, do you remember?"

Elodie didn't. She'd tried hard to forget everything and everyone but Ice. "I guess it could be the same one."

"I might look him up. He could prove useful if we need some local backup."

Elodie frowned. "Are you saying you can't protect her alone?"

"No, I'm not saying that. I'm asking if she has any idea what this guy has dragged her into. The informant who passed this info on has dropped a bag of fucking snakes in her lap. You need to let her know what I'm telling you. She needs to know I'm around, and she needs to let me protect her. I can't do it properly from a distance."

Elodie got it. She'd come across people like Therese Hunt in her old life. Madison was used to danger in her line of work, but this was something else. "Have you seen anybody around her? Do you know where this trafficker is right now?"

"She's based here in L.A. somewhere, but there's no way of knowing if they're on Madison's trail or not. It could be that they're completely in the dark and Madison's safe. But I *can* guarantee she won't be if she publishes that article before they get caught. No matter how fast the FBI shuts that shit down, you can be sure they won't rest until Madison's been taken care of."

Elodie shivered as if icy cold fingers had trailed down her spine. She'd finally found someone she could see more than just a few nights with, and she was in mortal danger. Elodie had no choice but to convince Madison not to write the article. "I should get her to give everything to the cops and let them handle it. The insider was worried someone in the FBI was involved, and since you're saying nothing's happening over there, he was obviously right."

"Not the cops, no. Get her to give everything to me. I'll pass it on to someone I trust implicitly. Let them deal with it, and I'll keep Madison safe in the meantime. She can write her big article after they go down."

"I don't think she'll give it up. I reckon she's already looking up the other four clients Santiago gave her details of."

Ice rolled her eyes and pushed away from the counter. "She'd be insane to take them on herself."

"I don't think she's insane." Elodie gave a half-smile. Madison had nerves of steel, as far as Elodie could see. "I think she might just have an unhealthy disregard for the value of her own life."

Elodie's phone ringing interrupted their conversation, and she answered it without checking the ID, hoping it was Madison. Ice had done an excellent job of putting her on edge and made her desperate to hear Madison's voice again. She had to know Madison was safe.

"Finally, you're answering your phone again. I've been trying for hours, but even your landline was off. I was beginning to worry."

Elodie sighed loudly. She did *not* want to speak to Paige right now. "What do you want?" All she could think about was Madison and her safety. Ice motioned to the door, waving the iPhone she'd given her.

Madison had accepted Elodie's Find My Friend app request laughingly, not knowing that Elodie's real motive was to give Ice a relatively cheap tracking device.

"I'm heading out. She just left Soho House," Ice said and left Elodie to deal with Paige.

"I've got the script for you for the first movie in the female 007 franchise. Do you want me to bring it over?" Paige asked.

"Not really. I'm kind of busy with something else." There was a small pause, most likely from Paige's shock at Elodie's lack of interest in the script she was offering.

"Are you okay? Is there something I can help with?"

"I'm fine, Paige. Just leave me alone." Elodie regretted her harshness, but she was so intensely worried about Madison she didn't have the energy to waste finessing her responses to Paige.

"Wow. Okay. I'll leave you to it."

Paige hung up, and Elodie slammed the phone on the marble countertop.

"Fuck!" Helpless was something she hated being. Deep down, a sickening ache in the pit of her stomach called for her attention. Elodie's phone rang again. This time, she checked who it was and sighed when she saw Madison's face on the ID. "Hey you." Elodie tried hard to control the emotion in her voice.

"Hey. What's up?"

"Nothing, why? I'm just missing you." And worried for her life. "You've been gone forever."

"You sound strange."

There you go again with that sixth sense. "I do? Must be how I sound when I'm lonely. Where are you? Are you on your way ho—back?"

"I am, but the traffic's bad as usual so I could be a while. I just wanted to hear your voice, but it sounds like something's wrong."

Elodie traced the trails in the marble. "It's nothing." She clenched her fist and knocked her knuckles to her head. She already hated lying to Madison. "How was your meeting? What was the offer of a lifetime?"

Madison tsked. "It doesn't sound like nothing, but fine, I'll play along and we'll talk when I get back to you. He had a book offer. Troy Donovan has a deal to produce a biography slash photo book, and he wants me to write it for him."

Elodie didn't care that much for Donovan. Madison had managed to make him almost likeable in her feature series, but in real life, he was tough to take, with his fake self-deprecation and false sense of humor. But it was his story about Madison that really bothered her. "Do you want to do it?" Elodie recalled him trying to impress her with tales of his conquests and had bragged about fucking the journalist and photographer in a New York threesome. Elodie already had a small crush on Madison, and the way Donovan spoke about her really pissed her off.

"I've signed the contract. I think it's a good move for me. And it keeps me in L.A. for a while longer."

"Am I not enough of a draw to stay in this hellish city?" Elodie couldn't decide if she was teasing or was half-seriously disgruntled at the prospect of *not* being a good enough reason.

"You know you are. But I need to work, or I'll end up bugging you all day, every day."

"That wouldn't be such a bad thing." Elodie took a stubby glass from the shelf and pushed it under the ice dispenser. Satisfyingly giant chunks dropped into the glass and made crackling fire-like noises as she poured Disaronno onto them. "Are you two okay after your New York liaison?" She took a sip of the sweet almond liqueur, and the fiery liquid slipped down her throat like a snake sliding across sand dunes. Everything felt too out of control, and she wanted a moment of calm before she talked to Madison about not writing the article. *About not doing her job. How would I feel if someone said it to me?*

"What do you know about that?" Madison asked, sounding a little concerned.

"Relax, sweet lady. I can hardly judge you about your exploits before me. Though I wouldn't have thought threesomes were your style." She took another hit of the fierce soother and tongued the sticky liquid from her lips. *Stop picking a fight. You want her here and this is a good reason. Don't be stupid.*

"Threesomes? What are you talking about? I haven't had a threesome since I was in college, and that was enough of a disaster to put me off them for life. What *have* you heard?"

"Donovan has a mouth on him. A while back, he took a lot of pleasure in telling me all about his wild night with you and your photographer friend, Geva Doyle. Sounded like fun…if you like boys." Elodie couldn't keep the distaste from seeping into her words. But if she didn't keep a lid on this, Madison wouldn't be coming back at all.

"Sorry to disappoint you, but that's all in his head. He made a pass at me one night, and we kissed. I was drunk, and he was partway through his transition. But I stopped it. And Geva wasn't involved at all. Maybe he doesn't need me to write his book since he seems to have such a vivid imagination. And since you're asking, I don't like boys or cock…at least, not real ones."

Elodie finished her drink and poured another, much larger one. "I'm glad."

"Glad I don't like cock?"

"Well, yeah, of course, that too. But that you didn't fuck him or that he didn't fuck you. He's a false Romeo, and he pisses me off."

"False Romeo? You mean he brags about bedding the number of women you've actually fucked?"

Madison's annoyance was clear, but Elodie wasn't sure if it was directed at him, her, or both of them. "I mean, he's all mouth and no action. Look, I'm sorry. I shouldn't have said anything. It's great you've got the job. I want you close to me." Another swallow floated Elodie's emotions dangerously close to the surface. How did Madison do this to her so easily?

"You do? Tell me why," Madison said softly.

Elodie heard the smile in her voice, and it made her sigh. Making Madison happy seemed to be her current priority. "You'll laugh. I'm too shy."

Madison did laugh. "*You're* too shy?"

"It's a little-known fact, but yes, I can be shy." She refilled her empty glass again, noticing the ice barely had time to melt.

"I like it. It's sweet. But still, tell me why. It's not as if you're having to tell me to my face. I know that's hard…for both of us."

Madison was right. Elodie wanted to be the most honest and open version of herself, but actually doing it was almost painful. To lay herself bare, to be this vulnerable, felt so alien, and yet she'd never felt more accepted. "You've got a one fifty-one IQ, so why don't you work it out?"

"Tell me."

Elodie sighed and took another shot. "I really like being with you. I like the me that I am when I'm with you. I like how everything and everyone softens in the background. I like you being my leading lady." Another drink, another truth. "I like our conversations, I like that we can talk about anything, and I'm really enjoying getting to know you. It feels…you feel right, like we've only just met but you've been there all along, waiting for me, waiting for this, waiting for us."

Elodie paused. There was utter silence from Madison. She looked at the glass and cursed its power to release the chain on her emotional drawbridge. "So traffic's bad, huh?"

"Baby…"

The way Madison said it made Elodie deep sigh again. *God, I love your voice.* "Let's talk when you get back. I'm going for a quick swim while I wait. Maybe it'll release some of this sexual energy."

"I've got a better way of doing that," Madison whispered.

"I don't doubt that for a second, but there's plenty of it to spare for the pool, trust me. I'll see you soon."

Elodie had already placed the phone on the counter, not wanting to hear Madison say goodbye. She never wanted to hear Madison say goodbye.

***

Head in, breathe out, stroke, stroke, stroke, head out, breathe in. Elodie loved to swim, and she loved water. It calmed her. When she'd made enough money to buy and develop her dream house, an Olympic-size swimming pool had been one of her first design considerations. Now, she swam every day.

She hit the edge of the pool after twenty laps and stopped for a brief rest. As she emerged from the water, Madison handed her a towel.

"Hey you."

Elodie lifted herself out of the pool and took the towel. "Hey you."

Madison leaned in to kiss her.

Elodie pulled back slightly. "You'll get wet."

"I'm already wet." Madison winked.

Elodie smiled. It was a comeback she'd have been proud of. "You're turning into a sex addict."

"Maybe I've always been one, and I just needed the right dealer. Make me high." She opened her arms.

Elodie pulled her close and soaked Madison's blouse. They kissed, hot and hungry, almost enough to make Elodie forget what she had to say. She broke away, needing to get the words out before she lost her nerve. "We have to talk. You can't write the organ trafficking article."

Madison looked bemused. "What? Why not?"

"It's too dangerous. You're going to get hurt, and I can't let that happen."

"Lots of my jobs are dangerous, Els." Madison squeezed Elodie's hand. "It goes with the territory. But I'm taking a break from it when I've finished this one. That's one of the reasons I've agreed to write Donovan's book, although your story has me questioning that decision."

Elodie took Madison's hands and led her to the poolside bench. "You don't understand. I think you're in danger. But if you hand that package over to Ice, you'll be okay."

"You sound like Ash. Has he called you? This is my story, Elodie. It's what I do. Carlos trusted me with it, and I have to make sure he didn't die in vain."

"What do you care about Carlos Santiago? You didn't even know him." Elodie felt the effects of the alcohol rise along with the volume of her voice and paused to control herself. "Your cop hasn't called. Ice looked into it for me because I was worried about you, and it turns out I have good reason to be. You haven't thought this through. You put your name to an article before they're in prison, and they'll come after you. My friend has contacts she trusts. Give her the package, and they'll do a proper investigation. When the gang's brought down, then you write your article. Santiago's dead. Now Powell. What if you're next?"

Madison looked like she might be considering Elodie's words. "How do you know you can trust your friend?"

"I told you. I trust her with my life."

Right on cue, Ice entered the pool house. "Evening, ladies. It's nice to finally meet you in the flesh, Madison, instead of just following you around like gum stuck to your shoe."

Ice was typically blunt, and Elodie flashed a shut-the-fuck-up look as best she could.

Madison narrowed her eyes and glared at Elodie. "What does she mean?"

Elodie sighed. "I hadn't gotten around to that part yet, Ice, but thank you."

"What're you waiting for?" Ice asked. "Time's not for wasting. I need to get your package to my guy, and we need to talk about me keeping you safe by being closer to you, rather than a few cars or tables behind you."

Ice was used to dealing with military types and politicians; she simply expected her advice to be taken, which was why she'd only done one movie consultancy. Elodie's director hadn't taken kindly to being ordered around by a tall, butch woman packing a Beretta.

"You've been following me?" She turned back to Elodie. "And you told her to?"

"Baby, this isn't a game—"

"No, it isn't. And it isn't one of your movies either. Who do you think you are, telling me how to do my job? I don't come on your set and give you acting directions. What gives you the right to tell me what to do? And having someone follow me? What gives you the right to infringe on my privacy?" Madison moved away, putting physical and mental distance between them.

Ice took a step closer and stood in Madison's eyeline. "I'm sorry that you think Elodie's overstepped the mark, Madison, but you need to understand who these people are. The man who sent you the package and ended up dead. He'd been with the gang for over a decade and was practically family. But still, Therese beat him almost to death, slaughtered his father, probably in front of him, and then burned him alive. This is a person who kills for sport. You're nothing to her, so how do you think she'll deal with you? Elodie was right to be worried about this, so you need to let me protect you. Give me the package so I can get a proper investigation started. I'm pretty sure they're already—"

"I don't even know who you are. How do I know I can trust you any more than anyone else?"

"You can trust her, Mads." Elodie rested her hand on Madison's leg, but she brushed it away.

"You had me followed, Elodie. What were you thinking? Why didn't you just come straight to me with this? Now how do I know I can trust *you*?"

Elodie ran her hands through her wet hair. "It wasn't like that. Ice was checking it out at the same time as keeping an eye on you."

"No, that's no excuse." Madison got up and ignored Elodie reaching out to her. "I won't let you treat me like a child. I don't need your protection. I've worked in countries where women and children are used as bait and shields, where there are people who wanted me dead from the moment I stepped off the plane until the moment I got back on it. And you think I don't know what I'm doing now? I'm a big girl, and I can look after myself, just like I've always had to. I need to get out of here. You're toxic, and I don't think I can be around that."

Elodie stood and grabbed her wrist. "Please, Mads, please don't go. I need to keep you safe."

Madison pulled away. "No. No, you don't. The only thing you need is control, over everything and everyone around you. I'm not another toy for you to play with as you see fit, and I sure as hell won't be controlled or told how to do my job." She turned to Ice. "And you, don't you follow me anymore in your scary black Escalade." She left without a backward glance.

"Dee?"

"Ice?"

"I don't drive an Escalade."

Chapter Twenty-Six

Madison couldn't get in her car fast enough. She kicked the gravel at her feet before dropping into the driver's seat and locking the doors. As pissed off as she was, she knew if she stopped, just for a second, she'd fall into Elodie's soft eyes and forgive everything. And she sure as hell didn't want to do that. Not yet anyway.

A lot of what they'd said made sense. Of course it did. But the deception, the control, that's what hurt. Her father had controlled her and didn't stop trying even when she was hundreds of miles away at Princeton. Now it felt like Elodie was trying to do the exact same thing. As though Madison wasn't capable of making decisions of her own, for her own good. They'd barely gotten together, and Elodie was already trying to call the shots.

Madison headed home. She needed to be alone. She was always better alone. She needed to shut the door on her apartment, switch off the outside world, get into a hot bath and think things through. Was she really in imminent danger? The serious woman Elodie had called Ice fit Madison's stereotype for a clandestine CIA agent perfectly. Brusque, no-nonsense, and built like a brick shithouse. Elodie was working with the TIP office, and the cartel couldn't possibly have every government officer on their payroll. Madison knew she should probably trust Ice, and the things she'd said about Therese made her skin crawl. Madison had never been able to grasp the limitless viciousness of some people, the pleasure they'd take in their violence. It wasn't news. Carlos had detailed several accounts of the way Therese dealt with informants, with competition, or just with someone looking at her the wrong way.

Madison slammed her hand against the steering wheel as she braked at a stop sign she registered just in time. Part of her had known nothing permanent could ever come from getting involved with Elodie. The other part reminded her how good she felt when they were together. Even though they'd spent such a short time in each other's company, on the phone and in person, Madison had begun to realize what love and happiness might be. Before…before, they were just words. Being with Elodie was giving her the emotions to go with the words. It seemed ridiculous to finally be feeling what love was all about when she was pushing forty, and yet it was tempered by this control issue. *Love or lust? Control or all-consuming concern?* Madison had always been independent, always looked after herself. When she was a child, she'd been the one to care for her mother. Her twin, Safia, had always been too self-involved to help or care about anyone other than herself. In relationships, Madison never allowed anyone to look after her, though she was sure they must've tried. But she'd kept everyone at a safe distance. If she only ever depended on herself, no one could let her down. Rightly or wrongly, it was a life edict really based on her childhood. Elodie's anxiety over her safety was alien, especially so because it might actually be welcome. *Kind of.*

The driver behind her honked their horn and pulled Madison from her musing. She held up her hand. She glanced at the rearview mirror and saw Ice's black Escalade three cars behind her. Anger and relief flooded through her. She pulled into a turnout a few hundred feet along the road and turned off the engine. The Escalade pulled in behind her, but Ice didn't get out. Maybe Elodie was in the passenger seat. Well, Madison was going to find out. She got out of her car and devoured the ground between them.

She rapped her knuckles on the blackened window, and her irritation began to build. The window lowered slowly, and Madison was greeted with the business end of a mini Uzi. She recognized it from the time she'd spent in Syria with rebel forces.

"Well, look at you, making our job so easy, Ms. Ford. Won't you get in?"

Madison looked beyond the barrel and into dark brown eyes. If she were at all religious, she may have been inclined to believe in evil, just from that glare. She recognized Therese's right-hand woman from Carlos's photos. "Natasha." Madison tried hard to project calm in her voice. Her chest tightened and breathing became hard. She briefly considered running, but her legs were leaden and heavy. *I can't outrun a bullet.*

"You've been expecting us?" The rear door opened, and another menacing woman stepped out, gun in hand. "Therese would like to meet you too, but you'll wish you hadn't been in such a hurry."

The other woman grabbed Madison's arm and pulled her toward the backseat. There were no other cars passing by, and there was nowhere to run. She climbed into the car, and another woman in the backseat pulled her in quickly.

"Jen, go check her car for the package. Let's tie up the loose ends." The front seat passenger nodded and got out of the car silently. "Rope her up, Blake, and strap her down. She needs to be in one piece for Therese to enjoy taking her apart."

The two women in the back forced Madison's head between her own legs and fixed her arms behind her back. They secured her wrists with paracord, before they slammed her back into the seat. The one called Blake fastened the seat belt across her waist.

Madison thought about her phone in her back pocket. Could she pull it out and manage to dial someone with these two goons on either side of her? It might be her only chance. She didn't expect them to be so stupid as not to search her at some point. Jen returned to the car with Madison's satchel in her hand and passed it to Natasha.

Natasha rummaged through it and quickly found the package she was looking for. "I hope for your sake you haven't shared this with anyone else."

Madison clenched her jaw and tried not to give anything away.

"Do you want me to search her, Nat?" Blake asked, her tone suggesting she might really enjoy that task.

Madison met Natasha's gaze in the rearview mirror, and the look made Madison feel physically sick. There was an unerring sense of malevolence, and she regretted her unusually quick temper at Elodie's house. She wished she were still there, debating on a course of action, considering letting Ice protect her, handing over the damned package to the authorities.

Natasha grinned and nodded. "Of course you should. And be really thorough."

Madison braced herself as Blake turned to begin her task. This was only the beginning. She was a journalist, not a soldier. Sure, she'd taken some hostile environment training and attended various kidnapping workshops, but what good was that training in the face of someone like Therese? It looked like she was going to find out. *I'm sorry, Elodie.*

Chapter Twenty-Seven

"What the fuck does that mean? I don't care what car you drive." Elodie didn't know whether to chase after her or let her be for a while so she could cool down. Madison had every right to be mad at her. She should have told her about Ice. *I just wanted to keep her safe.*

"Madison said she was being followed by a black Escalade," Ice said. "I hired a Yukon for this little expedition."

"She's not exactly a car aficionado, so she probably doesn't know the difference. What are you getting at?"

"What I was going to say earlier; they're already following her. I picked up their trail on the way to her lunch meeting. The Escalade wasn't subtle, that's why she saw it. I've been in the field for over two decades, and no one knows when I'm following them."

The penny dropped. Madison was being followed by Therese or someone in her gang. And now she was out there without Ice's protection. "We'll take my car."

Ice looked at Elodie, still wet from the pool. "You get some clothes on, and I'll pull the Aston around front."

Elodie set off to her bedroom, taking the stairs three at a time. She misjudged the last one, tripped, and sprawled onto the wooden landing, knocking the wind out of her. She picked herself up and stumbled to her room. She tried to steady her hard breathing as she quickly changed into a tank top, jeans, and sneakers. It wasn't the exertion. It was the fear. She'd read some of the documents in Madison's package. Therese was an abomination of a human being, the kind of person Elodie had sought to combat through her humanitarian work, the kind of person she'd battled against in Afghanistan. She'd never expected to experience it again this close to home.

She sprinted outside to Ice, who was loading a small bag into the trunk. Elodie was grateful for her presence *and* her portable armory, though she was wishing it was bigger. Of all the people Elodie knew, Ice was the only one qualified to deal with a shitstorm of this magnitude. There was no one she'd rather have by her side right now.

Elodie got in the car, started the engine, and accelerated along the long drive toward the electric gate. "Jesus Christ!"

"Who the fuck is that?"

She slammed on the brakes as another car entered the gates.

She couldn't maneuver around the offending vehicle due to the narrow drive. Elodie was out of the car almost before she'd brought it to a complete stop. "Fuck, Paige, reverse your car, and get out of here." Elodie smashed her hand on the hood of Paige's convertible.

"What's wrong with you? I came to see how you are. Something's obviously wrong."

Elodie gripped the car door tightly. It was that or Paige's throat. "You're in our way. I need you to move your car."

"No. I won't. Not until you tell me what's going on with you." Paige motioned at Elodie's hands, her knuckles white and veins popping out on her arms from the pressure she was applying to the door. "I won't be able to put my window up ever again. You're going to crush my door."

"It's got nothing to do with you. Reverse your car before I drag you out and do it myself."

Ice emerged from the passenger seat and pointed her trusty Sig Sauer at Paige. "Do as you're told."

Paige's eyes widened. "What have you gotten yourself into? Are you in trouble?"

Ice shot her gun in the air, and both Paige and Elodie jumped.

"NOW."

They'd driven wordlessly for five minutes, heading for Madison's. She'd been shocked at Ice firing her pistol, but it was better than Elodie pulling Paige from her car and throwing her into the hedge.

Elodie slowed slightly for the stop sign and only narrowly missed the car crossing the intersection.

"Fuck!"

"Calm down." Ice shook her head. "It missed us by a—"

"That's Madison's car." Elodie's words almost lodged in her throat, threatening to choke her.

Ice swung in front of the parked CR-V, and they exchanged a silent look before approaching it. Madison was nowhere to be seen, and the keys were still in the ignition. Ice did a quick sweep, and Elodie held her breath when she checked the trunk, worst-case scenarios beginning to cloud her mind.

Ice pressed her palm to the hood. "Engine's still warm. No sign of a struggle, Dee." She walked quickly up and down the turnout. "No blood, but it looks like she walked toward another car."

Elodie started to shake. She dropped into Madison's seat and placed her hands on the steering wheel. *This is my fault.*

"Is her phone in there?" Ice asked. She repeated the question and put her hand on Elodie's shoulder, firm enough to bring her back around.

"I don't see it. It's normally in the cradle." Elodie wrapped her hands around the steering wheel. "It's not there...she's not here. Ice, she's not here."

Ice pulled Elodie from the car into a tight hug. "We'll find her, Dee. We'll get her back for you."

Elodie pulled herself out of Ice's arms. "Promise me, Ice. Promise me."

"Pull yourself together, Dee. If we're going to save your girl, it's time for you to ditch the movie star and slip back in time."

Elodie knew what Ice was asking of her and what she needed to do. It'd been over a decade since she'd held a real gun and not a movie prop, but she'd have to pick one up again now to have any chance of getting Madison back. "It'll come back to you. Trust me."

"I trust *you*. I don't trust them."

Elodie pulled on her soldier persona like an old favorite coat. These people had no idea who was coming for them, and if they harmed Madison at all, they'd pay in far worse ways than even Therese Hunt could imagine.

Chapter Twenty-Eight

"You did exactly the right thing, Doc. That's why we have the lockdown procedure."

Sweat beaded on Dr. Blakeley's pudgy face, and his shirt had dark patches under his armpits. Everyone was expendable, no matter their skill set or their loyalty. If they stepped out of line, every member of the team knew the consequences. The extent of any punishment kept them wary of making mistakes. Therese simply didn't tolerate them.

"Thank you, Therese. It's the first time anything like this has ever happened. Reality's a lot tougher than all those drills we practiced."

They'd suffered losses in South America due to poor aftercare, and that's why she'd moved this part of the business to L.A., with American doctors and American drugs. "You've done well, Doc, relax." Therese smiled. He was a great surgeon, one she'd poached from USC. Remuneration was good there, but Therese offered him so much more. He didn't take much persuading, a good sign that he'd be in it for the long haul.

She looked at the monitor and saw Mr. Lucas cradling his dead wife in his arms. It was the kind of image that would move anyone. She felt nothing. All she saw was a problem that needed solving. But she had to act fast, since she had Madison Ford to look forward to. As if on cue, her phone rang. "Where are you?"

"We've got her. We're nearly at the airstrip. Will you already be on the island?"

"No, Nat. I'm dealing with the Lucas situation. The wife died from complications, and Blakeley had to lock down the facility. Lucas was freaking out and threatening to call the cops."

"Do you want me to join you?" Nat asked. "Jen and Blake can take Ford to the island."

"No. You do it. I don't want any mistakes. You're my girl, Nat, but don't touch her. Deal with our other little problem in front of her. Get her good and scared."

There was a pause. Therese could practically feel Nat's twisted excitement.

"How will you kill him?"

"How do you want me to kill him?" Therese lowered her voice to the guttural tone Nat loved so much.

"Do you have your Mistress with you?" Nat whispered.

Therese knew she'd be throbbing, and her hand would have already traveled in that direction. Nat was referring to the beautifully balanced Down Under hunting knife she'd imported from England as a gift for Therese long ago. She unzipped her duffel bag and pulled it out slowly. "I do."

"Cut him from throat to cock. He was an arrogant prick. He deserves to die nasty."

Therese slid the knife from its embossed leather sheath. She'd always liked the feel of the leather handle, and Nat kept the brass pommel and guard polished to perfection. It was an epic knife, the largest in her vast collection. It was also her favorite. "I'll put it in Saran Wrap for you to clean when I get back." Therese pulled a roll of plastic wrap from the bag and laid it on the table.

"I do love watching your wet work. I wish I was there."

"You've got an important job to do for me. Focus."

Nat exhaled deeply. It amused Therese that just one word could melt her.

"I'll be there soon enough." Therese turned the blade over in her grip. "Deal with our greedy boy, and then we'll work the journalist together… nice and slow."

"Okay. I can't wait."

"Later, sweet filth monger." Therese ended the call and turned to Blakeley. "Have you called the cleanup team?"

"I have." Blakely glanced at Therese's knife. "They're on their way. And I've arranged their transport back to Cuba. Another unfortunate pair of American tourists fall foul of local hoodlums."

"If only Kennedy had made a better job of the Bay of Pigs, Cuba would be a much safer place."

Blakeley laughed, although it seemed a little forced. "They should be here in thirty minutes. Is that enough time, or shall I get them to wait?"

Therese liked that her surgeon understood her penchant for making the most from an unfortunate situation. "That'll be the perfect amount of time, Doc." She hefted the Mistress from hand to hand, and it slapped reassuringly hard against her palm. "Time enough for me to do the hubby a favor and send him to join his wife."

Chapter Twenty-Nine

Wet work. Mokroye delo. Madison knew its etymology. The Spetsbureau 13 of the KGB were known for its "wet dealings." Assassination, murder, the spilling of blood. She was in the hands of some twisted women. Natasha had flushed during the conversation, clearly turned on by the thought of Therese cutting up some poor guy. Madison's recent encounter with General Dudko in Russia had scared her, but that had been child's play compared to this. These women were criminals with no boundaries and no laws governing the treatment of their prisoners. "Where are you taking me?" Madison had waited until their barbaric conversation was complete. She didn't want to enrage her captors and give them a reason to hurt her.

"I thought a journalist would be able to come up with a more original question than that." Natasha and the rest of her captors laughed.

Madison shifted, trying to get the feeling back in her numb hands. "What do you want from me?"

"Therese wants to ask you a few questions, reverse the tables on you. You were wrongly sent some confidential information by a recently deceased employee of hers. Therese wants to know what you've done with it."

Natasha was matter-of-fact and businesslike, as if they were talking about stocks and shares. *Recently deceased? Brutally murdered, more like.* What did they already know? They obviously knew she'd received an identical package to the one Carlos had sent out to the FBI. At least, Carlos had said it was identical, but how could Madison trust him? Dead or alive, he'd still been a vital criminal cog in Therese's operation. A sudden conscience didn't wipe away the things he must've been responsible for. Was Elodie safe? Ash, even? Did they know who she'd spoken to about it at all? *How am I supposed to play this?* Madison sighed, desperate to think strategically. There was no playing. This was no game. They'd ask questions, and if they didn't like the answers she gave, she'd suffer.

Painfully and for prolonged periods. Hostile environment training could never prepare her for this. "Knowledge dispels fear" had been their tagline. It didn't ring true. Madison knew exactly what this gang was capable of, but she still feared for her life. Not really her life, but how she was going to die. "Other than meeting with Powell, I haven't done anything with it. You've got everything I had." Madison met Nat's look in the rearview mirror again, affecting a resolute expression, showing she was in control. Inside, she was a mess of fear and despair.

"Enough with the small talk. Gag her, Blake, I don't want to spoil Therese's fun."

Blake took a bandana from her pocket, tied a knot in the center, and with the help of the other woman, stuffed it in Madison's mouth and tied it around the back of her head. Natasha watched it happen in the rearview mirror as Madison struggled to stay calm. She had to quell her fears. She couldn't let them see her absolute terror, but the anticipation of what was to come had her wishing for unconsciousness. All she wanted to show Natasha was resolve. Taking her voice away removed her ability to reason or bargain with them. What did that leave her with?

Nat had mentioned an island, and Madison figured it had to be San Nicolas, the one detailed in Carlos's package. It looked like Therese's dummy corporation, run by some guy called Peterson, had managed to convince the Native Americans to sell their land to a criminal organization. Madison could only hope that Elodie remembered some of the detail from the documents she'd shown her, so she and Ice could rescue her. Madison couldn't quite believe her one great hope was a movie star. *A movie star who's also a war vet.*

Unless Ash checked in on her because he was worried about this whole situation. She cursed her own stubbornness. It was that and her ego that had gotten her this deep into something she would never have wished to handle herself. Had it all been about trying to impress Elodie? To show her what her real work was about because she'd compromised it by doing her fluff piece? It wasn't like she had anything to prove to anyone else.

Maybe she was being hard on herself. "The price of truth can be high for those who dare to risk their lives on the front line." She couldn't recall where she'd heard that quote, but she'd taken it too literally. She'd lost sight of the bigger picture, and though she'd considered the dangers, she'd chosen to ignore them. Carlos's death showed the FBI was corrupt; it had to have been their agent who had told Therese what they'd been sent.

But Madison had decided it had to come out this way, so someone would act. So someone could stop this evil bitch and her vile gang. Dealing in human organs was abhorrent enough, but the pleasure they took in the vicious side of their operations made shutting them down even more imperative. So she had to risk her life. *It's what hardcore journalists do.*

The truth. Justice. It was a sacrifice worth making, and she'd always known the risks. The incident in Russia had reminded her of those risks, and she'd lost close colleagues before. She'd been lucky, but that luck had finally run out. She had to accept that, as well as the knowledge she'd brought it on herself, when she'd had several people warning her to back off. Now she had to hope that somehow, she'd live through it.

Madison tested the ropes around her wrists. She'd done as she'd been taught: kept them together while the rope was looped around, then pulled them slightly apart as the knot was secured. Blake had been too interested in groping her to notice. If they left her alone long enough, she could work them loose. She'd lose skin, and probably draw blood, but getting her hands free could be a step toward escape.

The Escalade pulled to a stop. Madison was dragged out, pulled across the asphalt, and hauled into a helicopter. Nat got in beside the pilot, and the backseat pair sandwiched her again. The front seat passenger, who'd never uttered a word, waved them off from the ground before getting back in the car and driving off.

"Nice work, Nat. The boss'll be pleased with you."

The female pilot was of a similar build and look to Natasha. They could've been sisters. Madison stored the detail. If she got out of this alive, she wanted to be able to identify as many of the gang as possible. She didn't acknowledge the nagging fear that they weren't worried about showing their faces to her because they knew she wouldn't be leaving the island.

"She made it easy for us, walked right up to the car and rapped on the window, all sassy-like." Natasha turned to Madison. "Why did you do that?"

Blake removed Madison's gag. She rolled her tongue around her mouth to garner some saliva before responding.

Blake cuffed the back of the head. "Answer the question."

"Touch her like that again and you'll be answering to Therese," Nat said. "So, why?"

"I thought you were someone else." Madison said no more. She didn't want to warn them that there might already be a rescue in progress. She hoped.

"You looked pretty pissy. Who'd you think we were?"

"An ex." Madison met her inquisitive gaze. *Don't break eye contact. Don't look anywhere other than straight at her or she'll know you're lying.*

"An ex whose car you don't know?" Nat narrowed her eyes.

Madison shrugged. "SUVs all look the same to me. I'm no car expert."

Natasha faced the front as the pilot started to take off. "Let's get her to the island, then you can come back and wait for Therese."

"Okay."

The pilot glanced over her shoulder, and Madison thought she saw something like sympathy in her eyes. Madison tried to calculate the extra time that would give Elodie and Ice to find her before Therese landed. It would be at least another hour. Madison wouldn't be able to hold out for any length of time in the face of Therese's methods. Once she was in the same room as Madison, it was all over. She closed her eyes and pictured Elodie. *Please. Come for me.*

Chapter Thirty

Ice motioned toward the interior of the car. "See if the keys to her apartment are still here."

Elodie nodded and looked back at Madison's car. The battered leather bag she'd never seen Madison without was nowhere to be found. *I won't lose you.* She searched the car's pockets and compartments for Madison's apartment keys. Maybe Santiago's package was there. Madison had shown her some of the pages, but she couldn't remember a damn thing that was on them. She'd just gotten a sense of the malevolence this gang was capable of. And Elodie had let them get hold of her. Bile rose in her throat, her imagination running wild with vile possibilities. She squeezed her eyes shut tight, trying hard to rid her mind of the visceral images that invaded.

She found the keys in a concealed pocket below the steering wheel. "I've got them. Let's go." Elodie got into the driver's side of the Aston and started the engine. "I'm going to call the cop Madison was working with. If she showed him the file, maybe he knows something about where they might've taken her."

Ice nodded. "Tell him to keep his mouth shut. We don't want the LAPD involved. I'll get some CIA bodies on high alert."

"Can I speak to Lieutenant Ash Coleman, please?"

"I'll see if he's at his desk," the officer asked. "Who's speaking?"

"Elodie Fontaine."

The officer laughed. "Sure you are. You know I can trace this call and bust you for wasting police time?"

"Feel free. You'll find it's registered in the name of Elodie Fontaine. Me. I need Lieutenant Coleman."

The officer cleared her throat, maybe recognizing her voice. "I'm sorry, ma'am. We get a lot of crank calls. Let me get him for you."

***

Getting by Madison's reception had been easy. As one of the most recognizable faces in the world, her fame afforded her a pass for virtually anywhere. All this trespass had taken was a signed copy of the article in *M* magazine. The reception guard had looked a little confused when she pressed her hand over the glossy pages, like she could connect with Madison through her words. It was stupid, but she couldn't help it.

Now she and Ice were sharing an elevator with a dad and his twenty-something-year-old son, both of whom were trying desperately hard not to stare, sure that it couldn't be "the" Elodie Fontaine in their building.

It was the son who finally summoned the words as they hit the thirteenth floor. "Are you—"

"No, I'm not. I get it all the time, but no, I'm not Elodie Fontaine."

"I told you she wasn't," the dad said.

She didn't care at all for his dismissive tone. The son looked down and sighed. The elevator slowed for Madison's twentieth floor apartment, the doors opened, and she and Ice stepped out.

"She checked me out when we got in. That's how I knew it wasn't that dyke actress," the dad half-whispered as the doors closed.

Had it been another time, Elodie would've turned around and hit the dad with some withering put-down. Lucky for him, her full attention was focused elsewhere. They advanced slowly down the corridor, mindful that Madison could've been brought here if they wanted the package. They drew closer. The door was slightly ajar, and Elodie stopped. She wished she'd picked up the Beretta 87 she'd bought after leaving the Corps or any of the weapons Ice had in her bag back in the trunk of her car. On cue, Ice pulled out her Sig.

The elevator pinged its arrival, and she turned to see a big guy bearing down on them.

He held out his badge. "Coleman."

Elodie put her fingers to her lips to signal something might be wrong.

He pulled his Glock and tried to wave Elodie and Ice aside. "Stay here," he whispered.

Elodie clamped her teeth shut and tensed her jaw.

"What do you think you are, the fucking cavalry?" Ice asked, blocking his path.

"I'm a police officer. I think I have seniority over a movie star and her buddy."

Surprisingly, not everyone knew her history. "We're ex-Marines, and she's CIA, so let's not get our cocks out."

Ice grinned. "And she's back."

She turned away and pushed the door open with her left hand, keeping her gun at the ready in her right. Elodie and Ash followed closely behind. A quick sweep of the apartment gave them nothing, but it was obvious Therese's gang had been there looking for Madison and the package.

Ice leaned against the doorway of Madison's study. "Is the paperwork still here?"

Elodie moved the papers on Madison's desk around but found nothing about the Hunt gang. She saw Madison's MacBook on the floor with its broken screen. She'd told Elodie that she'd only just replaced it from her last assignment. *She was right. This is the life she leads.* "It doesn't look like it. She was carrying it around with her most of the time. I was just hoping she might've made some copies or something. Anything."

She sank into Madison's office chair and squeezed its arms tightly. Dread bubbled in her gut. She was glad Ice had been with her when all this happened, but if she hadn't asked for Ice's help in the first place, it was possible that Madison wouldn't be in their hands right now. She would never have left the house. She would have been safe. *No, they would have come for her at my place.* This way gave them a fighting chance. She and Ice had specialized in extraction. If anyone could do this, it was her and Ice.

Coleman shoved some of the papers around Madison's desk and grunted. "She said she was going to leave this alone and let me do some digging. What the hell happened?"

"She was being followed." Elodie stood. "Ice has been tailing her for a few days because I was worried. Madison left my house about an hour ago, and we found her car abandoned about two miles from my place." Elodie felt like she was being interrogated, like *she* was the criminal. She couldn't feel any guiltier.

"You knew she was being followed, and you let her go alone?" Coleman stepped forward, reducing the space between them to an uncomfortable distance.

Elodie stiffened and stood tall, more than aware of the four-inch height advantage Coleman had on her, but she wasn't easily intimidated. "She was angry I'd had someone follow her. She's headstrong; you must know that. She didn't take kindly to me making decisions about her safety, and she ran off." Elodie flexed her shoulders and stood her ground.

Coleman leaned in. "Why didn't you follow her?"

Elodie wrinkled her nose at his rancid breath. "We *did*. But I had to get changed, and I guess that was all the time they needed, 'cause when we got to her car, she was already gone."

"Get changed?" Coleman snorted. "Can't be seen without makeup and designer jeans?"

"Fuck you." Elodie moved into the space between them and made it nonexistent. "It's not like you've been protecting her. She's been working with you, and you've already let someone else get killed."

"I've been tracking Hunt. The best way to protect Madison was to remove the threat. Maybe I should've removed you instead."

Elodie flamed, and she pushed Coleman hard. He stumbled back a step, and Ice stepped between them.

"Back off, Johnny Law. She'd wipe the floor with you, in retirement or not."

Coleman straightened his shirt and muttered something inaudible.

"Do you remember anything from the papers she showed you?" Elodie asked, having regained her composure.

"There was an island facility Hunt was developing for an American-based operation. It was an old Navy site the Native Americans sold to a developer for a quick buck."

Ice checked the iPhone Elodie had given her. "I'd guess they're taking her there. Her phone's still on, and it's just left the old aerodrome site. The signal's moving fast so they're probably in a chopper."

Elodie quelled the rise of hope. "What if she's not with her phone?"

"She's a smart girl, Dee. She'll have found some way to keep it on her. How do we get to the island?"

Elodie titled her head. "I've got a boat."

"I've got guns."

"Let's get battle ready, Ice."

Ice saluted. "Hell, yeah."

Chapter Thirty-One

"What the fuck is that?" Natasha pointed at Blake, who'd been tapping away on Madison's phone since she'd found it ten minutes ago.

"It's hers. I was checking to see if there were any hot photos of her or the movie star on it." Blake laughed but stopped when she registered the look on Natasha's face.

"Are you fucking kidding me?" She snatched the phone from Blake and smashed it onto the floor, grinding it into oblivion with her heavy boots. "Don't you know they can be traced? Do you want to explain to Therese how the cops found our little kidnap victim?" She pulled Madison from Blake's grasp and pushed her into the arms of the pilot. "Courts, take her down to join Dawkes while I have a chat with Blake about the consequences of fucking up kidnap etiquette."

Madison stole a look back as Courts opened the door to the main building with a key card. Blake was prone on the concrete floor, and Natasha was repeatedly kicking her in the gut. "Jesus Christ," Madison said.

"Keep moving. You need to worry about yourself, not other people."

She pushed Madison into a corridor that could easily have been mistaken for a top-class medical center. The mirror-shine white floor tiles were almost blinding. French green walls tried in vain to promote a calm she certainly didn't feel, and harsh disinfectant assaulted her nostrils.

"How is that okay with you?" Madison asked. Natasha's absolute lack of humanity terrified her. It was one thing seeing it in documents and photos; it was entirely another witnessing it. *I'll be feeling it soon.*

"She was stupid. Stupid has harsh consequences around here."

Courts led Madison down some stairs and through another set of double doors. She stopped at yet more doors, flashed a key card for entry, and flicked the lights on. Madison saw a man in the center of the room, naked from the waist up, and tied to a chair. His hair was matted, his body bruised and cut, and his face was a bloody mess. One eye was swollen shut, and he had a three-inch gash across his cheekbone where it looked like he'd been smashed in the face with a blunt object.

Madison's fear immobilized her, and her hopes of surviving faded like an L.A. sunset. "What kind of mistake did he make?"

Courts laughed. "He's a greedy contractor. He wasn't satisfied with Therese's generous commission for refurbing this facility, and he threatened to talk. Loyalty's everything to Therese, and she's not a big fan of blackmail, so this guy doesn't get the mercy of being rubbed out quick. He's paying for his gluttony with pain. A lot of pain."

She sat Madison in the chair opposite him, walked over to the guy, and snatched his head back with a handful of his hair. His mouth fell open, and Madison could see bleeding deep holes where his teeth used to be…and only half a tongue. He remained silent and unconscious.

"We've brought you some company, Dawkes."

"Have you…did she…cut out his tongue?" Madison retched a little and caught some bile in her mouth. She swallowed it down and her mask of calm began to slip.

"Observant, aren't you? Yeah, Nat did that. She doesn't take kindly to people threatening Therese. She took off all his fingers too, but you can't see that from where you are. I reckon the next thing to go…well, I think you can use your imagination."

She headed for the door just as it opened, and Natasha entered.

"Go clean Blake up."

"Sure thing, Nat."

She exited, giving a last, knowing look at Madison.

"Therese is going to be a while, and she wants to concentrate on you right away, so I'm going to amuse myself by taking care of this asshole." She pulled a knife from inside her jacket. "You'll have to wait. I've been told not to touch you, but you may want to use this time to figure out how bad you want to make this on yourself."

Madison looked away.

"What's the problem? Are you squeamish? I thought you'd have more of a stomach for this kind of thing, given your war background."

Madison didn't respond or look over. She tried to tune out the sound of his distressing muted screams, but they were too much to bear, and she parted with the remains of the Soho House beverages. As Madison doubled over in her chair, Natasha's boots came into view.

Natasha laughed. "Get it all out, girl. That way, you'll have nothing left when Therese starts on you. It's always more pleasant to torture someone who has an empty stomach," she said and returned to Dawkes.

Madison lost all track of time. The gut-wrenching cacophony of screams and deadened cries echoed around the sterile unit. She tried meditating, repeating mantras, zoning out to her happy place, but she retched so much there was nothing left but mouthfuls of forced air and the burn of bile at the back of her throat. "Please stop," she whispered, knowing it was futile, but not knowing what else she could do. She heard Natasha's footsteps come closer, but kept her eyes squeezed tightly shut. Natasha grabbed her hair and yanked her head up.

"He's dead. You can look now."

Madison tried to pull her head away, but Natasha's grip was tight at the roots and her struggles just made it hurt more. "Why can't you tell me what you want from me? I'll answer your questions. There's no need for… for anything else."

"You'll get your chance to answer Therese's questions. What's your hurry? You want to get back to your red-hot movie star lover? Can't say I blame you. I'd love to get my hands on her. I bet she looks even more beautiful when she's in agony."

Madison snarled. "Don't you—"

Natasha snapped Madison's head back and got in close enough that her breath was warm on Madison's face.

"Touch her? Fuck her? Hurt her? It always makes me laugh when someone in your position thinks they have some power. What do you think *you're* going to do to stop me from doing whatever the fuck *I* want to that sexy piece of ass? You're helpless. Tied up. Powerless. If Therese and I take a trip to her mansion in the hills to play with her, what can you do about it?" Natasha released her hair. "That guy thought he had power too. And he was in a better position than you are right now. Look what happened to him."

"I'll tell you whatever you need to know, just—"

"Don't hurt Elodie? Save your breath and your pleadings for Therese. She'll gladly listen to you beg."

Madison sagged in the chair and closed her eyes. If she couldn't see any of it, maybe none of it was real. Why hadn't she just stayed with Elodie?

Chapter Thirty-Two

Elodie stepped into the elevator, and Ice and Ash followed. "Coleman, you're not sure who you can trust, so we can't have the LAPD involved in this at all. You have to trust us. This is what I do…used to do, and it's what Ice still does. I'll have Madison call you as soon as she's safe."

"Let me come with you. You don't know how many of her gang you'll be facing."

Ice raised her eyebrows, as if considering his request, but Elodie shook her head. She'd never gone into battle without knowing her colleagues inside out, and that had served her well. It had been over ten years since her last conflict, and she needed to trust whoever she was doing this with Madison's life as well as her own. It was too important, and she wouldn't risk it. Coleman was in his fifties, and she had no idea of his pedigree.

She placed her hands on his shoulders firmly. "Stay here. If you don't hear from us within four hours, call it in." *Four* hours. Madison was tough for a journalist, not for a criminal. How long would she be able to hold out? What would they do to her, just for fun, let alone to get information? The thought of Madison being harmed by those animals was unbearable. She had to get there as soon as possible.

Coleman nodded as the elevator doors opened, and without speaking, Elodie and Ice began to jog back to the car. Madison had left in such a fury. She'd never given Elodie the chance to tell her how much she already meant to her…how much she loved her.

Elodie got back in the car and drove like a demon. It didn't take long before they hit the 710 Freeway South. She zigzagged from lane to lane and thought only of Madison. Every moment that passed, Elodie fought away vivid images of her being tortured, making it hard to concentrate on the traffic around her.

Ice placed her hand on Elodie's arm. "Let's get to your boat safely. We're no good to her as roadkill."

Elodie nodded and adjusted her driving slightly, but it still didn't take long before they pulled up in the private harbor. She popped the trunk and Ice retrieved her black duffel bag while Elodie boarded her boat and prepared to leave the dock.

Ice joined her and carefully placed her bag on the main deck chair.

"Doesn't look like much. What've you got in there?" Elodie asked before she pulled away at the requisite, and unbearably slow, speed.

"I don't tend to travel with a full arsenal when I'm supposed to be on vacation." Ice raised her eyebrows. "I've got another SIG in there, some C4, a hunting knife, and a few magazines of ammo. We need a stealth attack, and we pick up whatever weapons we find if we end up in a firefight."

"If our approach is good, we should be able to avoid that. A nice silent extraction, and let your team do the rest." Elodie didn't want to contemplate being too late, but she couldn't barricade her mind from morbid thoughts. "If they've hurt her though…I'll take them all apart with my hands."

Ice patted her on the back. "It's not going to come to that. We were the best extraction team the Marines had ever seen. We've got this."

Elodie clamped her jaw shut to prevent voicing any more negative thoughts and concentrated on getting them close to the island.

"Cut the engine, Dee," Ice said when they were close to the island. "We need to stay far enough away not to attract their attention."

Elodie cut the engine, came down to the main deck, and changed into a wetsuit. "When's our backup coming?" Elodie had immense faith in Ice, and she knew her own abilities, rusty as they might be, but they had no idea how many people they were up against. They could only hope that Therese didn't have an army of mercenaries.

"They're on their way. We probably won't see them. They'll come in whichever way is quietest." Ice hitched her air tank on her back. "We'll get Madison, and the cavalry can clean up the mess."

Ice handed Elodie a tank, and she secured the straps tight to her body. She stuffed their jeans, tanks, and shoes into a watertight gear bag, and filled another with the contents of Ice's travel bag. It wouldn't be anywhere near enough if they ended up in a shootout. It'd been a long time since Elodie had readied herself to kill someone. She had eight confirmed kills during her tour, but it wasn't something she'd gotten a taste for. She acknowledged its necessity in the line of duty, of course, but she'd never taken someone else's life lightly.

Her thoughts went again to Madison, and it steeled her to know this time, she was the reason Elodie was ready for battle. Madison was a special woman. Elodie had only known her for a short time but already, she couldn't entertain the thought of letting her get away. She was the kind of woman people spent their lives searching for. Elodie just hadn't known she was looking. Madison was in a class all by herself. And she had absolutely no idea, which made her even more adorable, and even more of a loss for anyone who let her get away. The age-old declaration of "I'd die for you," was for women like Madison, and Elodie was prepared to prove that point.

Ice climbed down the ladder into the ocean. Elodie clicked the carabiners onto the gear bag and water scooters, then lowered them down to Ice before she joined her. Madison might still be pissed off that Elodie had Ice follow her, but she was hoping that'd be canceled out by the fact that the two of them were coming to rescue her.

Chapter Thirty-Three

"Enjoy the company." Natasha laughed and left the room.

The door swung shut behind her.

Madison realized she was breathing quick and shallow, on the verge of absolute panic. She'd seen dead bodies before: men, women, even babies. She'd seen gunshot and knife wounds, compound fractures and severed heads. She'd walked between a sea of distorted corpses in a Somalian battlefield. But she'd never actually seen or heard the pain, the moment of death. She'd never witnessed the inhumanity and the ease with which one person could take the life of another, let alone with such carefree abandon and with such relish.

For a moment, she wondered what Natasha had been through to make her this dismissive of and detached from the value of human life. She didn't subscribe to the biological side of that nature/nurture debate. She had a belief in the basic kindness of human beings, but she'd witnessed the aftermath of too many atrocities in the world for it to be unshakeable.

She fought back her panic and tried to rein in her breathing. *Slow, deep breaths. Think.* But the stench of her vomit and his fresh blood were an unpleasant cocktail. She stood and moved to the tiny open window in the far corner of the room in an effort to garner some fresh air.

That's when she saw another exit, one meant to be nearly invisible against the back wall. Key card security, as were the rest, but she could see from the slit of light where the doors met their frame that it led directly outside. All she needed was a key card.

Dawkes had been a contractor refurbing the facility. He'd need a key card. She looked across the room to where he sat. On the operating table beside him was a tool belt and his shirt. She couldn't be that lucky, could she? Madison ventured over, trying hard to keep her eyes from straying to his dead body. With her back to the table, she managed to feel her way through the shirt and searched the pockets. Nothing. His tool belt had been stripped of anything useful or sharp, unless she could strangle her captors with a tape measure, which wasn't likely with her hands tied behind her back.

She stole a quick glance at Dawkes. Could they have missed something in his work pants? She balked. There were patches of khaki left, but they were mostly painted in his blood. Two side, two hip, and probably two pockets on his rear. Six pockets. Six chances. Like Russian roulette. She looked for latex gloves and saw a dispenser above the pre-op washing sinks. She almost laughed at herself, worrying about communicable diseases when her own mortality was at stake in a much more instantaneous manner.

All she had to do was get her hands in front of her. She sat on the floor, a good few feet away from the body. She lay back, lifted her legs in the air, and started to work her hands over her butt. The rope bit into her skin as she pulled it taut, trying to get a few extra centimeters of length. Now she wished she'd taken more yoga classes. If she could work her hands over her ass, looping her legs through would be easy. She'd been pretty good at this part in the Hostile Environment classes, and even when they'd tied her wrists tight, she'd gotten loose. Granted, it had been at the expense of a few layers of skin, some blood, and bruises that lasted for three weeks.

The knots slipped a little, giving her slightly more slack to pull her wrists farther apart. She was close. A little more wriggling. Her hands suddenly pulled over her ass, and her head hit the floor with the force of the release. She shook it off and dragged her legs over the rope. She lay back with the exertion and tried to catch her breath.

Moments later, she got back up and put the gloves on. Bright purple and too big for her tiny hands. *Suck it up, Mads.* Side pocket one. It squelched, and she forced back a retch. Nothing. Side pocket two. Slightly drier and something right at the bottom of the deep pocket. *Jackpot.* A Swiss army knife. She couldn't help but think Blake was responsible for that oversight. Madison flicked it open and awkwardly sliced her way through the rope between her wrists. She closed the knife, tucked it in her pocket, and went back to her gruesome search. Two hip pockets and nothing but a few crumpled dollars and a washed tissue. Tied to the chair, he was sitting on his back pockets, her last hope. She had no choice but to handle him. She took out the knife again and started to cut through his bindings.

She finally freed him of the rope, but Madison still had to move him to get to his rear pockets. She gripped the back of the chair with both hands and yanked it hard from beneath him. He splattered to the floor, still on his back, still denying her access to the uninspected pockets.

Madison held her breath. She knelt down, took hold of his belt, and pulled him toward her. His arm fell on her lap, and blood stained her jeans. She pushed herself backward and gathered herself again before reaching for pocket five. Her fingers touched a credit card-sized plastic form. *Please God.* She slowly withdrew it, half expecting an American Express card. She wiped away the blood with her gloved hand. It looked exactly like the one Courts had used.

"Thank you, Blake," she whispered quietly as she stood. She peeled off the ridiculous purple gloves, tossed them to the floor, and headed for the emergency exit. Madison tentatively offered the key card to the electronic panel on the wall beside the door. Relief coursed through her when the tiny red LED turned green, and the magnetic click released the seal. She pushed the door open a few inches and peered out. Was Dawkes the last of the contractors? How many of Therese's goons were dotted around this island? What if she ran straight into them? She took a lungful of fresh air and exhaled slowly.

What was the alternative? Waiting for a horrible, painful, and torturous death at the hands of those two heinous bitches? She pushed the door open enough to slip through and closed it behind her. She slipped the key card into her pocket in case she needed it again. She took the knife out of her other pocket and opened it up. She'd never struck a person in anger before, let alone stabbed someone. But this was her life, and she was in danger. She needed to find somewhere safe, hunker down, and hope for rescue. She hated the sound of that but had to face facts. She was out of her league and her life was on the line. There were worse things to hope for than to be rescued by two ex-Marines, one of whom she seemed to have fallen in love with. She only hoped that she'd get to tell Elodie how she felt.

Chapter Thirty-Four

Therese wasn't a big fan of helicopters or of flying in general. It involved a lack of control she wasn't comfortable with. When she bought this island, she'd quickly decided that she'd be getting there by boat whenever her presence was needed. The inconvenience of the Lucas couple ruined her plan to travel that way today. She had to get to Madison Ford and find out what she'd done with the information Santiago had sent her. What Nat had found in Ford's bag seemed identical to the package Reed had intercepted at the FBI, intel that could bury her and her whole operation if it got to the wrong people. She wouldn't let that happen. She'd spent years building this business, started at the bottom of the food chain, and worked her way up. She wasn't about to let some do-gooder, prize-winning journalist ruin her life's work or her ambitions. Organ trafficking was more popular than ever, and she was reaping the rewards of good business planning.

And a good business owner meets problems head on. Therese would have to kill her after she'd gotten the information she needed. Ford was a little too high profile, and Therese wasn't completely comfortable with making this one disappear. But she could see no other choice. Nat had been careful tracking and kidnapping her, and Therese was confident there'd be no evidence to trace Ford's disappearance back to her. Even if the cops did strike lucky, Nat would take the fall without hesitation. She would protect Therese at the expense of her own freedom, her own life, if necessary. She had a strong sense of loyalty, and she owed Therese. Nat took that vow as seriously as a Benedictine monk took their vow of silence.

Therese was still high on the Lucas kill, and that mellowed her discomfort with the flight. She was horny too and thought about fucking Nat before getting to Ford. The chopper landed, and Nat greeted her.

"You did good, Nat. Let's celebrate." Therese pulled Nat into the facility and slammed her against the wall. She exhaled a satisfied growl as Nat's eyes flooded with desire.

"I don't ever want to let you down, T."

Therese smiled against Nat's chest and ran her hands over her body like she hadn't been with her for months. She opened Nat's belt and jeans and shoved her hand inside, sighing deeply when she found Nat was wet and ready for her.

"Something got you all excited?" Therese punctuated her words with deep, hard thrusts. She wrapped her other hand around Nat's throat and squeezed firmly.

"No. Just you."

Nat dug her nails into Therese's shoulders as she pushed her closer to orgasm. It never took Therese long to get her there when she was this ready for it, which was another good reason for Nat to be her regular plaything. She rarely had the patience for women who didn't respond to her time schedule. If she wanted them to come in five minutes, that's how it should be. If she had time for a good hour of slow, deep fucking, they needed to be able to come multiple times. It wasn't rocket science.

"Oh my God. Yes, harder, T, fuck me harder."

Therese obliged, forcing her fingers in and speeding her rhythm until Nat contracted around her hand, almost crushing her bones with the power of her orgasm. She bit hard into Nat's neck and made her scream even louder, the mix of pleasure and pain musical.

Therese pulled out and wiped Nat's juices on her jeans. "Time to visit Ms. Ford. Where are you holding her?"

Nat fastened her jeans and belt as they walked. "In the downstairs operating theater with Dawkes. I had some special fun with him that meant I needed him over a drain."

Therese raised her eyebrow and smiled. "What kind of special?"

Nat shook her head as she opened the doors to the stairs. "It's a surprise. I didn't get to finish properly before he died on me though. I need to figure out a way to make them stay alive until I'm done."

"You've been practicing your skinning, haven't you?" Therese asked.

"I'm not saying. Wait and see." Nat flashed her key card and pushed the door open to display her handiwork.

The chair was empty.

Dawkes was dead on the floor.

Madison Ford was nowhere to be seen.

Nat lurched into the room, frantically searching under tables and in cupboards. She turned to face Therese.

"What the fuck?" Therese sneered. "Where the fuck is my journalist?" She grabbed Nat by the throat and swept her legs from under her. Her head hit the floor, inches away from Dawkes's dead body. "Have you really let her escape?"

"She won't be far. I'll find her. She can't get off the island."

Therese released her and took a deep breath to center herself. "For your sake, you better hope not."

Chapter Thirty-Five

Madison needed her iPhone. As well as the obvious advantage of being able to call for help, she could really use a compass right now. Every direction looked the same. She'd scrambled up the bank and could see the coast. It was a beautiful, bluebird-sky day, and she could see for miles. She could just about make out the mainland, and there were plenty of yachts and sailboats dotted on the ocean, tempting her to consider swimming. It was a relatively brief consideration. The Pacific was home to sixty different kinds of sharks, almost half of which were thought to have attacked humans. Death by shark wasn't how Madison envisaged her end, but then, death at the hands of the sharks hunting her on this island had never been in her thoughts either. If that was her choice, maybe a swim in the ocean would be a quicker and less painful end.

Unless… she could find the Lost Indian cave to hide out in. Geva had dragged her along to the Californian Islands Symposium in 2012 because she'd won their photo competition, and it was all over their promotional posters. Madison had sat through hours of lectures about this island and the others in the chain, and it had prompted her to read all about the Lone Woman, Juana Maria, from the Native American Nicoleno tribe. She never thought that knowledge would become handy. The island was about four miles wide, and she knew the cave was on the opposite side to the old Navy support area. That had to be her goal. She just needed to work her way across the scrub brush and cactuses and into the troughs and valleys that would keep her out of sight. And she had to be careful crossing the roads that ran like veins all over the island. As soon as they realized she was gone, those roads would be pretty busy.

Juana Maria had survived on this island for eighteen years. All Madison needed to do was lie low for…for what? Hours? Days? She had to believe Elodie and Ice were coming after her, and that they'd ignored her petulant tantrum. And even though she'd specifically instructed…*demanded* that Elodie stay away from her and that Ice stop following her, she had to believe they'd ignored that too.

She had to make a run for it, nonstop for as long as her lungs would allow, get herself away from the main buildings and deep into the scrubland. She scanned the area and saw nothing. The helicopter had gone too, so she expected Therese was on her way. She looked down at her feet and plucked a sunflower from the arid ground. *If this fucking flower and an eighteen-year-old kid can survive here, I'm damn sure I can.* She stuffed the flower in her pocket and ran.

Running had never been her strong suit, but the threat of inevitable death seemed to provide her with extra motivation. She ran until her throat hurt from the hot, dry air. She ran until her legs burned.

Then she ran some more.

She crossed the roads without detection and couldn't see any kind of a hunt being rallied yet. It seemed that they were only making use of a small portion of the island, so thus far, she hadn't seen another soul. When she finally paused for breath, she pulled off her thin cardigan. It was one of her very favorites, but she cut it to the right size anyway, hacking at it with her stolen pocketknife. *Can you steal from a dead man?* She wrapped it around her head to prevent sunstroke and used the rest of the material as a scarf to keep the sun off her neck.

The tutors at the Hostile Environment classes would be proud.

Eventually, Madison reached the shifting sand dunes and the valleys beyond the minimal man-made encroachments on the island. Somewhere along here was Juana's cave. If she could find it, and if they didn't know their Native American history, she'd be safe for a while. And maybe, if she was discovered, if there was only one of them, maybe she could overpower them…or slow them down with her knife. She shuddered at the thought. She'd spent her life reporting on genocides, revolutions, the Arab Spring, documenting countless lives wasted and destroyed by mindless violence. Yet, here she was, knife in hand, ready to…kill? Maim?

She climbed steadily down the dunes, jealous of the gulp of cormorants strutting the beach and able to come and go as they pleased. She headed right with nothing but a feeling that it might be the correct way. She looked back to make sure she was out of sight from the main mesa, pulled her makeshift scarf tightly around her neck, and continued with her search for Juana's hideout. She didn't know how much time she had left, but it sure didn't feel like much.

Madison focused on moving forward. Her pulse raced, and trekking through the sand fatigued her legs beyond belief. Her heart pounded in her throat, and the inside of her mouth felt like it was lined with cotton, while the bile from earlier continued to burn her throat. She kept halfway fit, but the heat and terrain were kicking her ass.

A hand clamped over her mouth, and an arm pulled her into a reverse bear hug. Madison tried to grab her knife from her pocket, but her arms were held tight to her body by a human straitjacket. She stamped her feet, trying to find those of her captor. There was a gentle laugh in her ear.

Chapter Thirty-Six

"Stop stomping like a wild stallion, baby." Elodie held Madison tight in her arms, not wanting to release her just yet. She hadn't wanted to say it out loud, but she hadn't been completely confident that she'd be able to do this again.

Ice moved into Madison's sightline, and she slumped against Elodie in obvious relief.

"When I let you go, keep very quiet," Elodie whispered.

Elodie released her, and Madison spun around. "You came for me?" She enfolded Elodie in her arms.

"Of course we did," Elodie kissed her. "I'll always go wherever I need to, to get to you." *Jesus, that was cheesy.*

Madison gave her a shy smile. "How did you get here?"

Ice held a finger to her lips. "Shh."

Elodie took Madison by the shoulders and turned her to face the ocean. "See that yacht at twelve o'clock about three miles out? That's mine. If you're going to get kidnapped, there are definite advantages to being the girlfriend of a boat-owning actress."

Madison smiled broadly, and Elodie's heart ached at the sight. She was never more beautiful than when her face lit up like that.

"Where were you headed?" Ice asked.

"I was trying to find the Lone Indian's cave." Madison rolled her eyes when Elodie and Ice exchanged a questioning look. "I haven't got heat stroke if that's what you're thinking. Don't you know your Channel Island history?"

Elodie shook her head, enjoying the schoolmarm version of Madison despite the serious danger she'd just been in. "Much as we'd love to discuss our rich Native American history with you, I'd rather we find a good spot to get you off the radar and to defend against the inevitable hunting pack. Ice, I'll take Madison up front, and you protect our back." Elodie took Madison by the arm, and they continued on her previous trajectory. Ice stayed thirty or so paces behind them, scanning for trouble. "How did you escape, baby?"

Madison pulled out a multitool and wafted it around. "I shanked three guards and stole a truck, but it ran out of gas a mile or so back."

"Wow. Brains, beauty, and now brawn. You're an amazing woman, Ms. Ford."

Madison laughed. "Not really. I know captivity is supposed to make you do some crazy stuff, but I'd only been there an hour or so. I got lucky with a key card."

"A key card?" Elodie didn't hold back a quiet chuckle. "Novice kidnappers then. We should've expected that though, given that they didn't de-activate your phone before they brought you here."

"The woman who made that mistake paid for that," Madison whispered and held onto Elodie's hand a little tighter.

She saw the distress in Madison's eyes. "You've seen things you want to unsee?" Elodie wished she could reach into Madison's mind and whitewash the ugliness.

"I've seen death and the results of genocide but witnessing that kind of brutality…" Madison shook her head like she was trying to shake away the memories. "It really rocks my belief in the basic goodness of people."

"You can believe in me…if you want." Elodie swallowed hard, still trying to quash the horrendous movie playing in her head. Everything was going to be okay. Madison was safe now. "I won't let you down."

Sadness flooded Madison's eyes, along with her tears. "But what if I let you down?"

Elodie frowned and rubbed her thumb across Madison's hand. Pulling her into a long, tight embrace wasn't ideal right now; they had to keep moving. "You couldn't possibly let me down, Mads. Why would you think that?"

"Because I'm never enough. For anyone. I wasn't enough for my father, and it's been the same with everyone else. Eventually, I disappoint everyone."

Ignoring the need to stay on the move, Elodie stopped and pulled Madison into her arms. Her unwillingness to explore their obvious connection made sense now. "Is this what you've been hiding? Why you've been holding back?"

Madison nodded against Elodie's chest and murmured something she didn't catch,

"You're perfect for me. Everyone else has been stupid and didn't realize how special you are. They didn't realize what they had. I do. And I want you, all of you."

Ice smacked her hands together behind them. "Pick up the pace, people. Those valleys ahead look like a good spot."

Madison went to move, lost her footing, and fell hard on some sandstone. Elodie heard something crack in Madison's wrist as she put out her hands to prevent herself from falling flat on her face. She screamed despite the absolute necessity for silence.

Elodie was by her side instantly, and she pushed the edge of her hand into Madison's mouth. "Bite down."

Madison did as she was told and bit hard. She wrapped her left hand around her injured wrist and cradled it against her chest.

"Scoop her up, Dee. We've got incoming."

Shit. Elodie's training kicked in. They'd survive this, and they'd get out alive. She wouldn't guarantee the same for Therese Hunt.

Chapter Thirty-Seven

Nat was acting like a genuine Native American tracker. Every quarter mile, she jumped out of the Jeep and checked the ground. At points, Therese was sure she was going to start tasting the dirt.

Nat came back to the Jeep, looking pleased with herself. "I found tracks. She's heading to the caves."

"We've got caves?" That was news to Therese. Not that they'd be any use to her operation, but she liked the idea of having her own personal caves to play in.

"Yeah, it's one of the reasons the Navy gave the island back to the Native Americans."

"As long as there's no speedboat hidden in them so she can escape. What now?" Therese was beginning to enjoy herself. It was like big-game hunting for humans.

"We head after her on foot. You and me. Petra stays here." Nat indicated to their driver, who nodded her agreement.

Therese got out of the Jeep and pulled her close by her shirt. "You know this is going to cost you, don't you? No matter how much fun you make this chase." She tightened her grip when Nat's eyes half-lidded, just the way they did when she was needy for something extra filthy. "It won't *be* enjoyable. It *will* be painful."

Nat nodded. "Whatever you have to do…"

"Petra, leave the Jeep here and head back to the facility." Therese waved her toward the main buildings. "We might be a while."

"Sure thing, boss." Petra jumped over the side and headed off, swigging from a water bottle.

"Shall we take some water?"

"Yeah and bring the ropes."

Nat's left eyebrow raised. "You're going to play out here?"

"What's the point in having your own private island if you don't make proper use of it?" Therese saw Nat's eyes glisten with anticipation. "Don't think she's going to be the only one I fuck up tonight."

It wasn't long before they caught sight of movement on top of the dunes.

"Hey, Maadisonn!" Therese wanted her to know they were close to recapturing her, wanted her fear to heighten. As she'd watched Nat seeking their quarry, she recalled the nineties movie about rich businessmen getting their kicks hunting humans for sport. She was starting to get an idea for an additional business to run from the island, though she'd have wealthy women stalking men for a million apiece.

Ford disappeared behind a particularly high dune and didn't reappear. She and Nat picked up their pace and closed the gap. As they rose over the dune, a bullet zinged past Therese's ear. They dropped to the ground and pushed back to cover. More shots kept them down. "What the fuck? How did she get a fucking gun?"

"There's no way. Dawkes wasn't packing. He was just a fucking builder. There was no gun in that room."

Nat peered around the rock atop the dunes. More shots forced her back. She looked guilty.

"What's wrong? What did you see?"

"Two guns firing."

If Therese could've summoned dark clouds to reflect her mood, she would've. "Two guns," she said, "as in two people or as in, she's got two guns and is using both hands?"

Nat bit her lip: she didn't have to answer.

"Two people, then." Therese took a moment to consider their position. She pulled out her Glock 18 machine pistol. Thirty-three rounds and a spare magazine. Nat only ever carried knives for close combat. They hadn't come prepared for a firefight, and there was no retreating. Who was here with her, and what did they have? "Fuck, Nat." She extended her arm over their cover and fired off two rounds. Triple came back at them, all close to their position. The shooters weren't fairground enthusiasts. "Since when do bleeding heart liberals shoot guns like professionals?"

"I don't think that's her. It doesn't fit. There was no sign of a gun in her apartment."

Therese rolled her eyes. "Remind me to save a bullet for you." She moved so she could shout over their cover. "Kind of rude to invite your friends to my island without asking, don't you think?" she shouted.

"No more fucking rude than kidnapping someone." The woman shouting accompanied her response with a shower of bullets.

Therese shrugged. She couldn't argue with that. "Which of us are Butch and Sundance?"

"I'm not a big fan of labels, but I guess that's gonna depend on who's got the most bullets."

More bullets emphasized the woman's point, and the way she was using them indicated they might have plenty. Therese shot a few back and looked at Nat. "Thoughts?"

Nat had the razorback Therese had bought her for skinning their kills in her hand. "Little premature. We need them to run out of bullets first."

"They will. No one saw their approach, so they must've got here by water, which means—"

"They wouldn't have been able to bring a whole heap of weapons and ammo," Therese said loudly over the staccato of shots.

"Exactly." Nat grinned and hefted her blade. "We'll all be out soon enough, and then we can make our move. There's only two of them; my guess is they weren't counting on—"

"Running into any trouble and were hoping to leave quietly without engaging us."

"Yeah, and Ford made it easy—"

"*You* made it easy by letting her escape." Therese glared at her. Hunting Ford down would've been a lot more fun without this complication.

Nat looked away, unable to keep eye contact. "I'll make it up to you."

"I know you will." Though their conversation was punctuated by gunfire, Therese heard Nat's sincerity. She knew she was at fault, and it was killing her. Her loyalty was the only thing Therese could count on. The only thing Therese had counted on for a long time. Nat would pay, but she wasn't about to kill her.

Therese returned some shots with no real hope of hitting anyone. Their opponents had taken good cover and were too clever to reveal too much of themselves. She and Nat would just have to wait it out and hope they ran out of bullets at the same time.

They were losing light, and Therese had one bullet left. They'd had a few more exchanges, but there hadn't been any fire from anyone for a while. One bullet could be all she needed, and she wasn't about to waste it. "Want to finish this the old-fashioned way?"

"You think we're stupid enough to come out to your Bolivian army tactics even if we *were* out of bullets?"

God, I'm looking forward to killing that smart-mouthed bitch. Therese lifted her hand into the air above cover, counting on them being out, and not being crack shots able to pierce her palm from thirty yards. "See? How about we toss our guns at the same time?"

"You first."

"Where's the trust?" Therese smiled at Nat. "The party's about to start now."

Nat nodded and edged closer to Therese.

"You've got two. How about a gesture of good faith?" Therese saw a hand appear, and a gun was tossed into the no-woman's land between them.

"Your turn," the woman shouted.

"Together." Therese clicked the safety on, so it didn't accidentally fire when it hit the ground.

"Is that a good idea?" Nat frowned. "What if they've got other guns?"

Therese shook her head. "They're the good guys, remember? They fight the good fight. They're honest."

"That's a pretty risky gamble," Nat said, not looking convinced.

"Not for me. *You're* going to stand up. Then we'll see if they're lying and use you as target practice."

Nat closed her eyes and rested her head on the dunes. She took a deep breath and blew the air out slowly through closed lips. She opened her eyes, sheathed her razorback, tucked it into the back of her jeans, and took one last, long look at Therese before rising to her feet slowly with her hands in the air.

"Together?" Nat shouted, her voice barely trembling.

Therese nodded, acknowledging her unfailing commitment and bravery. Maybe her punishment *would* be the kind she liked after all. She was making up for it now. Nat stepped over the edge of their cover, in full view of Ford and her mysterious rescuers. Therese wasn't convinced of their integrity, but with Nat still alive and no shots fired, it looked like she might be right.

One gun and the two warriors tentatively rose from Ford's position for Therese to get a good look at her opponents. "Is that Elodie fucking Fontaine?" Therese asked Nat, though the incredulous look on her face answered her question.

"One on one it is. Where's your gun, Hunt?"

Therese raised her gun and threw it to join the one they'd already discarded, making a note of where it landed. The third weapon was quickly added, and all four of them stood in an unusual and unexpected face-off. There was no sign of Ford, but Therese expected she'd have been told to stay back and out of the way. This was a battle to be fought with knives, not words, and Ford had no skills to concern them. They advanced onto the flat ground.

"Ms. Fontaine, I'm a big fan," Therese said. "It's going to hurt to kill you. Are you sure you want to die for the sake of a journalist?"

"I'd die for her in a New York minute if I had to." Elodie laughed. "But I don't think you're up to the task of killing me."

She's got courage. "I admire your spirit and your acting. But you're a movie star, not a killer. I could put you down in seconds, but I'm going to have some fun. I want to do all manner of filthy things to you before I kill you." Therese was already imagining Elodie hung by her wrists, her taut body twisting and writhing with every strike, every lash, every cut.

"I wasn't always a movie star, sweetheart," Elodie said and fist-bumped Ice. "I used to be a Marine. Taking me down is way beyond a street rat like you."

"I'm calling that bullshit. You're way too pretty to have survived as a soldier. I think you were just a nurse." Therese remembered when that tale hit the newsstands a decade ago. Pictures of Fontaine in desert combats and a sniper's rifle. It was a publicity stunt for a movie role, nothing more.

"I guess you'll soon know the truth either way."

"Isn't this the part where you're supposed to tell us what your grand evil plans for Madison are, once you've killed us? What do you care who we are?" The long-haired and surprisingly tall one asked.

Therese sneered. "And who are you in all of this?"

"I'm her wingwoman, Ice Hamilton, since you ask. Also an ex-Marine, and now CIA."

CIA? Fuck. "Ice? Good name. Did you give it to yourself? Did Mommy and Daddy call you Barbie?"

Nat laughed.

"How'd you guess?" Hamilton remained expressionless.

I'm going to tear your heart out with my fingers. "Enough with the pleasantries now I know how careful I've got to be disposing of your bodies. Any family, friends, or CIA shitheads know you're here?"

"No one knows we're here," Hamilton said. "So if you get lucky enough and kill us, you'll be home free."

Therese narrowed her eyes. Hamilton was cocky, and Therese didn't believe a gruff word that came out of her mouth. "Ah, you see, you've destroyed the trust you'd established by surrendering your weapons. I thought the good guys didn't lie?"

Elodie laughed. "Who said we're the good guys?"

"Then you've given us no choice. We'll have to torture you before we even get to her." Therese had seen Ford peer over to watch the proceedings and motioned toward her. "This is better than Christmas."

They looked at each other, obviously skeptical. "You think you've got the skills to break us?" Hamilton asked.

Nat pulled out her razorback. "I'm practicing skinning people alive. It gets people talking. I think you'll make a great subject. There's plenty of you to go at." Nat waved her knife at Ice from head to toe.

Ice took a step closer to Nat. "You, me, and your toothpick, then."

"Guess that matches you and me, Ms. Fontaine." Therese motioned between them.

"I was counting on that. I'm not a big fan of *your* work, so it'll be a fucking pleasure to take you apart. But please, we're about to be very intimate. You can call me Elodie."

Therese pulled her Mistress from its sheath, its edge cutting the sunlight perfectly. "You won't mind if I use this to defend myself." She lunged at her, but Elodie sidestepped and landed a punch across her jaw. Therese stumbled and thrust her knife out to defend against the follow-up, but there was only air.

Elodie just smiled. "I'm in no hurry."

They circled each other, Elodie hanging back and Therese swiping the air around her. She was quick, Therese had to admit that. In her peripheral vision, she could see Nat and Ice enacting a similar dance.

As Therese feigned a lunge, Elodie moved, and she flashed the knife across her body. It sliced through her tank and across her chest, and blood sprayed upward in an artistic arc. Therese followed up with a forearm smash into Elodie's face. She thudded onto her back, her head missing a nearby rock, and she scrambled backward as Therese advanced. "What's the matter, hotshot? Underestimated your opponent?"

Elodie got enough distance to get back to her feet. "I'm just warming up, that's all. I've been out of the field for a while." Elodie touched her chest wound without taking her eyes off Therese. "This is just a scratch. You got lucky."

Therese shook her head. "I don't believe in luck, Elodie. You make your own path. Reliance on luck, good or bad, is an excuse for the weak-willed."

"Two-bit philosophy from a fucking psychopath? You can keep that, thanks."

"You've got a foul mouth for a movie star role model. I've got a far better use for it. And after I've fucked your mouth, I'm going to cut that offensive tongue out and feed it to the island's dogs, along with the rest of you." Therese's anger boiled; there was no need for such disrespect. She thrust her giant blade toward Elodie's gut.

Elodie stepped aside and kicked at Therese's wrist. The impact loosened her grip, and the knife fell to the ground. Elodie kicked it away and followed up with a left jab to Therese's face, and a right hook to her kidneys. As Therese fell to her knees, pain shot through her, and she saw Nat thrown to the ground. Her arm twisted awkwardly beneath her, and there was an almighty, unmistakable crack of shattering bone.

Nat's face twisted silently in pain, but she looked directly at Therese, who could see she was beaten. Ice planted her knee between Nat's shoulder blades and fixed her forearm around Nat's throat, choking her. Nat's eyes flicked to the left, and Therese followed them.

Her gun.

One bullet left in the chamber.

She allowed Elodie to kick her in the gut, and she fell closer to her Glock. She scuttled crab-like across the sand, grabbed it, and swung it around as Elodie was upon her. Elodie froze, the barrel inches from her bleeding chest.

Therese grinned. "Sucker," she said and pushed the gun into Elodie's wounded chest. "Maybe I'll just forego my fun and kill you."

Elodie snatched at the gun and forced it away from her own body. "Safety?" she asked, and they fought to control it.

Therese managed to flick the safety catch with her thumb and tried to force the gun back toward Elodie, but she was trying to push her finger behind the trigger.

The gun fired its last shot, and they both followed its trajectory, knowing it was in the vicinity of Nat and Ice.

Ice released her grip.

Blood began to pool on the sand. Stark ruby liquid on golden silica crystals.

Therese looked into Nat's eyes.

They were blank.

No spark.

No mischief.

No necessary evil.

Therese saw where her bullet had entered Nat's skull, directly above her left eye.

She closed her eyes and opened them again.

Her girl was gone.

She vaguely felt her gun pulled from her grip. *Gone. She's gone.* Without her, was what she was left with enough?

She felt the strike against her forehead. Welcome darkness descended over her…

Chapter Thirty-Eight

The CIA team had arrived about half an hour after their encounter with Therese and Nat, which had ended in one unconscious and the other dead. They'd driven the Jeep back to the main compound after a short firefight between the CIA and the rest of Therese's gang. Without their leader, they gave up surprisingly easily and with no more loss of life.

Elodie and Ice had been busy with them since. Madison thought herself a battle-hardened journalist, but today she'd seen the death of two people and the savage beating of another up close and personal. It made her question herself and her job. She needed a break, a real break, or maybe she just needed some time writing this biography for Troy. She wasn't sure. After the day she'd had, she wasn't about to rush into any decisions. There was one thing she *was* sure of. Elodie.

Regardless of the fact that if it weren't for her, Madison would be dead, Elodie was all she could think about when faced with her own mortality. Elodie had been her motivating factor for escaping. Madison wanted to get off that island and back into Elodie's arms. Nothing else mattered. And though she'd doubted her, though she had misgivings about Elodie's ability to be in this, whatever this was, for the long haul, her actions had proven Madison wrong. It was Elodie who came after her. It was Elodie who really saved her. It was Elodie she needed to be with.

Madison lowered her arm and adjusted the makeshift cardigan sling around her neck. Adrenaline had kept her from feeling the break too intensely while Elodie and Ice had battled with Therese and Nat, but now her wrist throbbed with pain. Ice's backup was crawling all over the facility and grounds, and she could see Elodie and Ice barking orders. It was such a contrast to the calm and soft Elodie she'd been getting to know. She wondered how hard or easy it had been for her to slip back into military mode.

She thought about her own patterns and how she'd slipped into a world where she no longer truly interacted in anything other than a superficial way. She'd spent years denying herself connection with another, but she couldn't deny Elodie. This was something unique, a passion and emotion she'd read about but never experienced. Before Elodie, they were just words written by long dead poets and movie mavens. Now they were words Elodie had matched emotions to. And she'd knocked on her door so hard, Madison wasn't just prepared to open it, she wanted to build a new house around her.

Elodie left Ice and her group of agents and start to jog toward Madison. Her heart hammered at her chest, and her breathing quickened. Apparently, love felt like a fucking heart attack.

Elodie pulled her into a tight embrace, carefully avoiding her damaged wrist. "Hey you."

Madison smiled at what had become their familiar refrain. "Hey you."

Elodie looked tense and ready for action, ready to bolt. Madison figured it was a natural state of being for a soldier after a battle. Maybe it took time to come down. "Are you okay?"

Elodie laughed mildly. "Am *I* okay? How about you? You're good?"

Madison shrugged. "A broken wrist and a few scratches, but other than that, I'm fine."

"So you don't like to complain even when you're in obvious agony?"

Madison wrinkled her nose and briefly looked away, unable to hold Elodie's intense gaze. "You'll soon learn that."

"I want to learn *everything* about you," Elodie said.

Madison pulled the flower from her jean pocket. "This is for you." She handed over the squished, limp bloom and hoped Elodie would see beyond its marred appearance and to its allegorical value.

Elodie smiled at the flower and didn't look up. "You're ready for more than friendship?"

Madison placed her hand on Elodie's heart, careful to avoid her dressed wound. "The moment your lips covered mine, you claimed me."

Elodie's shoulders relaxed, and she looked relieved. "So, where do we go from here?"

"Where do you want to go?" *I need to know how you feel about me.*

"Back to my place?" She smiled and raised her eyebrow.

Madison saw something different from the trademark movie smile. Something deeper. But she had to be sure. "To fuck? Is that all?"

Elodie opened her mouth to say something but looked away.

"Tell me," Madison whispered.

"I'm scared. I want you. I want us, but I hurt people, eventually."

"I'm tough. I'm not going to shatter like a mishandled Christmas bauble." Madison took Elodie's face in her hand and kissed her deeply, trying to convey the depth of her feelings.

"There's so much at stake. I'm petrified of fucking this up and seeing you walk away from me."

"As long as we turn toward each other, and not away, we'll be okay." She could feel Elodie needed to say something else, something more. She wanted to open her mouth and pull the words from her throat. "Tell me…"

"Tell you?" A long, heavy pause. "If you don't know I'm in love with you by now, your emotional intelligence doesn't match your Mensa IQ."

Wow. "I don't think I've ever been insulted at the same time as someone declaring their love for me."

"Then let me take you home and apologize."

Chapter Thirty-Nine

It was bad form to disrupt a filming schedule, but Jules had been exceptionally understanding and had told Elodie to take as much time as she needed. The movie and her part would wait for her return. Elodie insisted Madison didn't bring her cell, laptop, or even a book. The cell and laptop had been relatively easy to wrestle from her; the demand of no books was proving infinitely harder to enforce.

"La dolce far niente," Elodie said. "The sweetness of doing nothing," Elodie pulled the books from Madison's hand luggage and put them on the edge of the bed.

"That sounds like some new age bullshit."

"Nope, not bullshit, truth. If you don't concentrate on anything else, your book or my movie contract, and if you don't listen to music or even the sounds around you, what surfaces is pure life. Your feelings of the moment, good or bad, joy or despair. Your true self emerges."

Madison grumbled and rolled her eyes. "What're your feelings right now?" she asked and smiled.

"Honestly?"

Madison motioned around them. "We're all packed. We're not doing anything else right now."

Elodie bit her lip. She could do this. "Gratitude. Euphoria. I feel complete. You fill in the pieces I didn't even know were missing."

Madison enveloped her in a snug embrace and kissed her chest, careful to avoid her healing knife wound. "You're getting good at this honesty thing."

Elodie kissed the top of Madison's head and took a step back. "One thing I would like you to take, *if* you'll accept it this time." From her hand luggage, she pulled out the Patek Philippe watch she'd tried to gift Madison after they'd first met and offered it again.

Madison put her hand over her mouth and shook her head. "Baby…"

"Don't tell me it's too much. I could give you all the diamonds in the world, and they wouldn't be enough." She took Madison's wrist and pulled her closer. "Please."

Madison bit her lip. "Are you *sure*? I'm so clumsy. What if I break it?"

Elodie laughed. "Then I'll get you a new one. It's just a thing, Mads. Every*thing* can be replaced, but you can't." She slipped the watch onto Madison's unbroken wrist and fastened it.

Madison shook her arm out. "Huh, it's a perfect fit."

Elodie frowned. "Of course it is. I had it adjusted for you."

"*Of course* you did. Thank you. It's beautiful." Madison held her wrist then kissed her. "Let's get to the airport, or we'll miss the plane."

Elodie chuckled and shook her head. "It's my plane. It doesn't leave the ground without me."

Madison rolled her eyes. "Show off."

Elodie wiggled her eyebrows. "I've got some other things to show off once I get you to myself."

***

"Do you realize how clichéd it is to have your own private island?"

"I'll have you know it's taken years of hard work to develop this imbued sense of cliché. And anyway, you don't seem to mind the seclusion it affords." Elodie patted Madison on her bare ass. She'd found the privacy immensely freeing and had taken to walking around completely naked most of the time, which made it so much easier to tumble into bed...or onto the huge suede couch...or into the beach cabana. Things they'd spent the past week doing a lot of.

Madison shifted slightly and grimaced.

"Your wrist?"

Madison massaged her forearm beyond the cast gently. "Yeah, it's pretty sore today."

"I bet finishing that article before we left didn't exactly aid its recovery." Elodie flipped Madison onto her back with ease and followed the curves of her body with her fingers.

Madison wriggled beneath her touch. "It had to be done. I didn't want someone else writing my exclusive."

Watching her squirm in such obvious delight turned Elodie on more than she could articulate. "God, woman, you're so fucking sexy." She sighed deeply and focused on the conversation. "No one else *could* have written that story. You're the one they kidnapped, *and* speaking of clichés, you lived to tell the tale." She pressed her lips to Madison's stomach and began a trail of light kisses down her inner thighs, all the way to her petite feet. "I seem to be developing a fetish for your feet," she whispered as she adjusted Madison's toe ring and kissed each digit. "No, scratch that. I'm just developing a fetish for you, period."

"You're just desperate, period, and it's contagious. You're making me feel like a horny teenager." Madison's hips rose from the daybed, and she sighed. "You know the magazine wanted the first instalment before Therese went to trial. I had to get it done."

Elodie worked her way back up Madison's thighs to her breasts. She straddled her and tenderly shifted Madison's stray locks from her eyes. Madison usually straightened her hair to within an inch of its life, but she had succumbed to Elodie's pestering and let her hair remain in its natural curls after she'd gotten it wet when they'd had sex in the ocean under moonlight. Elodie was discovering she had a romantic side that she couldn't control. "That trial will be a long way off. Ice said they're still tracking down everyone named in Santiago's documents, and the warden of the prisons where she was going to harvest the convicts' organs has completely disappeared. Add that to the additional charge of the first-degree murder of her cellmate, and it's going to take a while for the prosecution to get all their ducks in a row."

Madison laughed and tried to push Elodie off with her good hand, to no avail. "You're just showing off with your clichés now…and your rock-solid abs." She traced the ridges of Elodie's stomach with a look that was both appreciative and lascivious. "Ash said he'd keep me up to date, but now that I'm stranded on this island with you, I don't know what's going on."

"Ice will let us know what's going on. It's a federal case now, so Ash won't know much more than he already does." Elodie took Madison's hand and placed it over her heart. "But your words wound me. Do you feel like you're still a kidnap victim?" She smirked mischievously. "If it'd make you feel more comfortable in my custody, I could tie you down…"

"You're kinky…"

Madison closed her eyes for a moment, and Elodie knew she was picturing it. "You like me that way."

"And you?" Madison opened her eyes. "How do you feel about me?"

"I really like you."

Madison scoffed. "You better do more than really like me."

"Oh yeah? Why's that?"

Madison pulled Elodie close to her as best she could with one arm. "Because I'm giving you my everything, so *like* isn't really going to cut it."

Elodie nestled on to Madison's chest. She couldn't get close enough. "What if I told you I loved you and you didn't take it as an insult? What if I said I can see forever with you? What if—"

"What if you looked me in the eye and said it?"

Elodie lifted her head and stared into the depth of Madison's soul. *My soul mate*. "I want to lose and find myself in your eyes. I love you, Mads, like I've never loved before, like I never believed I could love."

"I love you, too… Kiss me and never stop."

Elodie cupped Madison's face in her hands and kissed her, hard and intense. "I'll never stop. All the kisses in the world are never enough, but these are the kisses with my heart in them. And my heart is yours, always."

Epilogue

Elodie opened the limo door, and the thousand flashing bulbs were blinding. "How do you put up with this?" Madison asked, like she always did whenever they went anywhere together. She took Elodie's hand and stepped out of the car.

"I can put up with anything if you're by my side." Elodie grinned and wrapped her arm around Madison's waist.

"God, you're cheesy." She grasped Elodie's other hand and held on tight. Tonight was huge for Elodie. She was up for a Best Actor Oscar for her role as Elya Charinov, the movie was up for Best Picture, and it had at least another five nominations. Elodie had successfully campaigned, along with a host of other actors and Hollywood heavyweights, to make the awards non-gendered. Actor and actress were no longer separate categories. It made the competition even more fierce, one statue for all actors, and Madison couldn't be prouder of her wife. She smiled widely. *Wife*. She still checked her wedding ring finger every morning when she woke.

"You make me this way." Elodie looked at her. "What are you grinning at?"

"You, wife. I love you."

"I love you, wife." Elodie squeezed her gently.

"Darlings." Elodie's agent, Paige, appeared from nowhere and ushered them along the south side of the red carpet to the first spot for official photographs and her first of a hundred interviews before they'd enter the Dolby Theatre to take their seats for the big event.

Madison smiled and posed as they made their way tediously slowly along the line. She played the supporting role just as Paige had trained her to do early on. Madison had been doing it for nearly two years now, but she still hated every second of exposure. After nights like this, she longed to be far away from the big city, looking up at a black night sky glittering with the stardust kind of stars instead of Hollywood stars, with Elodie holding her in her arms and only the sound of owls surrounding them.

"What are you wearing?" someone screamed out.

Clothes. But Madison said nothing and let Elodie tell them they'd been dressed by CK Larkly, an unknown, up-and-coming queer designer. All the top designers had *wanted* to dress Elodie, but since all their samples were size two, she made a stand for regular-sized women and turned them all down. Just like she'd done last year when they walked down this carpet together for the first time. And Elodie looked stunning in an intricately designed dark maroon tuxedo. CK had even managed to make Madison feel sexy in a matching long-sleeved, high-collared gown. It was a Christmas miracle they'd made it out of the house at all, and Elodie had been whispering explicit details about her own Oscar after-party activities in Madison's ear on the journey here. Madison usually couldn't wait to be home after these events, but now she was desperate for this to be over so they could get started.

Their honeymoon period was far from over.

Madison glanced back along the carpet to see Troy Donovan and Brad Carlton hand in hand, working the crowd. They'd published Troy's memoir earlier that year, and it had gone straight to number one on the New York Times Bestseller list. It hadn't budged since, and now FlatLine was making it into a movie, starring Troy and Brad. Madison had been in the meeting when the two of them met a month ago, and the sparks were instant and obvious to everyone in the room. She was happy for Troy. He seemed settled and in love. She caught his eye and waved, and Troy smiled and blew her a kiss just as Elodie turned to see what Madison was doing.

Elodie nodded his way and tightened her grip on Madison's waist. "He better keep his kisses on Brad's lips, thank you very much."

Madison laughed. "How can *you* be jealous of Troy? There's no one in the world that could turn my gaze from you."

Elodie grinned and looked a little shy. "Now who's being cheesy?"

Madison got on her tiptoes and kissed Elodie. The crowd cheered, and even more bulbs flashed.

"You'll ruin your makeup," Elodie said, breathless when Madison broke away.

"No, I won't. It's smudge-proof."

Elodie dropped her hand from Madison's waist and squeezed her ass. "We'll see about that later," she whispered.

They continued along the line and eventually took their seats on the front row, sandwiched between Anne Hathaway and Daniel Radcliffe. Madison had long admired both for being LGBT+ allies as well as great actors. She and Elodie clinked glasses of Fleur du Miraval champagne and settled in. Best Actor was the second to last award to be presented, but Elodie was presenting one too, so she'd disappear after half an hour. She touched her watch after checking it. Even after two years, she was still getting used to wearing it. She did love how the lights shimmered and reflected in the diamonds though.

Madison kept her drinking to a minimum. She wanted to be completely present for this one. Kristen Stewart gave a little spiel before announcing the nominees, and Elodie smiled brightly when the cameras focused on her, but also as each of her colleagues were named. She gripped Madison's hand tightly, and Madison kissed her neck. "I love you, actor wife."

Elodie looked into Madison's eyes, making her feel like they were at home on the couch rather than in front of thousands of people.

"I love *you*."

"Thank you," Madison said simply.

Elodie wrinkled her nose. "For what?"

"For being amazing. You're my world."

Kristen Stewart cleared her throat and opened the envelope. "And the Best Actor goes to…"

Time slowed. The sounds of the audience faded into silence. Madison closed her eyes.

Kristen clasped the card to her chest and smiled broadly. "My friend, Elodie Fontaine."

The volume went back up to normal, the crowd erupted, and Elodie pulled Madison into a rib-breaking embrace.

"I couldn't have done this without you," Elodie said and stood to approach the stage. "I love you," she said again.

Madison grinned as Elodie headed to accept her second Oscar. She wouldn't be satisfied until she had more Oscars than anyone else in its history, and Madison loved her for that drive and ambition. But mostly, Madison simply loved *her*, for everything. For all that she was, and all that she would ever be. And for being hers. Forever would never be enough.

What's Your Story?

Global Wordsmiths, CIC, provides an all-encompassing service for all writers, ranging from basic proofreading and cover design to development editing, typesetting, and eBook services. A major part of our work is charity and community focused, delivering writing projects to under-served and under-represented groups across Nottinghamshire, giving voice to the voiceless and visibility to the unseen.

To learn more about what we offer, visit: www.globalwords.co.uk

A selection of books by Global Words Press:
Desire, Love, Identity: with the National Justice Museum
Aventuras en México: Farmilo Primary School
Life's Whispers: Journeys to the Hospice
Times Past: with The Workhouse, National Trust
Times Past: Young at Heart with AGE UK
In Different Shoes: Stories of Trans Lives
From Surviving to Thriving: Reclaiming Our Voices
Don't Look Back, You're Not Going That Way

Self-published authors working with Global Wordsmiths:
E.V. Bancroft
Addison M. Conley
AJ Mason
Ally McGuire
Emma Nichols
Helena Harte
Iona Kane
James Merrick
Karen Klyne
Robyn Nyx
John Edward Parsons
Simon Smalley
Valden Bush

Other Great Butterworth Books

Dead Pretty by Robyn Nyx
An FBI agent, a TV star, and a serial killer. Love hurts.
Available on Amazon (ASIN B09QRSKBVP)

An Art to Love by Helena Harte
Second chances are an art form.
Available on Amazon (ASIN B0B1CD8Y42)

Caribbean Dreams by Karen Klyne
When love sails into your life, do you climb aboard?
Available from Amazon (ASIN B09M41PYM9)

Nero by Valden Bush
Banished. Abandoned. Lost. Will destiny reunite her with the love of her life?
Available from Amazon (ASIN B09BXN8VTZ)

Warm Pearls and Paper Cranes by E.V. Bancroft
A family torn apart. The only way forward is love.
Available from Amazon (ISBN 9781915009029)

The Helion Band *by AJ Mason*
Rose's only crime was to show kindness to her royal mistress...
Available from Amazon (ASIN B09YM6TYFQ)

That Boy of Yours Wants Looking At by Simon Smalley
A gloriously colourful and heart-rending memoir.
Available from Amazon (ASIN B09HSN9NM8)

Judge Me, Judge Me Not by James Merrick
A memoir of one gay man's battle against the world and himself.
Available from Amazon (ASIN B09CLK91N5)

LesFic Eclectic Volume Three edited by Robyn Nyx
A little something for all tastes.
Special edition raising funds for the DEC Ukrainian appeal: available from Amazon (ASIN B09V39LW2W)